GRAHAM CAWLEY joined Lloyds Bank in 1954, in South Devon, eventually retiring as senior manager of St James's Street branch in London. He has had numerous financial articles and short stories published, and has written two self-published novels, Chain of Events and Fatal Retribution. Each novel features bank manager, David Goodhart, while Avarice deals with his promoted role of bank inspector. All three books depict little-known-about banking crimes and also feature Graham's love of jazz and football.

GW00586659

GRAHAM CAWLEY
AVARICE

A DAVID GOODHART MYSTERY

To Roy

With my very best wishes

Graham

SilverWood

Published in 2013 by the author using
SilverWood Books Empowered Publishing ®

SilverWood Books
30 Queen Charlotte Street, Bristol, BS1 4HJ
www.silverwoodbooks.co.uk

ISBN 978-1-78132-095-2

British Library Cataloguing in Publication Data
A CIP catalogue record for this book is available from the British Library

Set in Garamond by SilverWood Books
Printed on responsibly sourced paper

For Shelagh, Ian, Lisa, Katie and Lucy,
plus my ever-supportive great friend, David Trower

Chapter 1

Bank inspector David Goodhart heard the news at eleven-thirty. It should have been half an hour earlier.

He had only put one highly-polished black shoe inside the room before Trevor Smith leapt to his feet, his youthful eyes fired with rare concern.

"Where have you been, sir?"

David stared back at the lad. What was this all about? Being admonished? By a fledgling assistant? But this was so unlike the Trevor of old; something must be seriously wrong. And David now felt it in the pit of his stomach. Yet, on checking his watch, he had only been away from the branch for forty minutes.

"What's going on?"

Trevor had been working at a decrepit pre-war desk and he now leaned against it, his lean fingers splayed on the pock-marked and ink-stained work surface. Though only small, the desk still managed to dominate this tiny, claustrophobic room. When they had arrived here a week ago, David had wondered if it had been a deliberate move by the branch manager: give the inspectors the smallest room in his bank for them to carry out their inspection.

"Regional Office phoned," Trevor blurted out, his patience clearly at stretching point. "At eleven. Where were you, sir?"

He then looked a little shamefaced, pink spots appearing below his high cheek bones. Did he now realize his words had been laced with reproof?

David cast narrowed eyes down to the desk. It was completely clear of its normal jumble of papers. In the middle of the morning? It was as if Trevor had been deliberately tidying up for an imminent departure.

"We've got to go," Trevor then said, confirming David's fears. "Right away. To Lamberhurst."

David grimaced.

"Lamberhurst?"

It was the last thing he needed. Here in Tenterden, he was already way behind schedule with his inspection.

Trevor now looked distraught.

"Something's happened there."

David glowered at his assistant and made no attempt to disguise his impatience.

"Come on, Trevor. You can do better than that. Something's happened?"

He contemplated the slender young man who he still considered to be a lad, despite his now being twenty-four. Trevor simply shook his head. Was it in frustration? Or was his defensive mechanism simply clicking in?

"I'm sorry, sir. That's all Regional Office told me. They said there's been an incident at the sub-branch in Lamberhurst. They must have known more, but they wouldn't tell me. It was as if they didn't trust me. As if they didn't believe I'm your assistant."

David now seethed.

A few moments ago, he had simply been irritated. Not only was he already behind schedule with his inspection, but there was something odd going on at this branch. And he needed to be here to explore further. He could not put his finger on it, but he knew from experience not to ignore his inspectorial nose. So the last thing he needed was to be dragged away on a jaunt through the Kent countryside to the village of Lamberhurst.

That was a few moments ago.

Now his irritation had turned to anger, his wrath focussed directly at Regional Office. How dare they not trust his assistant with further information! And he had no need to ask Trevor who had actually made the call: the Regional Manager's deputy -the self-styled High and Mighty – Angus McPhoebe.

"McPhoebe, eh?"

Trevor nodded, though appearing reluctant to incriminate a

man who was so much more his senior.

"He said you must ring him when you got in."

Must? David pulled back the sleeve of his jacket to look at his watch. It gave him good enough reason to defy McPhoebe's command from above. It was far too late to make such a call.

"There's no time to do that. Come on. We're off."

He felt completely at ease with his decision. Three years into being a branch inspector, he had metamorphosed into an independent spirit. It went with the territory. National Counties Bank had effectively said this when they promoted him back in 1957. They were not looking for yes men. And they did not expect their inspectors to acquiesce under pressure. Such as from those who might want to exert undue influence – based on some personal agenda or another.

Just as Angus McPhoebe might do.

But was the man playing this game now? David could well imagine McPhoebe rubbing his hands at having discovered an inspector having apparently gone AWOL. In the middle of a Monday morning? Yet something serious might well have happened at Lamberhurst.

"We should have been on our way long ago," Trevor muttered, as if still seeking an explanation for his boss's absence from the branch.

On reflection, David agreed. But this was not the moment to admit to having been enjoying a quiet pint in the nearby Red Lion.

Yet he certainly regretted not having been here to take McPhoebe's call. For three years, it was the sort of call he had awaited – though not wanted. Raids or hold-ups, though infrequent, did arise in banking and inspectors always attended and investigated such crimes which might occur in their respective regions. So far, David had not received such a call.

Until now.

Yet McPhoebe had only said there had been an incident at Lamberhurst. It might be something or nothing. But despite his misgivings about McPhoebe's possible motives, David was not prepared to take a chance. And he needed to appease Trevor.

"All right, all right," he replied, smiling at the lad. "Don't go on about it. Let's just get everything packed into our bags."

His ready acceptance of Trevor's concern seemed to calm the lad down. He became more like his normal, controlled self. Yet something was clearly still troubling him.

"I've already done most of that, sir. You reckon we need to take the bags with us?"

David glanced at the floor where two large Gladstone-like bags lay, stuffed with papers, folders and reports. These monstrosities had to be carted round with them from branch to branch.

"Yes, better take them. We might not be coming back here today."

In normal circumstances, the locked bags would be deposited in the branch's strongroom overnight, but if something significant had arisen at Lamberhurst, an early return to Tenterden was unlikely.

They quickly donned their overcoats – plus trilby, in David's case – and left the branch by the front door. They were unable to tell the manager they were leaving; he was interviewing a customer. The sub-manager, clearly curious as to what might be going on, said he would pass on the news of their departure.

David had parked his Ford Consul about a hundred yards down the High Street and he was now thankful it was not further away; their loaded bags were becoming heavier by the yard. On reaching the vehicle, he put his own bag down on the pavement, took the ignition key out of his pocket and unlocked the driver's door. Reaching inside, he then unlocked the rear door.

"Now, let's get these bags into the back."

"Not in the boot, sir?"

David shook his head. He now realized he had not passed on to Trevor a new instruction he had been given that morning.

"No … sorry. Forgot to tell you. Had word this morning about a Brummie inspector. He'd parked his car – right in the middle of

Walsall. The boot was locked, but some rogue levered open the lid. Then made off with the bags."

Trevor looked wide-eyed.

"Is nothing sacred?"

David grinned, but it would not have been a laughing matter for the inspector concerned.

"Anyway, the boot's off limits now. Must use the rear footwells. Just got to make sure we lock the rear doors."

And after getting into the front of the car, they both stretched behind them to trigger the rear locks. David then turned the ignition over, dabbed the accelerator pedal and the engine roared into life.

Before he put the car in gear, he glanced sideways at Trevor, knowing this was always a moment of some apprehension for his assistant.

"Now, Trevor, we're both agreed? Speed is the essence?"

Trevor nodded, if rather reluctantly, and David engaged the clutch. The car surged forward and he sensed an intake of breath at his side; Trevor had duly confirmed his unease over his boss's driving.

But this was not of concern to David now. He was starting to experience nasty feelings about what might have happened at the Lamberhurst sub-branch. A little while ago, one of his inspector colleagues had actually become involved with a murder case – a gruesome one, at that. God forbid anything like that may have happened this time. How would he be able to handle something so appalling?

He tried to shake off his concerns. He had to be realistic. The chances of anything really traumatic having happened were minimal. McPhoebe had called it an incident. Something worse than that and he would, surely, have told Trevor. Or, at least, called again.

Yet the sooner they got there, the better.

To this end, he decided the secondary roads ought to provide the quickest route – provided farm vehicles did not hinder their progress. In Tenterden, itself, traffic was light and on reaching the outskirts, he swung right on to the minor road which would take them through the picturesque villages of Sissinghurst and Goudhurst.

"Do you think it might really be a raid?" Trevor asked, hastily gripping his seat as a Vespa scooter sped across their path to gain right of way at the next junction.

It was not so much the question as the way it was asked which shook David. It was as if a stiletto had pierced right though him.

How could he have forgotten? Was senility setting in? Yet he was still only 43.

All right, it had been over five years ago, but he should have remembered. What Trevor had experienced then would stay with the poor lad for ever.

"I simply don't know," he replied, hesitating over what more he should say. Trevor's head must have been in turmoil since he took that call from McPhoebe.

The lad remained quiet with his thoughts and David instinctively slowed down. He realized he was now clenching the steering wheel. For Trevor's sake, he must try to relax and maintain his composure.

"Don't worry, sir," Trevor then said, as if reading David's thoughts. He then smiled, though rather ruefully. "I'm fine. They say there's no accounting for experience."

David glanced at Trevor and returned his smile. The response was typical. It was a good example of why Trevor was now here in Kent as his assistant.

"I think we need to be prepared for anything," David said. They had now reached Sissinghurst and Baden-Powell's motto seemed increasingly apposite.

"Or nothing, sir?"

Bearing in mind Trevor's state of mind, the question seemed laced with wishful thinking.

"Perhaps."

From the corner of his eye. David could see that Trevor had become unusually pallid. The lad turned towards him, shaking his head.

"In which case, sir, why would Regional Office have called?"

That was certainly true. But Trevor had not yet met Angus McPhoebe. He did not know how that man's arrogant mind worked.

"At least we're making good time, Trevor."

And at least they had not encountered any tractors on this country road. Even the bottleneck entrance to the village of Goudhurst soon proved to be free of other vehicles.

They were now only five minutes away from Lamberhurst and David felt his chest tightening. He could sense the empathy from Trevor. That was good. They both needed to be on full alert.

But as they left Goudhurst behind them, they immediately encountered a road worker boldly displaying a red STOP sign. Half the road in front of them had been blocked off and, round the next bend, a plume of black smoke belched above the high hedgerow. It could only come from the tall funnel of an Aveling-Barford steamroller. Although David had spent much of his childhood ogling traction engines and steamrollers, the last thing he needed was to see one now.

He drummed his fingers on the steering wheel, willing the workman to twist his sign round to display the green GO. Even Trevor muttered an uncommon oath, as if to encourage the man into positive action.

At last, the sign allowed them through. And with the aroma of newly-laid tarmacadam wafting through the car, they soon reached the A21 which would take them into Lamberhurst.

But diversion signs had been set up ahead of the road down to the village, followed by wooden barriers marked 'Road Closed'. David grimaced. He had to get to the sub-branch. At least the roadblock was unmanned and, despite a protest from Trevor, he nipped out of the car and moved one of the barriers to give his car just enough space to slip through. When he got back in he found Trevor looking aghast.

"Should you have done ..."

"Needs must, Trevor," David said, stopping the lad in mid-sentence and then immediately getting the car moving again.

At first, from a distance, everything seemed normal in the village centre and David wondered if McPhoebe's 'incident' had, in fact, been just that. Then he noticed a solitary policeman standing on the pavement outside the sub-branch. Two other men in civilian clothes were working in the road and David could now see the adjacent area had been cordoned off with police tape.

It seemed his worst fears were now confirmed.

Chapter 2

Some three hours earlier, Alfie Templeton had gazed furtively across the main thoroughfare in Tunbridge Wells.

He shook his head sadly. Sitting behind the wheel of his Clarendon-grey Morris Oxford, he could only wonder how it had not happened before.

The fools! They make it so easy; the routine never varies.

He drew deeply on the Woodbine which he cupped in his right hand, his nicotine-stained first finger and thumb holding the weed to his lips. In this day and age – for goodness' sake, it was now 1960 – there was enough organized crime to make even the most unsuspecting bank take simple precautions.

They might not yet have heard of the Krays – never mind the Richardsons. Templeton already knew of them well enough. And it would only be a matter of time before their nefarious activities came to general light. But, even now, no one should succumb to that tired old syndrome: it will never happen to us.

Some people would never learn.

He stubbed out the half-finished cigarette into the fascia's ashtray and automatically lit another, flicking the discarded Swan Vesta out of the door's open window.

But why should he care? This bank's laxity would help to make five years of planning more than worthwhile.

He had been taught that patience was a virtue and he had certainly proved that old adage correct. At first he had never thought he had such restraint in him, but taking on a partner had made all the difference. It was the benefit of teamwork: pooling thoughts; sharing ideas and plans; being prepared to listen to each other. And, despite his basic distrust of partnerships, this one had worked like a dream.

Until yesterday.

The dream had then turned into a nightmare. But there had been no alternative. Otherwise, the whole operation would have disintegrated. Five years of planning would have proved worthless. As for the resultant jail sentence … or worse.

Perhaps he should have stuck to working alone. It had always worked in the past. It was about being in full control and not exposed to the vagaries of others. And he had never been greedy. But, despite the obvious benefits, it had become too constrictive. It had narrowed his horizons.

It had now been thirty years of narrow horizons; thirty years of petty crime.

All those years ago, Woolworths had been to blame. They made it so easy to nick toy cars and sweets; the best that Dinky and Rowntree's could produce. It had been the ideal apprenticeship for his future career.

But now, he needed to move on. Though not into the big-time; he could leave that to Reggie and Ronnie. But he had to stretch out and achieve one big one – his one and only big one. And then he could retire; and live the life of Old Riley. Yet for that big one, he needed a partner. Only it had to be the right person; someone he could trust (in this game?); and someone who could also be patient.

Controlling a shiver, he exhaled smoke into the early morning March air and reflected on how Tunbridge Wells was the perfect location. The south-east town bisected Kent from Sussex, while highways and byways stretched afar to all compass points.

He could not resist licking his thin lips – and not just because they were dry from anticipation. In a nutshell, his getaway options were unlimited.

In other ways, he also reckoned Tunbridge Wells and its surrounds to be an admirable choice. It was such a quiet town, genteel almost. Nothing exciting ever happened in Tunbridge Wells. The retired colonels and their gentlewomen would have it no other way. The most stirring thing that ever arose from the town was the occasional carp to the letters' page of The Times –

missives that decried the falling standards in modern-day life.

Templeton sucked hard on his cigarette and inhaled with bated anticipation. Soon those same people would have something else to contemplate over their evening G and Ts.

It was so different back home in South London. Almost all his life he had lived in the Holmesdale Road, adjacent to Selhurst Park, home to Crystal Palace football club. Being so near he had no option but to become a supporter. He had never regretted it.

But this was cloth cap territory, a million miles from Tunbridge Wells. Or Royal Tunbridge Wells, as the local gentry liked to call it. These people had probably never heard of the round-ball game. Any sorties to London were more likely to be in the direction of jolly-old Twickers.

He shook his head again – this time in despair. Such toffs would never have savoured the magic of the Matthews Final; nor the artistry introduced into the game by the magnificent Hungarians; nor, even, Palace's Budgie Byrne mesmerising opposing defences at Selhurst Park.

But this was not the time to dwell upon such cultural niceties.

He felt inside his jacket for the comforting feel of his revolver. He could still not believe how he had come to acquire it. Never before had one been on his agenda. And he had no intention of firing it; just showing it, pointing it at its target, ought to be enough to concentrate the mind of any potential victim. He had even considered not loading it, but had soon dismissed the idea. He might not have any intention of firing the gun, but it was an effective form of insurance.

He had parked his Morris Oxford in Mount Pleasant Road. This wide, continental-style avenue stretched from the top of the town down to the railway station. Despite it being well past nine o'clock, he could see some dilatory commuters still heading for their trains. Not that he had any interest in these people. His prime focus of attention was the bank across the road.

Mount Pleasant was the home to three of the major banks.

Lloyds, the largest, occupied the principal corner site opposite the cinema, while the Midland stood down the hill towards the station.

But neither of these was his target.

He was parked midway down the street, opposite the town's branch of National Counties Bank. This was the smallest of the three banks. And the most vulnerable. Insider information assured him of that. How could a bank be so lax in its security arrangements?

But this was not his concern. If the bank could not act professionally, it deserved all it got.

He patted his revolver again. Just insurance. He had to convince himself of that.

He lit up a third cigarette and pondered, drawing upon his old habit of nibbling at his finger nails. It was curious that banks did not experience more raids than actually seemed to happen. They were, after all, such soft targets. Just the space of a banking counter separated a would-be raider from what could only be described as a good pay day. The simple act of pushing a threatening note across the counter, while only hinting at a concealed weapon, should coerce the most intrepid cashier into handing over the contents of his till.

Yet there were risks. Customers could get in the way. Even a cashier could choose to become incautiously brave. And successful crime had to be foolproof – free of any risk. For him, there were three essential elements to that particular theory: planning, planning, and planning.

That was why yesterday had been so appalling. Suddenly, his self-imposed abhorrence of violence had been laid bare. How could he have done such a thing? It had never been part of their plan. But at least they could now move on. They were back on stream. And today's operation would be as perfect as the smoke-ring he had just blown out of the car's window.

Digging into his pocket for a fresh packet of Woodbines, he realized how tired he was. During the last few weeks, he had covered hundreds of miles, visiting towns of which he had hardly been previously aware. He had chosen his targets meticulously. Each town had to be large enough not to draw attention to himself and all must have a branch of National Counties Bank, each one sited conveniently for ease of parking and a quick getaway.

Thank goodness for all that planning; it had paid off to perfection – literally so.

The operation of each heist had proved to be as smooth as the crisp new bank notes which now occupied much of the boot space of his Oxford. His only subsequent fear had been the possibility of a puncture or breakdown. To have to retrieve tools from underneath all that loot, especially in the company of an AA motorcycle patrolman, could have proved most embarrassing. But it was not to be and, as a precaution, he had now stowed the tools behind the front seats.

Templeton looked at his watch. Almost time to go. He stubbed out his cigarette, flinching as a spark nipped the top of his finger.

Sure enough, at 9.20 precisely, the bank's front door opened. Templeton pursed his lips. Idiots! It was the same every day. They deserved all they got.

First to appear was the head of a man who looked about a hundred, but was probably nearer seventy. After glancing up and down the street, he turned round and nodded at someone behind him. The two then emerged from the bank, slamming the door behind them.

It was a joke … really. For God's sake, the old man was supposed to be a guard. Yet, clearly, any ability to perform such a function had long since gone. The man even walked with a pronounced limp. All right, he might still have the bearing of an old soldier, but his effectiveness as a guard must be non-existent.

That was just as well – for what was about to happen.

The other man was younger, in his mid-forties. He certainly looked the part of a senior bank official – smart three-piece suit and pristine white shirt, its detached stiff collar holding in place a neatly-knotted military-style tie. Being a dry spring day, he had chosen not to wear a top coat, but a stiff breeze caused him to raise his left hand to keep his silky fair hair in place. His other hand held on to a large brown leather suitcase which appeared to be crammed to capacity. It was good to see he was clearly struggling to cope with its weight and it was just possible to see the end of a chain attached to the case's handle, the length of chain then appearing to extend up the man's jacket sleeve.

The two men made for an old Austin car which the driver had managed to park right outside the bank. The younger man had no option but to get into the back of the car; his case was too bulky for him to do otherwise. Once he was in, the old soldier, with some difficulty, climbed into the driver's seat and started the engine.

Templeton's eyes narrowed and he gritted his ill-maintained teeth. Time to go. He turned his own engine over, slipped the steering column's gear lever into first and got the car under way. That old apology for a guard could have no idea that the grey Morris Oxford would follow him all the way to the bank's Lamberhurst sub-branch.

CHAPTER 3

"You ready, Barney?"

It was enough to make Barney Wilson sigh. He was always ready. He had been trained for always being ready – no less than forty-five years ago. As a batman in the Great War, it was more than his life was worth not to be ready.

"Of course, sir."

"No need for that."

"No need for what, sir?"

"That sirring business. And springing to attention."

Barney pursed his lips. Easier said than done. Old habits die hard. At least he had got out of the habit of calling everyone in the branch 'sir'. Not the girls, of course. Yet Mr Fairweather was different.

"But you're the boss, sir."

"No, Barney. Colonel Fawkes-William is the boss. I'm still a simple cashier."

Mr Fairweather being humble? Not everybody on the staff had seen this side of his character.

"But you're my boss, s …, Mr Fairweather."

And that was certainly true. As the cashier in charge at the Lamberhurst sub-branch, with only his trusty guard at his side, Douglas Fairweather was definitely the boss. After all, he was effectively manager at Lamberhurst, all bar the title.

"Anyone would think you're still in the forces, Barney."

If only. But he had been invalided out decades ago. Yet he loved his present job in the bank. And it had the same chain of command. Colonel Fawkes-William was effectively the commanding officer – and he still used his old army title, Gawd bless him. But Mr Fairweather was, well, the officer in charge at Lamberhurst – with yours truly as his batman.

So, why not call him 'sir' and be at his beck and call? That had been his training – all those years ago. It had been his calling, dear old Ma had always said.

"And incidentally," Mr Fairweather continued, actually smiling, "no extramural activities today. We've a busy day ahead of us."

"You know that only happened at Rusthall, sir."

Mr Fairweather's smile now broke into a grin.

"Just thought I'd remind you."

But extramural at Lamberhurst? Mr Fairweather knew full well such things only arose at the much quieter sub-branch in nearby Rusthall.

It had started there in a small way. The sub-branch only opened on Monday and Friday mornings. Barney was proud to stand guard in the public space, the cashier being positioned behind his counter. In the wild west, he would have had a shotgun; in Rusthall, all he needed was his natural gift of the gab and his love of the geegees. Well, there was no bookie in Rusthall. So, it was no trouble to collect customers' bets on Friday, take them to the betting shop in Tunbridge Wells, and bring back any winnings to Rusthall on Monday.

How about that for a banking service? Some days he even seemed to have more customers than the cashier. But thank heavens Colonel Fawkes-William knew nothing of it.

Then it came to an end. He was made guard at Lamberhurst, instead. This sub-branch opened five days a week and Mr Fairweather was a stickler for doing things by the book. And there was no mention of bookmaking in banking regulations.

Yet, now, Mr Fairweather making a light-hearted comment? So soon after appearing humble?

Most of the staff had probably not seen this side of him. He seemed to be different when he was one-to-one with Barney. Others complained that he was dour and rather arrogant. But was this a cover for basic shyness? Barney had seen it before in the army. Arrogance could be used to impress them up on high. Was Mr Fairweather simply trying to prove to Colonel Fawkes-William that he was on top of his job? That he had the in-built self-confidence to become a branch manager?

But not everyone was impressed.

Barney recognized jealousy when he saw it. At least two people thought Mr Fairweather was kowtowing his way up the promotion ladder. And they did not like his undoubted good looks. Unlike Mary in the machine room. She had actually confessed to Barney about her crush on the cashier. She was smitten with his fair hair and complexion, not to mention his physique. She reckoned he was the spitting image of Hollywood heart-throb, Aldo Ray.

But, whatever else, Barney remained loyal to his man. Just as he had in the war.

Yet Mr Fairweather's levity was short-lived.

"What a palaver this is."

As usual, the cashier was grappling with a length of chain. This needed to be wrapped around him under his jacket, with the end of the chain then being fed down the sleeve of the jacket and locked on to the sub-branch case, loaded with the cash needed for the day. And, as usual, he refused Barney's offer of any help.

This was one difference from being back in the army where Barney would have been expected to help. And he had loved it. As he had in bulling his officer's shoes until his fingers ached. Then, buttons, brasses, webbing and pistol had to be cleaned, buffed and polished to perfection. And he had enjoyed every minute of it.

"Better to be safe than sorry, sir."

Mr Fairweather nodded, if rather reluctantly, and finally clipped and locked the chain to the case.

"God, this case is so heavy. You'd better do the donkey-work today."

Another bit of levity from the man? My, he was in a good mood today.

Barney felt the same every day. He revelled in his job at the bank. Now nearing 70, he was lucky to have a job at all – especially without a qualification to his name. Poor East End schooling and leaving at fourteen had seen to that. How different from the others here in this office. Education and qualifications almost seeped from the pores of each man, lad and occasional girl.

It showed up in so many ways.

If only he could cast up vast columns of pounds, shillings and pence. If only he had dextrous fingers to flit all over the keys of the new-fangled adding and accounting machines. As for the way they spoke …

But doing Mr Fairweather's donkey-work was not on.

"If I took the case, sir, who'd do the driving?"

Not Mr Fairweather, that was for sure. Barney could never envisage him getting behind the wheel of his battered old Austin.

"You wait, Barney. When I'm full-time manager at Lamberhurst, I won't need you to drive me there each day. Then what'll you do?"

Although Mr Fairweather said this in jest – why was he in such a good mood today? – Barney's heart sank. He had already feared the worst. But he tried to appear cheerful.

"You'll miss having good ol' Barney with you, sir."

Not that Mr Fairweather ever called him that. Other staff, yes, but not Mr Fairweather.

"But think of all those extra staff I'll have with me instead."

And that was Barney's big worry. It was no secret that, with or without Mr Fairweather's possible fawning, Colonel Fawkes-William was grooming him for management – specifically at Lamberhurst. Years ago, the cashier had been manager of a bank in India, but had to return to England for health reasons. No wonder he was seeking to work his way up again.

And he certainly seemed to have the ear of the manager. Barney tried to keep out of office politics, but, on more than one occasion, he had seen Mr Fairweather and the manager coming out of the Conservative Club together. Others might feel this was a step too far in the cashier's quest for promotion.

Yet, if Lamberhurst was made into a full branch – with or without Mr Fairweather in charge – what would happen to Barney's job? He was still fit and strong, but his age was against him.

And there was always his gammy leg.

What a 'mare that had been, not least because it had meant having to quit his beloved army. He still had bad dreams over what had happened. But a life was a life. And his action had been subsequently recognized. Though he had always kept that under wraps.

But would the bank, like the army, use his gammy leg as a reason for dispensing with his services?

Mr Fairweather checked his watch and, with some difficulty, lifted the case from the floor.

"Come on, Barney. It's 9.20. Let's be off."

Barney led the way to the front door. He opened it carefully, with the security chain still in place. Seeing no one immediately outside, he slipped the chain off its catch, pulled the door open and looked up and down the street to ensure all was clear.

He was always meticulous with this task. He treated his job as guard with the seriousness in which he had bulled his officer's shoes. He then turned back to Mr Fairweather to beckon him out, leaving the office junior to replace the security chain until the bank opened for business at ten o'clock.

Barney had managed to park his banger of an Austin right outside the branch, much to Mr Fairweather's evident relief as he eased himself and his heavy bag into the back seat.

"Thank God, Barney, we didn't have to trek right down Mount Pleasant."

Barney could only agree. But that was because of his leg. It was bad enough struggling to get behind the steering wheel, without having to hobble any distance to the actual car.

Once in, he triggered the starter motor. Relief. The engine started first time. He put the car in first gear, eased off the handbrake and the car rolled gently down the hill towards the station.

Moving up the gears he was soon heading for the Pantiles, before climbing up Frant Road towards Lamberhurst.

He really enjoyed this journey; the area was such a contrast to where he was brought up. Foliage versus concrete and brick. And the air! It was as if he could actually smell its sheer freshness. Could you Adam and Eve it? It was a far cry from the Mile End Road. Thank goodness he had eventually moved to this part of the country. Every day he felt that life could not get any better. Yet, it always did.

He crossed Forest Road and made his way past the golf course towards the hamlet of Bells Yew Green.

Mr Fairweather tapped him on the shoulder.

"Watch out for golf balls."

Barney grinned, but had not done so last week. Despite the shelter of a line of Poplar trees, a golf ball had sailed over from the adjacent fairway and hit the bonnet of the car. He shuddered to think what would have happened if the ball had gone straight through the windscreen.

Apart from the threat of passing golf balls, this particular country road was usually relatively free of obstacles and heavy traffic. This morning, the only other car he noticed was a grey Morris Oxford in his rear view mirror. That was fair enough, but he was curious as to why such a larger, more powerful vehicle should dawdle far behind and make no attempt to overtake.

Within about ten minutes, they approached the outskirts of Lamberhurst and Barney pointed the car down the steep, winding hill into the centre of the village. Three such approach roads descended towards a medley of centuries-old shops, houses and pubs, plus a resplendent oast house, so typical of those dotted around this hop-growing countryside.

The River Teise was the only potential downside of the village. This passed through its centre and, at times of heavy rainfall, could flood the main street and shops. Fortunately, the bank had, so far, managed to avoid such damage.

He parked the car right outside the sub-branch and noticed the Oxford draw up behind him. The driver then got out and approached the car. Barney shook his head; another geezer losing his way. No wonder, with the road signs around here. Barney found it easier to find his way around London than some of this Kent countryside.

The man reached the Austin and Barney made to get out to offer his help.

But the other driver immediately shoved his door closed. Then Barney gasped in shock. Right in front of him through the open window there was the glint of light on metal – a form of metal he had spent so many hours polishing, those many years ago.

"Out!" the man screamed, not at Barney, but at Mr Fairweather in the back seat. "Get out and into my car. Else your driver gets it in the head."

Barney heard a stifled cry behind him, but he could not take his eyes off the barrel of the revolver. It was pointing straight at him, no more than six inches away from his face. But gun or no gun, he was not going to be intimidated by this upstart.

"Get down, sir," he shouted back to Mr Fairweather.

He still kept his eyes on the revolver, but also took in the features of the gunman. He knew from his experience back in the war that eye contact could be essential. What was really going through the man's mind? Was he deadly serious? Was he in control? Was he bluffing? Or was blind panic dictating his every move?

"Get out of the back!" the man screamed again.

This time he turned his head to peer into the rear of the car. Barney immediately seized the opportunity and forced his door open. His action automatically thrust the man's arm into the air, his revolver pointing impotently at the roofs of the adjacent properties.

"What the ..." the man cried out, clearly astonished at Barney's reaction.

But he was only off-balance for an instant and his free arm grabbed hold of Barney, dragging him from the car. He immediately wrapped that arm around Barney's chest and swung him round so that they both faced the rear of the car.

Using the force of someone who clearly meant business, he then rammed the barrel of the revolver against Barney's temple.

"Get out!" the man again screamed at the cashier. "I'll only count to two …"

"No," Barney shouted into the back of the car. "Stay there, sir. I can handle this clown."

He did his best to yank his head away from the gunman and swing him round. But what with his useless leg and his good one twisted under him, he did not have sufficient strength. For the first time, fear then gripped him. Was it the gunman's reaction at being called a clown? Or was it because things were not going according to plan? Whatever, the man's breath suddenly felt hot against the back of Barney's neck. It was the last thing he felt as a deafening report from the gun shattered the quiet Lamberhurst air.

Chapter 4

David felt the bile rising in his throat.

At the best of times, he abhorred the sight of blood. Not that it was blatant gore that now confronted him. But the outspread dark stain on the road was sufficient to turn his stomach.

Yet his disquiet and inner turmoil ran far deeper than this.

The victim must have been a banking colleague; not someone he was likely to have known, but a colleague, nonetheless. And the victim would have been an innocent official – carrying out normal banking duties. But, apart from the tragic end result, what else must that person have endured in the moments before being gunned down?

One thing for certain: David had now discovered his reaction on being confronted with such an heinous crime. He was both incensed and nauseated.

A rough chalk outline showed where the body had lain. It was not unlike blackboard drawings David had composed as a child. It certainly represented a human torso, but the limbs appeared as uncoordinated as those sketched by a five-year-old.

Doing his best to control his unsettled constitution – and how a shot of brandy would help him now – David stared down in disbelief. A steady drizzle had started to fall and the chalk lines were already beginning to fade. Not so the ugly, grim blemish which defaced the road. He could only ask himself one question: how could this horrific sketch, and what had lain within it, possibly represent a murdered member of the bank's staff?

"You all right, sir?"

David barely heard Trevor's words. He remained dumbstruck – appalled at what must have happened.

"Sir?"

David now raised his head. Trevor's greyish-green eyes betrayed the young man's thinking. And his concern seemed to be genuinely as much for his boss as for himself. Yet, those five years ago, it had been he who had been looking right down the barrel of a raider's gun.

"I'm okay, Trevor. But what about you?"

Trevor pursed his lips and nodded.

"I'm okay, sir."

David glanced back at the sketch in the road.

"Which is more than can be said for this poor fellow."

Until now, David's job as a bank inspector had been to travel around branches, inspecting ledgers and accounts and assessing the abilities of managers and their staff. When required, he would also conduct special investigations into alleged misdemeanours committed by staff or customers. Now, after three years, the final piece had been inserted into his inspectorial work-load jigsaw.

And, already, he did not like this added dimension to his job.

"Why couldn't we have been forewarned?" he muttered, through gritted teeth.

He was not questioning the motives of the gunman; a would-be assassin could hardly be expected to give advance warning of his intentions. But McPhoebe must have known more. An incident? Some incident!

"He probably didn't know," Trevor replied, correctly gauging the object of David's displeasure.

Anger now effectively shook David out of his stupor. At the same time, it seemed to be calming his stomach.

"Then he should have!"

He could not accept that, once again, he had been given an inadequate brief. Only last week, a McPhoebe-inspired bogus briefing had resulted in a wild-goose chase to investigate an alleged contretemps at Ramsgate. Apart from anything else, it was a prime reason why the inspection at Tenterden was behind schedule. Here in Lamberhurst, though, it had been anything but a wild-goose chase.

If only it had been.

He had feared the worst when he had driven down the hill into the village. Charming peg-tiled cottages lined the street and a typical Kent oast house stood at its bottom. They may as well not have been there; he only had eyes for the police tape which stretched across the road.

After parking the Consul, they were stopped in their tracks. One of what seemed like a two-man forensics team barred their way. He was clearly not pleased to be disturbed.

"Back where you came from. Can't come through here. You blind or something?"

David sighed and produced his identity card.

"We're from the bank – to investigate."

"A bit late for that."

The man was not endearing himself to David.

"That may well be so. But please … can we come through?"

The forensics man was now the one to sigh and he reluctantly raised the tape.

"If you must."

He then displayed where his priorities lay by brusquely turning away to get on with his forensics work.

David raised his eyebrows at Trevor.

"Straight out of charm school?"

A young, uniformed constable was the only other police presence. He was stationed at the front door of the closed sub-branch and had made no attempt to get involved in the discussion at the tape. It was as if he had been instructed to stay at his post, no matter what. Yet standing by the door seemed to be a futile gesture. The bank was clearly locked up and if the shooting had taken place in the actual road, it was more than likely the sub-branch had never been opened that morning.

Now, having drawn away from that dreadful depiction in the road, David turned his attention to this young policeman.

"What actually happened?"

The constable's demeanour and hesitancy in replying revealed an immaturity in the job. Or was he, as with the forensics man, just wary about these strangers arriving on the scene?

"I think I'd better see your card first."

David sighed again and reached into his wallet. The policeman then, duly satisfied, said a member of the bank's staff had been shot in the head, just before the sub-branch opened at ten.

David glanced back at the sketch in the road.

"And our man was shot down right there?"

The policeman nodded.

David raised his eyebrows.

"But apart from you being here – and those two over there …"

His words tailed off as the policeman put up his hand.

"Everyone else has gone. We had to act quickly. You might imagine, sir – gawping onlookers. There's always morbid curiosity."

The policeman might be over-embellishing his experience with such matters, but David could understand what he meant. It was the same at any motor accident. On a dual carriageway, those moving on the other side – with no obstacles in their way – would always slow down and gawp at the crash scene opposite. It was a wonder they did not cause another accident.

When he made no comment, the constable appeared spurred on to elaborate further.

"Moving the victim quickly was paramount. And the car has just been towed away."

"The car? You mean the bank's car?"

David knew it was more than likely the person attending the sub-branch would use his own car. Sub-branches did not necessarily operate full banking hours. For the required part of the day, a cashier would be seconded from the main parent branch – in this case, Tunbridge Wells, some eight miles away. Public transport would not normally be a feasible option, hence the use of private cars.

The policeman now looked unsure of himself.

"I suppose so. I wasn't actually told whose car it was."

David this time stifled his sigh. But something else was now bothering him. There must have been two people in the car. The cashier would have been accompanied by a guard, or another clerk.

What had happened to this other person?

And what about the money? Sub-branches did not normally have their own cash safes. That meant day-to-day cash requirements would accompany the staff in the car. Had this money been stolen? Had it been an armed robbery, or was the actual shooting the only factor in this appalling episode?

David looked hard at the policeman.

"What about the other person in the car? There must have been two people. And the cash? Was anything stolen?"

The policeman actually gulped before answering.

"I'm terribly sorry, sir. The cashier was abducted – by the gunman."

David felt he had been hit in the solar plexus. Abducted? The cashier had been abducted? So whose body had lain here in the road? It must have been the driver. The sub-branch guard?

But the policeman had not finished.

"And the money went with him. The bag containing the cash was chained to the man."

"But the chain could have been unlocked," Trevor butted in.

In other circumstances, David might have clapped Trevor on the back. It was a point well made. A sub-branch bag was always strapped to the bearer with a chain. This was then locked to the handle of the bag. It was a most effective deterrent to an opportunistic snatch.

But this was not, surely, an opportunistic snatch. The more David thought about it, the more it had the hallmark of earlier planning.

Yet, part of the plan could not possibly have been to take the man still strapped to his bag. It would have been far easier to demand the unlocking of the chain.

Especially with a loaded gun pointing at the cashier. A gun that had already been fired?

David immediately pursued Trevor's point with the policeman.

"Why didn't the gunman force the cashier to unlock the chain?"

Despite his rawness, the constable was confident enough to make no pretence at expressing his exasperation. It was clear he did not appreciate being expected to know how the gunman's mind had been working.

David quickly acknowledged that he had asked the impossible of the man. But who had been gunned down? Had it been the guard?

The policeman did not know and he was also starting to look irritated at this continuing inquisition. David took the hint, but there was one more thing he needed to establish.

"What about the gunman? He got clean away?"

The policeman nodded.

"Before anyone realized what had happened, the car was disappearing round the bend at the top of the hill – the way you came into the village."

David could imagine the speed of the whole operation, but the absence of witnesses was disturbing. He could also see there must be myriad routes for an escaping car to take.

But this was a matter for the police – as was the actual murder investigation.

For his own part, there was important business for Trevor and him to do – not here, but in Tunbridge Wells. Although his queasiness had disappeared – without the need for that brandy – he felt distinctly unsettled. How would the manager and his staff be handling the trauma of the murder of one colleague and the abduction of another?

And what was more, could the whole tragic episode have been prevented?

CHAPTER 5

Alfie Templeton rammed his right foot down into the floor of the car. The rear tyres squealed in protest. Even inside the Oxford, he could smell the distinctive odour of burning rubber.

The road ahead was a blur. All he could clearly see was that expression in the man's eyes. He would never forget that anguished look. For God's sake, why had such an apology for an old soldier taken it upon himself to be so brave?

Why could the man not accept that the money would be stolen – no matter what he did to try and prevent it?

Templeton's knuckles gleamed white as he gripped the steering wheel. His Morris Oxford screamed in torment as it raced up the hill out of Lamberhurst. The tank-like car had not been built to be driven like this. Even in his present high state of anxiety, Templeton could appreciate the irony. He had acquired the car simply because of its copious boot space – not for its ability to mimic a racing car.

He tore past a speed restriction sign which boldly displayed 30, but what did that matter? After what he had done, they would hardly nab him for a speeding offence.

Thank God there was no other traffic. But why should that be? On the main A21 down to the coast? Perhaps there was an accident ahead. That would be all he needed. It would be just his luck to beat his retreat right into a posse of policemen – officers who would be far better employed back there in Lamberhurst.

But accident or not, he needed to get off this main road quickly.

He knew exactly what to do. He had got to know the area well in the last few days. His judicious planning would now reap its reward. The next turning would take him towards the village of Horsmonden. From there, various options would be open to him – none necessitating the use of the main highways.

There was still no traffic coming the other way and the sooner he reached the turning the better. At least the absence of other vehicles meant there were no possible witnesses of his speeding Oxford. He had already been riding his luck; there had been no pedestrians on the hill out of Lamberhurst. And to the best of his knowledge, there had been no eyewitnesses at the bank itself – apart from him in the rear seat.

Almost immediately, the turning was upon him. He took it so quickly he had visions of overturning the car. What a catastrophe that would have been. He immediately slowed down, necessitated anyway by the narrower, winding road. An unusually warm spring had already coaxed growth into the beech and hawthorn hedgerows and, even at the lower speed, the nearside of the car came into contact with spiky sprigs. Not that Templeton cared. He had not chosen this car for long-term use. And with what was stashed in the boot and in the case on the back seat, the last thing he was thinking about was any re-sale value in the car.

Then, even above the roar of the engine, another sound compounded his agitation: piteous sobbing from the back of the car.

Templeton glanced in the rear view mirror, adjusting it downward to take in the rear seats. His passenger was certainly doing as he had been told: crouching low to avoid being seen through the windows. That was something, but Templeton could well do without the resonant blubbering.

"Shut up!" he snarled back.

He needed all his faculties to concentrate, without such audible intrusion from the rear seat. And especially with that vision of the guard still firmly implanted in his mind. Why could the man not have obeyed the bank's rules?

Templeton, himself, knew full well what was required. So why not the guard? For a start, there must be no heroics. Faced by a gunman, bank staff must do as they are told. Cash can be replaced. Dead bodies are terminal. So what was the old man thinking about?

And the guard's final words still echoed in Templeton's ears:

"Stay there, sir. I can handle this clown."

Clown? Imbecile, more like it.

Templeton could still not believe what he had done. How could he really expect to get away with it this time? As he held the steering wheel, he could actually see blood on the sleeves of his jacket. It must also be all down his front. For all he knew, his face could be splattered. He looked at himself in the rear view mirror. There was nothing obvious, but even the most minute spot would not escape close examination. One thing for sure: he could not afford to let anyone get close enough to make such an inspection.

He had better slow down even more – especially as Lamberhurst was now several miles behind them. He could not afford to draw attention to the car. And what could be more innocent than a Morris Oxford moseying along country roads? It should hardly bring overt attention to itself.

Perhaps it was the reduced pace of his driving. Perhaps it was the distance he had put between the car and the village of Lamberhurst. Whatever, for some reason he was starting to calm down. Yet he knew the nightmare would never die.

Killing that guard, or even hurting him, had never been part of the plan. Why had he done it? Never before had he fired a gun. Why had he chosen to do so now?

As for the after effects …

He had been so ill-prepared for the outcome. In films, it was totally different. The gun would be fired, the bullet would hit the target and the body would fall to the ground. There was never any blood. Yet, back there, it had spurted from the old man like a burst water main.

Templeton instinctively wiped the back of his hand across his face. He must, surely, be splattered with blood. If it had sullied his clothes, his skin could not have possibly escaped. And he now remembered feeling it at the time – hard to imagine, but wet and warm. Ugh! Somehow, somewhere, he needed to stop and clean up.

He looked in the mirror again. What was going on in the back?

"Get down! Get out of sight."

The last thing he needed was for someone to see a passenger sitting up in the back of the car. A slip like that could come back to haunt him.

The only response, apart from ducking down, was further heart-rending sobbing. Templeton felt like screaming. How could he concentrate on all his problems with that going on behind him?

Then his heart almost stopped beating. It was the sound he hoped never to hear: a bell – reverberating stridently, somewhere in the distance.

But from which direction? Was it coming from behind, or in front? The road was now winding back and forth sharply and the high hedgerows made the sighting of another vehicle impossible.

He looked in the mirror, expecting to see a black Wolseley to confirm his worst fears. But nothing appeared.

He then realized the sound of the bell was coming towards him and the top of a white ambulance came into view above the hedge just beyond the next corner.

He almost veered off the road as the ambulance flew round the bend, but it did not prevent his grinning in relief. Not the police. Just an ambulance heading for the A21 – to that accident he had been wondering about? Templeton could only hope that such an incident would concentrate the minds of all the police in the area. The fewer who were left to go after him, the better.

Chapter 6

David normally enjoyed being behind the wheel of his Consul.

When he was promoted from manager of Barnmouth branch to the inspection staff, the bank had provided him with the car. For him, it had been an admirable arrangement; he had been able to sell his previous Hillman Minx. The resultant cash had certainly eased the financial burden of moving up from South Devon.

But, today, any enjoyment at driving the car had deserted him. In his role as an inspector, he could not imagine being in a worse case scenario.

The journey from Lamberhurst to Tunbridge Wells would take about fifteen minutes. It was little enough time to take in the enormity of what had happened and what they would now face.

He sensed Trevor felt the same as the lad glanced across at him.

"What do you reckon, sir?"

Reckon? This whole affair was beyond David's calculation. He had not been prepared for it. It was as if he were in alien territory.

And he knew there would be so much to do – without his full team complement. For a week his senior assistant, Phil Matthews, had been down with flu. It was another reason why they were behind schedule at Tenterden. Trevor was good, but he was still raw. Would he be capable of what would be required at Tunbridge Wells?

"One thing's for certain. I reckon we've got our hands full."

"Phil might be back tomorrow."

That was a possibility. But you never could tell with flu.

"Let's hope so. If not …"

Trevor remained quiet for a moment. Then he started humming *Singing the Blues*.

Despite the circumstances, David smiled. It almost lightened his mood.

"That might be spot on."

Back in their Barnmouth days, he and Trevor had shared two passions: football and jazz. In the case of football, now that he lived in Kent, a round trip of nearly five hundred miles to see Torquay United was clearly not on. So he had to spin a coin for the best local team: Crystal Palace or Charlton? Palace had won and he had supported them for the last three years. All he had to do now was to persuade Trevor to transfer his allegiance to the Glaziers.

As for jazz, David only listened, but Trevor played a mean tenor saxophone. He was good enough to play professionally and his move to the London area was to give him more playing opportunities in his spare time. David could only hope that National Counties would not ultimately lose him to the likes of Ronnie Scott's. And just thinking of one of the capital's premier jazz clubs was making him feel thirsty.

"The blues," he continued, "might prove good enough reason for us to have a drink by the time we're done today."

At least there were some good hostelries in Tunbridge Wells. It was one reason why he was glad to have bought a house in the town. It had not been high on his darling Sarah's priorities; she had been more concerned about nine-year-old Mark's schooling.

For the remainder of the journey, they remained silent with their thoughts.

At Tunbridge Wells, David rounded the corner at the railway station and just hoped they would find a convenient parking space in Mount Pleasant. Those heavy bags in the back still occupied his mind.

He immediately spotted one small space, but had to pass it by. It was big enough for a Minx, but not the Consul.

Just when he was envisaging a weary trudge from one of the car parks, a Humber Super Snipe eased away from the kerb, right opposite the branch of National Counties. David immediately reversed into the vacated space, drawing forth from Trevor a nod of satisfaction. But was this an acknowledgement of skilful parking or simply relief at not having to traipse far with a heavy bag?

Now, finally at the branch, what were they about to discover?

They unloaded the bags from the back, locked the car and made across the road. David then saw that the front door was closed for business. A man was reading a hand-written notice that was pinned to the door. He then turned away, clearly frustrated at what he had read.

David was not surprised the bank was closed, if only temporarily. Even if the police were not inside, the staff were unlikely to be in the right frame of mind to carry on as normal.

They reached the front door and David rang the bell.

"When we get in, Trevor, I want you to sort us out a room – a lockable one, for our bags. I'm going to go straight to the manager. While I'm with him, nose around the general office. But keep a low profile. The staff will be feeling bad enough, without having the inspectors on their backs. Just try and get their perspective on what's happened. It's likely to be only hearsay or rumour. But you might get a different slant on things. Different from what I hear from the manager."

It was a good role for Trevor to play. Although he was inexperienced in the job, he was still a branch man at heart. He would have empathy with the others. He should also be able to gain their confidence.

Which was something David was unlikely to achieve with the manager.

David remembered him well : Mr Fawkes-William – or Colonel Fawkes-William, as he still liked to be called.

Three years ago, David's first inspection had been at Tunbridge Wells. He had been only too aware of his inexperience, but he could have done without the Colonel openly questioning his greenness.

The manager had clearly seen himself as an old warhorse and had no time for sprogs. That was the trouble with men like him: they had short memories. They failed to recognize that they, too, had once been found wanting in experience.

But it had been worse than that with Colonel Fawkes-William.

Throughout the inspection, he had attempted to influence David's operations. He had tried to point him in certain directions and away from others. Even with David's inexperience, alarm bells had started to ring. Was the Colonel trying to hide something? Was he attempting to suppress possible transgressions? Trying to put David off the scent?

Yet, by the end of the inspection, David had discovered nothing untoward going on. So, was it just the Colonel's arrogant attitude that had got under his skin? Or had he missed something?

Now, three years later, he had to face this loathsome man again.

They were let into the bank by the office junior. And thank goodness he actually made proper use of the security chain before allowing them in. This was certainly not the day to break rules on security.

Leaving Trevor to make acquaintance with the sub-manager, prior to his enquiries around the general office, David made for the stairway. It led to the investments and securities department, set alongside the manager's room. The door to that room stood open and Colonel Fawkes-William sat opposite, behind an imposing mahogany desk. David remembered his being about five foot six, but the desk made him appear even smaller. When he became aware of David standing in the doorway, he raised his eyes over his pince-nez.

"Ah, Goodhart. And about time, too. Where have you been?"

David took a mental step backwards, before moving into the room. This was not a good start.

"Good afternoon, Colonel Fawkes-William. You were expecting me then?"

David had considered addressing the Colonel as Mr, but resisted the temptation. He firmly believed some ex-army officers desperately clung on to their service titles with questionable justification, though others fully deserved to maintain their ranks into civilian life. In case Colonel Fawkes-William belonged to the latter school, David decided to give him the benefit of any doubt.

Colonel Fawkes-William remained seated and made no move to shake David's hand. His mood was dark, emphasizing the lines etched into his haughty face. But, no wonder, after what had happened to his staff. And David knew his mood would be even blacker if he had not been addressed as Colonel.

"McPhoebe phoned. Said you were at Tenterden. But couldn't reach you. Left you a message. Seems it caught up with you."

David recalled this staccato way of speaking from three years ago. The clipped words and sentences were almost a parody of how some army officers might be depicted in films. Perhaps the film makers had got it right. Did officers and gentlemen really speak like this?

But David was not simply irritated by this man's mannerisms and his less than hospitable welcome; he was not best pleased with McPhoebe's clear indiscretion. But he would not respond to the Colonel's use of this particular bait.

"Caught up with me? Apparently so."

David remained standing in front of the desk. He was being deliberately made to feel like a naughty schoolboy. The Colonel eventually waved him to one of the two chairs opposite him.

"So you've come from Tenterden? Via Lamberhurst?"

David nodded.

Colonel Fawkes-William pursed his lips and stroked his pencil-thin moustache.

"I'd have gone myself. But you know how it is, what?"

Really? Lamberhurst was only 15-20 minutes away. Had the man not even tried to get there?

"A bad business," the Colonel added. "A truly bad business. God knows how this might affect my branch."

Affect his branch? One man murdered and another abducted. And the manager was worried how it might affect his branch?

This was certainly a time for counting up to ten. Yet David's attempt to conceal his astonishment had been ill-disguised. The Colonel started to huff and puff.

"I had to close the branch here. Couldn't keep it open. For further business, you know. The police agreed. They've gone now. Much more for them to do elsewhere. I can't believe Fairweather's been taken."

"Fairweather?"

"Douglas Fairweather. Our man. Our cashier. But he was far more important than that. That's what's so tragic. He's such a good man. I've been grooming him for management. He's been abducted. By the gunman."

Colonel Fawkes-William paused, as if reluctant to elaborate. But he then decided to continue.

"Not only abducted, but with all the cash."

Although David had already learnt this from the policeman, he was shocked at the Colonel's apparent train of thought. By his own admission, the man's concern appeared to relate to the effect of it all on his branch, while the loss of the cash seemed to be as significant as the actual abduction of Fairweather. Or was this a deliberate ploy on his part? No, this was hardly the time for ploys to be used, but David would not put anything past a man who had still to make any mention of the man who had actually been murdered.

He stared hard at the manager and posed the question.

"So who was it that was killed?"

It was now the Colonel's turn to display astonishment.

"Killed?"

"Yes, the driver of the car."

The manager actually leaned back in his chair, relief embracing his face.

"The driver was Barney Wilson. Our guard. No, he's not been killed. He's in hospital. The Kent and Sussex, up the road. Intensive care, you know. Unconscious. But he'll pull through."

"But I saw the sketch in the road. The one the police drew around the body."

Colonel Fawkes-William smiled smugly. It was as if he relished being one step ahead.

"The police got it wrong, what? Goodness knows how. Must have assumed the worst. Wilson lying in the road. Shot in the head."

David could hardly believe what he was hearing. The police got it wrong? It would seem the young constable outside the sub-branch was not the only inexperienced officer on the case.

But the Colonel's matter of fact account of what had happened almost over-shadowed David's relief that the guard was still alive. Where was the manager's compassion? Where was his concern for a man in hospital, quite clearly critically injured? What possible justification did the manager have in making his throwaway assessment that Wilson would pull through?

"Have you been to see him?"

Colonel Fawkes-William looked at David as if he were mad.

"See him? I just said, he's in Intensive Care. No one can see him."

"Are the police with him?"

"Of course they are! He's a prime witness. If he comes round."

So there was a doubt.

"Tell me more about him."

"Wilson?"

The man was now being obtuse. It went well with the way he continued to peer over his pince-nez.

"Yes. You say it was Barney Wilson?"

The Colonel nodded.

"He's been a guard here for about 10 years."

"Not a young man?"

"Late sixties. Ex-army. First world war. Invalided out. Don't know why. He was only a batman."

Only a batman? What had that got to do with it? Would the Colonel be more sympathetic if Barney Wilson had been an officer?

"You say he was invalided out. But he was fit enough to do guard duties here?"

"Yes, he's been fit enough. Got a limp. Some sort of war wound, I suppose. But it wouldn't have been front-line stuff. As a batman."

What made men like Colonel Fawkes-William tick? How could he differentiate so disparagingly between individuals based on a role and rank basis? It was out-of-the-ark stuff. Was this how he managed his branch?

"Does his limp affect his work? As a guard? He could clearly drive, but …"

"No, it's not that pronounced. Wilson can do his job all right. It wasn't as if he'd got it by going over the top."

David, somehow, kept his anger under wraps.

"It must have been the equivalent of going over the top this morning."

Colonel Fawkes-William either missed the sarcasm, or chose to ignore it.

"At least he's still alive. As for Douglas …"

The manager certainly had every right to be concerned about the welfare of Douglas Fairweather, but it did seem to be in some contrast to how he felt about his guard. Perhaps David was reading too much into this and he certainly needed to learn more about the cashier.

"You said you were grooming him for management. Here?"

Colonel Fawkes-William nodded and seemed to swell with pride. He leaned back in his chair and clasped his hands to the back of his head.

"Douglas is my number three here. That's why his disappearance is so tragic."

Because of being number three? What if he had been a junior? Or the guard, even?

"If he's so senior, why was he acting as your sub-branch cashier?"

The Colonel smiled in self-satisfaction.

"It may only be a sub-branch now, what? But I'm getting it upgraded to sub-manager-in-charge status. When that happens … well let's just say my branch here will also be upgraded."

David was well aware of the bank's system and the Colonel may well be right, but it was odd hearing him talk about it in this way.

"And your Douglas Fairweather would be the sub-manager?"

The Colonel continued to be well-pleased with himself.

"That's been my long-term plan. As I said, I've been grooming Douglas. Getting him involved with the Lamberhurst set. It's a wealthy village. Good people, what? Douglas is just the man. I actually recruited him, you know."

"You what?"

Recruitment of staff was not down to branch management. That was the preserve of regional staff managers.

Colonel Fawkes-William puffed out his chest, removed his pince-nez from the end of his nose and started to polish the lenses with a voluminous handkerchief he had removed from the sleeve of his jacket.

"It was about five years ago. I met Douglas in the Conservative Club. He'd just come back from India. He was a manager there with Grindlays. In Calcutta. But he'd had ill health. Something to do with the climate. I sized him up immediately. Just our type. And I needed someone with his qualities."

"But what about the RSM? He should have done the recruiting."

"Oh, he was no trouble. I can wrap him round my little finger."

It was now all coming back to David. He could remember Fairweather from his last inspection. And the manager was right. Fairweather had been an able man. But his capability had not been his only attribute. His appearance had been so striking. With his silky blond locks he must have come from Scandinavian stock. He could certainly do with some Viking blood now – to see him through his present ordeal.

But David had no idea the Colonel had actually recruited him. It was surprising he had not boasted about it at the time.

Colonel Fawkes-William replaced his glasses on the end of his nose and looked down at David.

"Anyway, the RSM was impressed with the reference I got. But there was no vacancy here for a sub-manager. If he was to become a manager, he'd have to do that job first. Couldn't have him step into my shoes straight away, what?"

He paused, as if waiting for David's approval of his witticism. When this failed to materialize, he carried on with his explanation.

"So I've been biding my time … grooming Douglas in the right way. Getting him involved with interviews at Lamberhurst. Lending money. And it's worked out perfectly. He'll be ideal as sub-manager-in-charge."

"Except that he's now been abducted."

Colonel Fawkes-William now looked stunned. It was as if he had temporarily forgotten what this meeting was all about. How could that be possible? What drove him on? His guard nearly murdered and his cashier having been abducted, yet the man could only crow about his plans for the upgrading of his sub-branch and his selection of the person to run it. These points must now have hit home. He could not hide the increasing discomfort which lurked in his eyes as he struggled to reply.

"And abducted with all that cash."

It was now difficult for David not to view the manager with contempt.

"Colonel Fawkes-William, surely the loss of a few pounds is the least important consideration."

The Colonel immediately rose and moved to the window which overlooked Mount Pleasant. David frowned. How odd. It was as if the manager did not want to talk about the money that had been stolen.

Eventually, still with his back to David, the Colonel deigned to reply.

"It wasn't just a few pounds in the sub-branch case. It was well over £50,000."

Chapter 7

"£50,000?"

David was shocked. He thought back to the time he had bought his house in Tunbridge Wells. It had cost £5,000. Even though this was three years ago, it had probably not increased much in value since then. It was simply extraordinary how many such houses the contents of the sub-branch case could buy.

Colonel Fawkes-William returned to his desk and David tried to make eye contact with him. But the manager was concentrating on his hands. They rested on his desk, fingers intertwined.

"Colonel Fawkes-William?"

The manager kept staring down at his hands.

"Colonel Fawkes-William? You can't really be serious."

The Colonel now looked up, shook his head, but remained silent.

"Why so much, Colonel?"

The manager slumped back in his chair and removed his pince-nez for yet another polish. He then raised his eyes to the ceiling, as if summoning inspiration from on high.

"Wages, I suppose," he eventually muttered.

But this was a Monday, in the middle of the month. In any case, a village like Lamberhurst could not possibly muster sufficient large employers to warrant such a high wages bill.

"At Lamberhurst?"

Fire now returned to the manager's eyes and he glowered across the table.

"I just told you. There's good business at Lamberhurst. That's why it'll be upgraded."

No. That was not good enough. How many people would be employed around the village? 100? 500? 1,000? Taking the unimaginable figure of 1,000, with each person paid about £10 a week, the wage bill would be an absurd £10,000. It would have been bad enough having that amount in the sub-branch case. Yet there was over £50,000 in it.

David eyeballed the Colonel.

"I think you'd better elaborate. I don't remember any large businesses in Lamberhurst at my last inspection. And they'd need to be huge concerns to justify such high wages."

As he spoke he noted the Colonel returning to his innate self. This was a man who clearly deemed it his rightful place to be the one to exercise control of a situation – especially with this upstart of an inspector in front of him.

"Things have moved on since then, Goodhart. South-East Pharmaceuticals started up in Lamberhurst a couple of years ago. And Kentish Provident have moved from Tunbridge Wells. And don't forget the farmers. It's big hop growing country, you know."

Except that it was still only March. It would be months before the invasion of the army of hop pickers. As for the other businesses … Most of their employees would be paid monthly into bank accounts or, at least, by cheque. Weekly cash wages would only be minimal.

No, the Colonel's explanation was flawed. Or was he trying to lead David down a blind alley? Deliberately?

"But, Colonel Fawkes-William, you're saying the money would be needed for wages. Yet, just now, you seemed to be reluctant to admit there was £50,000 in the sub-branch case."

The Colonel smiled knowingly.

"That's before I'd really thought it through."

"You mean you just accepted it when you were told how much?"

"You might imagine, Goodhart, I had other things on my mind."

That was fair enough, but there was no doubting the relevance of the vast sum that had been stolen. And the Colonel had been distinctly uneasy when he had made the admission of the amount. This was not, then, the moment for David to be directed back to those 'other things'.

"Your first cashier told you the amount?"

The number one, or first, cashier was in charge of a branch's overall cash resources. He maintained control of how much each cashier retained in his till and would certainly be aware of the cash requirements at the sub-branches.

"Well … no … not exactly. He didn't turn up for work today."

"He's ill?"

"I don't know. He just didn't turn up."

David took a deep breath. He readily acknowledged there were different ways in which to manage a branch. What might be appropriate in one place might not necessarily work elsewhere. But effective man-management needed to apply everywhere. And if anyone simply did not turn up for work, let alone someone as significant as the first cashier, it should not be beyond the wits of any manager to ask why. Apart, it seemed, from Colonel Fawkes-William.

The manager read David's incredulity correctly and started to bluster.

"I don't think, Goodhart, that you have grasped the enormity of what has happened today. Have you any idea of what it's been like? To have someone gunned down and another abducted? The absence of my first cashier – probably because he really is ill – hardly rates highly in the significance of what's happened."

"So who's your acting first cashier? Did this person tell you about the £50,000?"

Fawkes-William sighed deeply.

"Goodhart, my dear fellow, I can see I've not made myself clear …"

"Colonel Fawkes-William, on the contrary, you have made yourself perfectly clear. Except that you have still not said who told you about the money."

Yet again, the manager removed his pince-nez and polished each lens vigorously before replying.

"I think it must have been Barnett."

"Barnett?"

The Colonel nodded.

"My sub-manager. And I hope you're not going to grill him like this. He's got far more important things on his plate."

David could only assume the Colonel believed he had come to the branch on his own. Was it too late to get word to Trevor downstairs not to grill the sub-manager? Not that Trevor would operate in such a manner. But one way or the other, he could well be having more success than his boss as to what had been going on in the branch – before and after the actual hold-up.

CHAPTER 8

Trevor had taken a deep breath when he entered the branch. A cocktail of excitement and apprehension mixed uneasily with a slice of indignation. He was, surely, too young and inexperienced to carry out such a task. Mr Goodhart should have realized that. It was a job for a senior assistant. Yet his boss had been given no choice; Phil Matthews was still down with flu.

On the other hand, Mr Goodhart must have faith in him, otherwise they would not be working together now. It went back to their days in Barnmouth, yet that was three years ago. Time enough for people to change. But Mr Goodhart appeared to be much the same, although his penchant for beer had definitely increased. No doubt this accounted for his expanded girth. Yet at nearly six foot, he could carry some extra weight without it appearing to be excessive.

One other difference was that Mr Goodhart had become a stickler for attention to detail. That, of course, went with the territory as an inspector, but he seemed to be constantly correcting Trevor, one way or another. "Must maintain standards, Trevor," was an all too familiar refrain. Written reports, in particular, had to be grammatically correct, not to mention punctuation. In this respect, Trevor repeatedly erred with the ubiquitous apostrophe, either leaving it out, or putting it in the wrong place.

It had been a particularly bad moment when, in one report, he had to refer to their London branch in St James's Street and he had left off the final s in James's. Mr Goodhart had not been impressed. Nor when Trevor had then pointed out that Newcastle United's ground at St James' Park did not include such an s. That duly brought forth, "two wrongs don't make a right, Trevor."

So, Trevor was determined to be meticulous as he prepared to delve into the reaction around the general office. And, despite his inexperience, he would do his best to exhibit self-confidence, especially after the faith Mr Goodhart had put in him.

He strode into the branch, excitement starting to take over, though still mixed with apprehension.

But why not feel some disquiet?

At twenty-four, he must be one of the youngest inspector's assistants with National Counties. Young and inexperienced. And he was miles away from his previous South Devon comfort zone. Applying to come to the London area had seemed a good idea at the time – if only to become embroiled in the jazz world. But, with banking, everyone up here seemed to be so much more worldly-wise.

He knew that his early promotion was due largely to the part he had played in a criminal investigation back in Barnmouth. But this new job had made him patently aware of the gaps in his technical knowledge and training. Time had simply not been on his side.

And now he must face a far more experienced sub-manager and his staff.

Yet these people were not to know about his own relative inexperience – unless he made it obvious by a naivety in carrying out his investigation. Taking another deep breath, he was determined this would not be the case.

Weighed down by his two laden bags, he immediately spotted the likely sub-manager. The man was seated behind a large desk at the back of the office. Low glass screens around the desk set it apart from the other long desks where much of the branch's routine work would be carried out.

The sub-manager, though sitting down, appeared to be a small man, his ill-fitting shirt collar and jacket making him seem emaciated. He looked to be about sixty, in which case, he must be nearing retirement. If so, what an appalling retirement present this hold-up and its consequences would prove to be.

The man's pallor and demeanour spoke volumes about how he must be feeling. He sat slumped at his desk, staring into space, and he seemed oblivious of Trevor's approach.

Placing his bags on the floor by the desk, Trevor quietly cleared his throat.

The sub-manager turned to him, his dull eyes hardly registering the presence of a stranger. Yet word must already have been passed to him by the office junior that inspectors had arrived. A man of his experience would also have been expecting such visitors.

Trevor held out his hand.

"I'm Trevor Smith, part of the inspection team."

The man extended his own hand, which then lay limp in Trevor's grasp, but he said nothing. A little unnerved, Trevor felt he had no option but to persist.

"I say team, but, at this stage, it's only two of us. Mr Goodhart's the inspector and he's gone straight upstairs to see the manager. And you are?"

In the circumstances, Trevor would have preferred not to ask such a direct question, but the man's silence gave him no choice.

"Barnett," the sub-manager eventually replied. "I'm sorry, sir … it's just that I can't believe what's happened today."

Sir? Trevor could not have wished for a better boost to his self-confidence. It was the first time he had ever been called sir – anywhere. Having said that, it was clearly his position with the bank that was earning the sub-manager's respect: the bank's man from Head Office. Trevor's main task now was to ensure that he, as a person, should deserve such high regard.

"I think that must be an understatement, Mr Barnett. We've just come from Lamberhurst and …"

"Poor old Barney."

"Barney?"

"Barney Wilson, sir. Our guard. Gunned down. He's now fighting for his life. Up at the Kent & Sussex."

Trevor's mind flashed back to Lamberhurst

"Your driver? You mean he wasn't killed?"

Relief coursed through him as the sub-manager recounted what he understood to have happened. The sketch in the road had certainly not prepared Trevor for any good news, whatsoever.

"We're all praying for Barney," Mr Barnett continued. "He's the salt of the earth. So popular with everyone here. Perhaps not with him upstairs. But Barney would do anything for anyone. He just doesn't deserve to have …"

His words tailed off and his eyes filled with tears.

Trevor looked away. He had never seen a grown man cry; he was experiencing so many firsts today. Perhaps now might be the time to sort out a room for the bags.

Mr Barnett seemed relieved at the change of subject and led Trevor through a door at the back of the office. They immediately passed the main strongroom on the right and Trevor drew in his breath. Although it was normal for the outer fortified door to remain open during the day, the inner grille must always remain closed and double-locked, unless staff were present inside the safe. This grille was wide open, with no one inside.

Before he could say anything, he was led further down the passage. They passed the staff rest room and then came to a final door at the end of the corridor. The sub-manager opened the door to reveal a box room, no bigger than the room they had left earlier in Tenterden. Perhaps there was a conspiracy in branches to minimize hospitality towards visiting bank inspectors.

At least the door had a lock, into which a key was already inserted. The sub-manager withdrew the key and handed it to Trevor.

"Will this room be suitable, sir?"

Trevor nodded. There was clearly no alternative. He entered the room and placed the bags alongside one of two small desks. He immediately turned tail to leave the room and locked the door behind them. He was anxious to learn more about the abduction of the cashier and his cash, but not here. It was not inconceivable that Mr Barnett might break down completely within the confines of this small room. Even with his new-found confidence, Trevor was not sure how he would cope with that.

They retraced their steps along the passage and reached the

unlocked strongroom. Trevor decided it would be a dereliction of duty to overlook this major lapse in branch security. He pointed at the wide-open grille.

"What's going on here, Mr Barnett?"

The sub-manager now looked flustered. He had clearly not noticed this negligent oversight.

"That's the casualness of youth, damn it."

Trevor was as much surprised to hear the mild oath as to the blame being put on the shoulders of young staff. This was not what he would expect from a sub-manager on top of his job.

"I don't follow you, Mr Barnett. The casualness of youth?"

The sub-manager now looked dejected. He clearly realized he had no escape from this black mark from the inspectors. He leant heavily against the strongroom's outer door.

"Oh, God. Everything's gone wrong today."

Trevor was not sure how to react. Was the man on the point of losing it? On the strength of an open strongroom grille door? It was certainly an unforgivable oversight, but in the context of a shooting and an abduction?

Mr Barnett then gave a shrug of resignation.

"Grimshawe didn't turn up this morning."

"Who's Grimshawe?"

"Our first cashier."

"Is he ill?"

"We don't know."

"Have you rung his home?"

The sub-manager nodded.

"No one answered."

"Is he married?"

"Yes. But Mrs Grimshawe couldn't have been there, either."

Trevor frowned. This all sounded rather odd. Never mind it being on top of everything else.

"What about his keys? Does he hold one for this strongroom?"

The sub-manager sighed.

"He does. So we had to get out the duplicates. The sealed packets are all held at Lloyds."

That was normal. It was the procedure all the banks used. If such a system of obtaining duplicates was not in place, the bank would not be able to open. But timing at this branch could be critical. With sub-branches in operation, their staff and the cash had to be underway long before normal branch opening time.

"Did that create a time problem?"

The sub-manager shook his head.

"No. Grimshawe always gets in by eight-thirty. We gave him quarter of an hour and then rang Lloyds. Fortunately their keyholders had turned up and we got our duplicates by nine. But what a start to such a bad day. And now this."

Mr Barnett pointed at the open grille as he eased himself away from the door.

But Trevor was still puzzled.

"So what's this about the youngsters?"

The sub-manager looked contrite.

"I had to give Grimshawe's duplicate strongroom key to a junior. And the other key was also held by one of our young staff. I had no choice. No one else was available."

"What about yourself?"

Mr Bartlett actually recoiled at the suggestion, as if the holding of such keys was beneath the dignity of someone in his position. Had Trevor opened up a wound in the man's psyche? Without waiting for a reply, he decided to pursue the point.

"At the very least, you should have kept your eyes on what's going on. Especially if you're concerned at the so-called casualness of youth."

But Trevor immediately regretted his stance. He had broken the promise he had made to himself three months ago. Never would he play the role of archetypal inspector's assistant. He had seen them in the past – treating branch staff as if they were second-class citizens. It was certainly his job to ensure security procedures were properly in place, but he should not overlook the bigger picture. And nothing could be bigger than what had happened to this branch today. The sub-manager and his staff deserved some respite after all that had occurred.

"Come on, Mr Barnett," he said, putting a comforting arm around the sub-manager's shoulders, "let's get back to your desk."

When they reached the general office, the sub-manager described what he knew about the abduction of Douglas Fairweather, the Lamberhurst cashier, and his sub-branch case. But it was no different from what Trevor already knew. Mr Barnett had also been through it all with the police and he was resigned to the fact that there would be no happy ending to this dreadful episode.

Leaving the sub-manager to sort out the keys to the strongroom, Trevor decided to get the views of some other staff. He felt distinctly uneasy about Mr Barnett. There was something not quite right. The man had only shown real compassion for Barney Wilson. He was genuinely upset about this popular guard. But as for everyone else? It was as if he simply couldn't care. As for 'him upstairs'…

Chapter 9

The exquisite head was enough to make David salivate. Just gazing at its perfection was almost as good as it gets. Almost. On this occasion, the end result would be better than the anticipation. But it was good to relish the before and the after.

He and Trevor were sitting quietly in the lounge bar of the Kentish Yeoman, a popular hostelry in Grove Hill Road, at the bottom of Mount Pleasant. Two foaming tankards of Harvey's best bitter lay before them. Even Trevor had chosen this tipple, dismissing his usual choice of a non-alcoholic beverage.

It seemed they both needed this pick-me-up.

David raised his glass to Trevor and then to his lips. He dug deeply into the nectar and then, with the back of his hand, wiped away the resultant white froth from his upper lip.

"Well, Trevor, what have we got ourselves into?"

Trevor sipped his own beer and pulled a face.

"I don't know why I ordered this."

David pursed his lips. These young boys. What was the world coming to? On the other hand, his own partiality to real ale was relatively newfangled. Back in Devon he had stuck mainly to proprietary brands; Watney's Red Barrel had been a favourite tipple. But up here, hop fields abounded. On their way to and from branches, they passed one such field after another. It was enough to whet anyone's appetite for the real stuff.

Though not, apparently, Trevor's.

"Just persevere, Trevor. That's the answer. You'll soon conquer your doubts. But getting back to the branch. What do you think?"

Trevor placed his tankard on the small table in front of them and frowned.

"I reckon there's more to this branch than meets the eye. But how did you get on with the manager?"

Trevor had posed this question back in the branch, but David had resisted answering. He had been concerned about the lack of privacy; there were too many ears around. The alternative was to be ensconced in the small room the sub-manager had allocated to them. But that was not an option.

There had been so much to do – and no time for any discussion.

After carrying out their respective investigations, they had to count all the cash – apart from the first cashier's. In his absence, this remained locked in his personal cash box and safe in the strongroom.

For the time being, David decided to leave it like that. Otherwise, he would need to resort to Lloyds Bank and get out the duplicate keys for the first cashier's till. Yet, he had no reason to believe this till would have any bearing on the stolen money. So, he restricted their cash check to the remaining money in the branch. That was bad enough. With only two of them, it had been a long haul.

Without having been forewarned by the manager, he would never have anticipated the outcome. £52,076 had disappeared – more or less equating to the manager's estimate.

At the start of the count, David had told Trevor of the likely outcome. The lad had been visibly shocked, the sub-manager having made no mention of it to him earlier. Why should that be? Had the man deliberately held back information which might reflect badly on himself?

Now, in the pub, with all that behind them, there was much to discuss and Trevor's question made a good starting point. David was still disconcerted over his meeting with Colonel Fawkes-William.

"Let me just say, Trevor, that the manager is not a role model you should aspire to."

Trevor raised his eyebrows and appeared shocked at this statement.

"That doesn't sound encouraging."

"I met him three years ago. My first inspection was here in

Tunbridge Wells. I didn't believe the bank still had such managers."

"In what way, sir?"

"For a start, he treated me like a novice. I suppose I was, in a way, but there was no need to rub my nose in my inexperience."

"Especially when you were inspecting his branch. Doesn't seem very sensible to me."

"He's that sort of man. Still calls himself Colonel. He's probably a great proponent of feudalism. It makes you want to speculate on his real background. And I wonder what he actually did in the army?"

Trevor took a sip of his beer.

"Sounds as though he might have a chip on his shoulder."

"Yes, but why? For some reason he certainly believes himself to be a cut above the rest. And he was so disparaging about Barney Wilson – about his being only a batman in the army. As if he didn't matter. Yet Barney Wilson's now lying unconscious in hospital. And all in the line of duty."

Trevor looked disgusted.

"That's terrible. It sounds as though Barney Wilson deserves a medal – not disparagement. He certainly has the sub-manager's sympathy. He spoke really highly of him. But …"

David looked sharply at Trevor.

"Go on"

"I'm not at all sure about Mr Barnett. There's something funny there. He certainly made great play about all the problems of the day – and no wonder – but the only compassion he showed was for Barney Wilson."

"Perhaps Barnett was also a batman. No, sorry, Trevor. This isn't a time for flippancy."

Trevor seemed to agree. He remained deadly serious.

"Mr Barnett spoke so highly about Barney Wilson. Salt of the earth, he called him. How he always helps out. How popular he is. Except…."

Trevor paused, as if hesitant about continuing.

David frowned.

"Get on with it, Trevor."

"Well, sir, it was a throwaway line by Mr Barnett. About Barney Wilson's popularity with everyone. Then he added perhaps not with him upstairs."

"That's interesting. Dissention in the ranks?"

"Sounds like it, sir. It's not the sort of thing he should let slip in front of me."

David frowned again. It might not have been an unwitting slip. Perhaps there was an ulterior motive. Could this be the start of a blame game being played out? So far, no one seemed to want to admit to anything going wrong.

Yet, rational thinking could hardly be expected today of all days. Everyone must be shell-shocked.

He drained his tankard and looked across to Trevor's glass, still three-quarters full.

"Another one?"

Trevor shook his head.

"I'm fine, sir."

"Does that mean you're playing tonight?"

"I wish I was. I actually got my sax out last night. There's a place up on the Common. It puts on Sunday jazz. The first time I've been there. I reckon it went down quite well."

David was not surprised. Trevor played excellent tenor sax, much in the style of Coleman Hawkins and Lester Young. The first time he heard the lad was at the Walnut Grove Club in Torquay. David had been in the audience when Trevor had astounded him by suddenly stepping up to the bandstand. He then blew up a storm on *Autumn Leaves*. But at the end of the set he had been mortified to discover his manager there. The taking on of additional employment – even by being paid to play the saxophone – was strictly prohibited by National Counties. But he need not have worried. David had been only too pleased to find a kindred spirit; there were not many of those in the jazz-starved community of Torquay. So why not turn a blind eye? Especially as Trevor's playing was restricted to weekends.

"So what are you doing tonight?"

"Back to my digs. Beans on toast, probably."

David recalled his own time in digs. It did not bring back happy memories. He had endured his fill of baked beans. Such a meal did not compare with the hotpot Sarah had promised him for tonight.

"Come round to us. Sarah's doing a hotpot. And she'd love to see you."

That was certainly true. Sarah had been particularly thrilled when Trevor had moved to Kent. Back in Barnmouth, she had always had a soft spot for him. On one occasion, she had even spoken glowingly of how she saw him as a younger version of her husband. David had not been sure whether to be pleased with that or not.

"That's very kind of you, sir. But another time? I'd really planned to get on with some composing tonight. I'm trying to expand my repertoire. On the other hand, I don't think I'll get today's events out of my mind."

David rose to get himself another pint, dwelling on Trevor's words. It would be the same for him. So much to think about. When he returned to his seat he brought up the question of the first cashier.

"What about this chap Grimshawe? The Colonel said he just didn't turn up. Then he said he was probably ill."

"Mr Barnett didn't think he was ill. They rang his house, but there was no answer. If he was ill, his wife would have picked up the phone. It seems neither was there."

"So where is he?"

Trevor shrugged.

"Do you think we should go round to his house?"

"I'm beginning to think so. I know he's only been absent for one day, but it just seems a bit odd. If he's not in tomorrow, I think we should go round. And if there's still no sign of him, I reckon it's a police job."

"I might be well off beam here, sir, but … but do you think his disappearance might be connected to the hold-up?"

This had already crossed David's mind. And the more he now

thought about Grimshawe, the more this became a possibility. And another thing was now troubling him. Had he lapsed in not getting the duplicate keys out to check the first cashier's till? If this man was connected in some way, David would have the reddest of faces should Grimshawe's cash box and safe turn out to be empty. He could now visualize this particular thought keeping him awake for much of the night.

"Sir?"

"Sorry, Trevor. I wish you hadn't just asked that."

He explained what had been going through his mind. Trevor was not convinced.

"Realistically, sir, how could it be connected? It's not as if Mr Grimshawe could possibly turn out to be the gunman."

That must be true. Such thinking was far too fanciful. And totally unrealistic. It was the stuff of films.

"I think we're going off at a tangent here, Trevor. But I still think we need to know more about Grimshawe. We'll do that tomorrow. If he doesn't turn up, we'll get his address and go round first thing. I also want to check out the hospital and see how Barney Wilson's coming along."

Trevor now looked perturbed at mention of the guard.

"I can't believe it, sir. All this talk about Mr Grimshawe, never mind the manager and Mr Barnett. It's as if we've put Barney Wilson on the back burner. That's terrible. And what about Douglas Fairweather? What must he be going through?"

Trevor was, of course, spot on. But no matter how compassionate they might feel, the investigation of the attempted murder of Barney Wilson and the kidnapping of the cashier must, primarily, be down to the police. In-branch problems were another matter. Quite properly, such things were within their own domain. And their reporting lines were to Regional Office and the bank's chief inspector in London, rather than the police. That meant an early visit to see Angus McPhoebe to put him in the picture. No doubt, McPhoebe would not be shy in coming forward with his views on how they were handling the investigation.

"We also need to know more about Douglas Fairweather," David replied. "And why did he have so much money in the sub-branch case? Mind you, was it in the case? I've been assuming it was, but could it have gone missing elsewhere? Put it this way, the money's missing and Grimshawe's missing. Is this the connection?"

"But the gunman must have targeted the bank's car for the money. And he must have planned it. Was this because he knew it would be a good haul? Did he have inside information?"

Trevor was making a habit of putting forward pertinent suggestions. An inside job? And with a missing first cashier? On the other hand...

"He might not have needed inside information. Maybe he'd just been keeping his eyes open. Casing the joint. Checking out possible lapses of security."

"The strongroom was left wide open this afternoon."

"What?"

Trevor described what had happened. It was not good news. David's mind now raced ahead.

"If the branch is so lax about locking the strongroom, where else have they been falling down? Have they been varying the route to the sub-branch? What about proper control of cash? Just think about it. We had so much cash to count today, but most ought to have been under the control of the first cashier. Our missing Mr Grimshawe. Had he allowed cash to build up in the other tills because he knew he wouldn't be in today? What other lapses in security have been taking place? Such as with keys? Has dual control of safes always been properly adopted?"

Trevor leant back in his seat and stroked his chin.

"I think I know what I'll be doing tomorrow. I didn't notice much else today when I chatted to the other staff. Incidentally, I didn't really get anything meaningful out of them. They were all too upset. As with Mr Barnett, they seemed to think the world of Barney Wilson. I even saw a Get Well card doing the rounds."

David liked the sound of that. It indicated encouraging *esprit de corps*. Did such team spirit actually stem from the manager, or was it despite him?

"Did they say anything about Douglas Fairweather?"

"Not a lot, sir. They were naturally upset, but the warmth wasn't there. Unlike with Barney Wilson. I got the impression they were a bit wary of Fairweather's seniority. And there may be a little jealousy there. I actually heard one of them refer to him as the manager's pet. That's a bit odd, isn't it?"

"Not really. The Colonel actually gushed when he talked to me about Fairweather. He thinks of him as his rising star. And they're certainly close. They have some connection with the Conservative Club. That could get up the backs of the other staff."

Trevor nodded his agreement at that, but stayed silent. Could it be his mind had strayed back to Barnmouth? Back there he had also shared club activities with his manager.

"Anyway, Trevor, tomorrow I think I'll go to Grimshawe's house on my own – and to the hospital. That way you can get on with looking at possible lapses in security. If there's more laxity, it might well have a bearing on all that's happened. I certainly have the feeling we're only at the start of something here."

Trevor now looked as disconcerted as David was feeling.

"One thing's for certain, sir. I don't think I'll be writing much music tonight."

Chapter 10

Alfie Templeton could not believe it. Scrupulous planning had always been his forte. So, how could things have gone so horribly wrong?

By now, he should be ensconced in his end-of-terrace in the Holmesdale Road. He ought to be miles away from that God-forsaken village of Lamberhurst. Instead, he was no more than fifteen miles away, still deep in the heart of Kent. And he felt like a rabbit caught in the headlights of an on-coming car.

He had never before seen the inside of a barn. They did not have such things in his South London suburb. And this one was nothing like the ones he had seen depicted in films. Loving couples would not cavort among hay ricks in this particular barn.

Yet, as a hiding place, it could not really be better. Not only did it appear to be isolated from any form of human habitation, but the barn's dilapidated state indicated that no one had been near the place for years. In effect, it appeared to be the ideal place to hole out until all the excitement had died down.

And any prior planning of his could not have averted his present predicament. How could he have planned for that accident on the A21? And he could not have anticipated nearly suffering a heart attack at the sound of the bell from that approaching ambulance. Those things had been bad enough, but it had got worse.

As he had approached the junction in the centre of the village of Horsmonden, he had to jam on the brakes. Some two hundred yards ahead was the vehicle he had expected to see just now instead of that ambulance. A gleaming black Wolseley police car straddled the road.

His first thought was that it was a road block – set up just for him. But, on reflection, how could that be the case? Only about ten minutes had elapsed since he had carried out his heist. The police could not possibly be so on the ball.

But, whatever the reason for the police car's presence, he had no alternative but to come to a halt. What on earth was he to do?

One policeman sat in the car, while another was on point duty. This one appeared only to be concerned about traffic coming from the opposite direction. For this reason, he seemed oblivious of the Oxford.

Templeton's initial panic had infiltrated every bone in his body, but it now started to abate. If the policeman on point duty was looking away from him, he and his colleague could not possibly be there on his account. If they were intent on not allowing cars to come in his direction, it must be because of that accident. It had been way behind him and must have been bad for the police to close the entire approach road and force all vehicles to take an alternative route.

He tried to think back to the way he had just come. Should he try and re-trace his steps? Had there been any turnings he could have taken to avoid Horsmonden? No, he could not think of any. If he turned around, it would just take him back to the A21. The accident would then bar his way from travelling north towards Tonbridge. He could be forced back into Lamberhurst itself. That would be disastrous.

What was he to do?

Oh my God! The policeman now turned in his direction. And even from the distance between them he could decipher a frown crossing the man's brow.

Templeton froze in his seat.

"What's going on?"

Templeton closed his eyes in frustration. He could well do without any inquisition from the back of the car. Especially as he was now even more conscious that he might be splattered with blood. What if he had to come face-to-face with this policeman?

"Shut up!" he snarled. "And keep your head down."

The policeman then waved his arm for the car to approach the junction.

Templeton felt helpless. If he turned tail and made back from where he had come, any suspicions the policeman might be harbouring would be well and truly confirmed. Yet if he moved forward, as he was now being directed, the game would be up.

What on earth should he do?

He immediately recognised that he had no option but to proceed. The policeman, with his hands now on hips, clearly meant business. His full attention was directed at the Oxford. Templeton bit hard on his lower lip. Some quick thinking was paramount.

"Sit up," he hissed, glancing over his shoulder. "Now close your eyes. Pretend to be asleep. And lean against the handle of the case. Make sure no one can see the chain."

With that, he slipped the car into gear and moved forward towards the policeman. In no time at all, the officer was standing against the off-side door.

Templeton wound down his window.

"What's up, officer?"

The policeman stared at him hard. Had he spotted any tell-tale signs of blood? Apparently not. Instead, he scanned the interior of the car.

"There's been an accident, sir. On the A21. We're re-directing all traffic. Where're you heading for?"

"Ashford." It was the first town Templeton could come up with.

The policeman nodded and pointed to the back of the car.

"What's up with your friend?"

Templeton smiled, a resigned smile, one which he hoped might engender understanding from the policeman?

"He's out for the count. I've just picked him up from London Airport. Flown in from the States."

"Jet lag?"

Templeton shrugged his shoulders.

"It seems so."

The policeman frowned and moved towards the rear door. Instinctively, Templeton felt for the revolver inside his coat pocket.

Yet using it must be the last thing he should do. His mind flashed back to his last cinema visit – to see *The Blue Lamp*. Dirk Bogarde's reckless delinquent had confronted George Dixon and then gunned the policeman down. The actual killing had been shocking enough, but Templeton had never forgotten Bogarde's sheer panic in carrying out the act. Yet he, himself, had effectively re-enacted that part back in Lamberhurst. God forbid he should be faced with a re-run now.

He then heard a shout. The policeman in the car was holding a walkie-talkie to his lips. He clearly wanted his colleague to join him.

Relief swept through Templeton as his own policeman turned away to return to the Wolseley.

"You better get on your way, sir," the officer said over his shoulder. "Turn right. That'll take you towards Ashford."

Templeton took a deep breath and set the car moving. The sooner he got on his way, the better.

After making the turn towards Ashford, he glanced in his rear-view mirror. Having talked to his colleague, the policeman was staring after the car. But it was not only the Oxford the man had obtained a good look at: Templeton knew that his own face must now be ingrained in the policeman's memory. Somehow, Templeton had managed to pick himself the worst possible witness as to his whereabouts: an on-duty policeman.

He would need to change his plans – quickly.

There was now far too high a risk in staying on the open road, either here in Kent or getting back to South London. Once those policemen got wind of the hold-up, road blocks would be set up everywhere. And he and his Oxford had been seen by them no more than a few miles from the scene of the crime.

His heart then missed a beat. That other policeman had been on his walkie-talkie. Had it been about the hold-up? That could well be so by the way his colleague had stared after the departing Oxford. Templeton now knew he was in deep trouble.

They would be looking for a car with a passenger in the back seat. How many cars, other than his, would that apply to? Most passengers would sit alongside the driver. And had the policeman noticed the case – never mind whether he had seen the chain attached to it?

Templeton hit the accelerator hard. He needed to get some miles between him and Horsmonden. He might have said he was heading for Ashford, but the police would probably take that at face value. If they put two and two together they would hardly expect a raider to give away his planned destination. But this particular road did head for Ashford and Templeton needed to get off it as quickly as possible.

As far as he was aware, Marden was the next village and that would pose another problem. He had been through there only last week and it had been particularly busy. If it was the same this morning, he could encounter witnesses by the dozen. He must avoid that at all costs.

But what was the alternative?

Within seconds of posing this question to himself, he came across a farm track, on his left. It must have been about half way between the villages of Horsmonden and Marden. But as far as he was concerned, it seemed to be in the middle of nowhere.

His speed had taken him past the opening and he screeched to a stop. Flicking the gear lever into reverse, he roared backwards, narrowly avoiding a ditch which ran alongside the road. He quickly re-assessed the narrow track. Yes, it was worth a try.

Although it appeared to be a farm track, there was no evidence that anything, farm vehicles or animals, had used it in years. Overgrown hedgerows had reduced the width of the track to about five foot and he now had doubts as to whether the Oxford would be able to get through.

But desperate times needed desperate measures.

Twigs and overgrown foliage scraped both sides of the car as he inched his way down the narrow track. Potholes shook the car every few feet and Templeton feared for the survival of the car's suspension system. The rocky ride also drew forth violent protests from the back as to what was going on.

But Templeton shut his ears to what was being said behind him. He needed to exercise his full concentration on what lay ahead.

He had no idea as to where the track was leading. But he knew it was taking him away from the arm of the law. And that particular limb must now be in hot pursuit.

After a few hundred yards, the track started to peter out. Surely not to a dead end? But then Templeton saw the barn, not that at first sight the ramshackle structure appeared to be a barn. Yet, as he neared the building he realized this could be an ideal hideaway.

Although it looked dreadfully dilapidated, the building did have four walls and a roof. More importantly, double doors stood wide open in the front. It was as though they were inviting him to drive the Oxford inside. Provided he was then able to close the doors behind the car, no one would have any idea of what lay concealed within the barn.

It was another matter as to how long they would need to be holed up there. But Templeton's relief at being hidden away from the highways of Kent far outweighed any concerns he might have about his new-found accommodation.

Chapter 11

First thing next morning, David's mind had been in a quandary. Trevor's questioning had not helped.

"Do you think it'll do any good, sir? If he was there, he'd have answered the phone."

That was logical enough. So should he make the journey? Was he overreacting to the first cashier's continuing absence? Or should he leave it in the hands of the manager?

"We can't just do nothing, Trevor. And going to his house … it's just possible something might come to light."

Trevor nodded, but did not look convinced. Perhaps he wanted some support here at the branch in his task at looking into possible lapses in branch security. So, should David, himself, get involved in that mission? Any branch that allowed a strongroom to be left wide open was clearly capable of other security transgressions. In which case, would such deeds have had some bearing on what happened yesterday? Trevor certainly had concerns over Mr Barnett, while David's meeting with Colonel Fawkes-William hardly inspired confidence. But the missing Mr Grimshawe was worrying and David really needed to pursue this line of enquiry. So, yes, he would leave Trevor to continue the in-branch investigations. He was a sensible lad and deserved to be given the opportunity to play a full part in trying to establish what might have been going on.

Decision made, David would now try to discover first hand why Grimshawe had not turned up again. Was there some innocent reason for his absence? Had he had an accident? Or was it possible the cashier had, indeed, been associated with yesterday's hold-up?

But if he had been involved, why? And how?

So, where better to start an investigation than at Grimshawe's house?

And leaving the visit in the hands of the branch could be ill-advised. Colonel Fawkes-William would certainly not want to demean himself by looking into the whereabouts of one of his clerks; he would delegate such a task to someone else. Yet the attitude of underlings was likely to be one-dimensional. It would not cross their minds that skulduggery might be a factor. They would simply be enquiring about a missing person. Lateral thinking would probably not be considered.

As he made his way to his Consul, David's mind was working overtime, but he was well refreshed from an unexpected good night's sleep. Perhaps that was the result of a generous nightcap, accompanied by dulcet sounds from his latest Ben Webster LP. More likely his evening discussion with Sarah had put him in the right frame of mind for an undisturbed sleep.

Fourteen years of marriage had not diminished David's devotion for his soul mate. Her luminous smile had hooked him on their first date; it had never waned and epitomized a warmth of personality to which others could only aspire. And David was not simply thinking of Colonel Fawkes-William and Angus McPhoebe. But Sarah's strengths ran deeper than this. In particular, she had always been a good sounding board. Being also employed by National Counties helped. She had enjoyed a break until Mark had reached school age and she now worked part-time at Tonbridge branch. Her practical knowledge of banking routines and her innate good sense were always a great help. This had been the case back in Barnmouth. His staff might have felt he had all the answers, but little did they know. And now, having moved from manager to inspector, he and Sarah continued to prove that old adage of two heads being better than one.

This had been the case last night. Sarah had been appalled at the day's events, but she had relished their speculation on possible scenarios. And she had been a clear advocate of this trip to Mr Grimshawe's house this morning. Apart from the grimness of what had happened, her only personal disappointment last evening was Trevor's absence from the supper table.

It was just after nine-thirty when David got under way. He made for the A21 which would lead him to the Grimshawes' house at the south end of Tonbridge. The journey would take no longer than fifteen minutes and Mr Barnett had given him directions to the actual house.

He needed to make for a quaint pub, intriguingly called The Cardinal's Error, and then turn into the next road on the right, Cardinal Close. This turned out to be a compact estate of some thirty semi-detached properties of varied design. The estate had been built in a wide oval, houses straddling each side of the road. The Grimshawes' house was half-way down on the left.

Although it was a small property, constructed in a chalet style, David reckoned there would be three upstairs bedrooms. It looked as if one reception room stretched across the downstairs front of the house and, behind this, there was probably a kitchen/diner. Alongside the house, a short drive led up to a single detached garage.

To remain inconspicuous and to get a good view of the property, David parked across the road, a few doors away. He was immediately impressed by the neat and tidy appearance of the house.

Even though it was still only March, the small front lawn had already been given its first cut and the edges had been finely manicured. The curtains at the front of the house were all drawn back and the whole property had a normal lived-in feel about it. If the Grimshawes were not there now, it did not seem as if they had been absent for very long.

Apart from a man tending his roses a few houses down, there was no activity in the Close. David got out of his car and crossed the road. He walked up the short driveway to the front door which was positioned at the side of the house and rang the bell.

There was no answer. He waited a few moments and rang again.

It was clear the house was empty and David decided to look round the back. An open side gate seemed to be an invitation to investigate and he was soon by the back door which led straight into the kitchen/diner. The glass in the door was frosted, but the window alongside gave him a clear view into the room.

As with the outside of the house, everything in the kitchen was neatly in place. Beyond the sink, four upright pine chairs flanked a small, matching Formica-topped table, similar to the one Sarah had chosen in Barnmouth. It was clear of crockery and utensils. No doubt these were stored away in a chest of drawers and wall units sited at the back of the kitchen.

Nothing seemed to be out of place and, clearly, no one had left in a hurry. It was almost too normal to be true.

"Can I help you?"

David's heart missed a beat.

It was not just a reaction to someone else's presence when he had felt entirely alone; the innocent enough words had been laced with accusation and admonition. They demanded to know what David could possibly be doing, staring through the kitchen window at the back of this house.

He turned round and faced the man who had been working on his roses. And this man now appeared far larger and more aggressive than he had seemed in his garden across the road. David took a deep breath.

"It's not what you seem to …"

The man took a step forward and David hastily reached into his jacket pocket for his wallet. This was clearly a time to produce his credentials.

"Look. This is all above board. I'm from National Counties Bank. An inspector. We're concerned about the whereabouts of Mr Grimshawe."

The man immediately relaxed, any intimidation disappearing.

"Well that's all right then. You'll understand …"

"Of course. I must have looked most suspicious. Sorry."

David then held out his hand.

"I'm David Goodhart. I've come from Tunbridge Wells."

The man returned his grip and then lifted his left hand to his mouth.

"It's not to do with that hold-up – at Lamberhurst? You're not saying Mr Grimshawe …"

His words tailed off and genuine concern etched his face. David quickly shook his head.

"No. He wasn't there. But he's not turned up for work. Neither yesterday, nor today. We couldn't reach him on the phone. That's why I've come round to his house."

"He was here on Saturday. I saw him cutting his lawn. I live nearly opposite and he puts me to shame with his garden. To tell you the truth that's why I've been working in my own garden this morning."

"So he was here on Saturday? And Sunday?"

"I didn't see him on Sunday. I was out most of the day – visiting my in-laws. But he always goes fishing on Sundays."

"What about Mrs Grimshawe? Is she around?"

The neighbour frowned and then snapped his fingers.

"No, I remember now. She went to her mother's on Friday. Up in Northampton. She's not been well."

"And Mr Grimshawe didn't go with her?"

"No. I don't think he gets on with his mother-in-law. And he doesn't let anything get in the way of his fishing on Sundays."

David was already forming a picture of the cashier. The evident *esprit de corps* in the branch might have nothing to do with this particular man.

"This fishing of his … would that mean staying away from home?"

"No, never. He only goes to a small lake near Eridge, between here and Crowborough. That's no more than ten miles away. And he never goes for the whole day."

"You didn't see him come back?"

"No, as I said, I was at my in-laws. I'm lucky. I get on well with mine."

It was becoming clear this man was not going to be able to shed any light on Mr Grimshawe's disappearance. But what about

Mrs Grimshawe up in Northampton? She might well know of her husband's whereabouts.

"Do you reckon I could get in touch with Mrs Grimshawe?"

The man shook his head.

"I don't have her number. But she normally comes home on Tuesday."

That was good news, anyway.

David reached into his pocket for his notebook and fountain pen. If Mrs Grimshawe was returning from Northampton, she should be back some time this afternoon.

"In that case, I'll leave a note for her to contact me. And if you also happen to see her …"

The neighbour nodded, as if satisfied at the arrangement, and then bade farewell. He was clearly anxious to get back to his roses.

Left on his own, David wrote out his message and put it through the letter box. He meticulously screwed the cap back on to his pen, had a final glance around the house and then returned to his Consul. As he got underway, he checked his rear view mirror. The neighbour did not take his eyes off the departing car. Perhaps he was not entirely convinced as to the credentials of this bank inspector.

David re-traced his route past The Cardinal's Error. This pub certainly looked worthy of a visit and it was just as well it was not yet open. He had too much else to do.

In the meantime, where was Mr Grimshawe? All had been apparently well with him on Saturday and going fishing on Sunday hardly conjured up any matter for concern. Perhaps when he returned home, he decided to follow his wife up to Northampton. She had probably gone by train and maybe he had a guilty conscience to go and bring her home by car. But if he had done this, he would have let the bank know. Unless they had suffered an accident up there.

No, that was unlikely. But there was nothing more to do than await Mrs Grimshawe's return. David could only hope she would have some pertinent information about her husband.

Until that happened, if indeed it did, David felt no further forward. There had simply been nothing suspicious about his visit to the Grimshawes' house. Its air of normality had been effectively confirmed by the neighbour. That man's evident concern had only been about the stranger poking his nose around.

David's next port of call was the Kent and Sussex Hospital. The bank staff had already put in hand a Get Well card for Barney Wilson and the least he could do was to put in an appearance. He doubted if he would be able to see the guard, or even get near him, but he could certainly try.

He had already built up a picture of what this man was all about. For this he partly had Colonel Fawkes-William to thank.

If ever there was a case for having empathy with an underdog, this was it. The manager's castigation of Barney Wilson's war service was enough to put anyone on the guard's side. And the views of the staff must, surely, bear greater pertinence than those put forward by the manager.

David had seen such staff support before. Guards had no axe to grind. They were not in competition with the clerical staff; there was no vying with them for promotion. So often, they simply provided support, help and friendship, with an inborn sense of duty. Barney Wilson seemed to have these qualities in spades.

And, apparently, he had displayed one further attribute: outstanding bravery.

David made his way down Pembury Road into Tonbridge and turned left to go up Quarry Hill towards Southborough and then Tunbridge Wells.

Traffic was light and he reached the hospital in about ten minutes. He managed to find a parking space and was soon inside the building. An antiseptic aroma hung in the air and reminded him of twelve years ago when Mark had been born. It might have been a different hospital, but the smell and the corridors with their floor-to-ceiling tiles were the same as here.

A young nurse directed him to the Intensive Care Unit, but warned him that he would probably get no further than the reception area. He fully accepted this and would be perfectly satisfied just to hear, first hand, how Barney Wilson was coming along.

The ambience in Intensive Care turned out to be so different from downstairs. Colourful blinds and curtains eloquently set off the pastel walls, while the tidiness of the Unit and the calm authority of the nurses quite belied the traumas which must dominate the wards each and every day.

Not unlike Sarah, a petite nurse, her auburn hair drawn back into a neatly-formed bun, greeted him with a warm smile. This was just the sort of person he would like to have around in these surroundings. But the nurse downstairs had been right; it would not be possible, sir, to see Barney Wilson.

Yet the news was encouraging. They were perfectly happy with his progress. He was very seriously ill, but his condition was not worsening. He was, in fact, expected to regain consciousness shortly.

David felt elated. He was so pleased he had made the visit. And Colonel Fawkes-William had been wrong; there was no police presence. Perhaps they were simply waiting to hear when they would be able to speak to the guard. They clearly did not expect any retribution from the gunman, fearful at having been recognized by the guard.

David went downstairs with a spring in his step. There was now every chance that, in due course, he would be able to meet this man whom he had already come to admire. It was not a feeling he shared with the next person on his agenda.

As far as he was concerned, there was nothing to admire about Angus McPhoebe.

CHAPTER 12

"Out of the way! Down on the floor!"

Trevor would never forget those screamed demands. He had stood rooted in his till position, his eyes fixated on the barrel of the gun. It pointed at his face, no more than a foot away.

Nothing had prepared him for such a moment.

Yet, despite his rawness, his mind had worked overtime.

"Down on the floor!"

The gunman brandished his weapon, wild eyes now locked on Trevor.

No question, Trevor needed to act quickly. But no heroics. The bank would not thank him for that. Yet he had to do something.

He immediately fell to his knees, his arm stretching upwards to the underside of his till, just out of sight of the gunman. But with his fingers only inches away from the alarm button, he was knocked flat on his face, the gunman having leapt over the counter.

Within seconds, the man had scooped up all the notes from Trevor's till, stuffing them into a canvas bag. He then swung himself back over the counter and fled from the branch.

It had all been over in less than a minute.

Trevor shivered as he recalled the immediate aftermath. No one moved. Total silence. Then a piercing scream from the girl at the next till.

Now, five years later, he knew he would never expunge that previous black day at Chagford from his memory. He had only gone there from Barnmouth for a week. Yet, two days into his stint as a relief cashier, he had come face-to-face with death.

Then yesterday. No wonder his knees had quaked when he took Angus McPhoebe's telephone call. And with good reason, after what they discovered at Lamberhurst.

Poor Barney Wilson. It had been so much worse for him. Would he ever recover from such an experience? Would he ever recover?

Yet one aspect was ironic. Way back in school, he had wanted to be a policeman. He had been tall enough: five foot nine. And not even the mods and rockers had put him off. Looking back, were they really warring factions? The locals who strolled along Torquay's sea front might have thought so. And those two-wheeled hooligans did cause mayhem in the local cinema which chose to show Bill Haley's *Rock around the Clock*.

But jobwise, reason had prevailed; by way of Mum and Dad who suggested that National Counties would provide good pensionable employment.

So, he became a bank clerk. And had done his best to master double-entry book-keeping. Some people revelled in making sure that every debit had a credit, but ...

Anyway, he had been lucky.

Mr Goodhart must have seen something in him. A kindred spirit, maybe? With jazz, yes. And at work, the manager had involved him in the kind of investigative tasks which had originally attracted him to the police force. His subsequent banking career had then proved to be anything but routine.

Because of crime.

At Barnmouth branch, he had encountered criminal deeds of which he had been previously unaware. And he had been enthralled by the cut and thrust of investigation into corrupt practices.

Now, he was on the inspection staff. Those past experiences should, surely, help him.

Here in Tunbridge Wells, his brief was clear enough: to look into all aspects of branch security.

And he feared the worst.

The strongroom grille having been left wide open yesterday had not been a good start. If the branch got such a basic requirement wrong, the scope for further laxity was immense.

The bank's general rule book comprised some three hundred

closely-typed pages. Each rule and regulation was there for a purpose: primarily to protect the bank's property, its financial dealings with customers and, of course, its staff.

Trevor would never forget one basic lapse back in Barnmouth. The first cashier had left his unlocked till unattended. It had only been for a few moments while he went to the back of the office. But in that time, £5,000 was stolen. As Tommy Cooper would say: just like that.

So, this morning, whatever else he might be checking up on, Trevor would keep a constant close eye on how the cashiers controlled their respective tills. A loss of £5,000 in Barnmouth had been bad enough. But yesterday? At Lamberhurst, it had been over £50,000. This might well have been by way of an armed hold-up, but had there been contributory factors here in the main branch?

But what to do first?

Should he immediately seek out Mr Barnett? Or simply nose around and get a feel of the place? Could it really be that yesterday's strongroom lapse had been a one-off? He doubted it. And so did Mr Goodhart.

Better, therefore, to nose round first. In any case, in Mr Grimshawe's continuing absence, Mr Barnett would have his hands full organizing the office. At least there was plenty of cash in the other tills ready for opening time at ten o'clock. Trevor and Mr Goodhart had learnt that to their cost yesterday; there had been so much to count.

As he started to wander around the office, Trevor introduced himself to one or two members of staff. Inspectors were never the most welcome visitors, so he expected some apprehension. But there was no antagonism. Not that they would realize he was scrutinizing them for possible lapses in security. Nevertheless, they ought to be fully on their guard.

Yet, he immediately came across a problem.

And it must be down to one particular person.

Every branch had a small, lockable metal code box. This would have two keys, one each held by the manager and the sub-manager. The box contained a variety of code cards, inscribed with letters and numbers. Whenever significant balances or funds needed to be transferred to other branches, the transactions would be encrypted by use of these code cards. Only the manager and sub-manager could do this and the locked code box would remain under the control of the sub-manager.

This box now lay in front of Trevor, unattended on a back desk in the general office. Any control over it by the sub-manager was non-existent. Mr Barnett sat several yards away, head down, in his sub-managerial enclosure, oblivious of what might be going on around him.

But it got worse. Trevor tested the lid. The code box was unlocked.

He shook his head in despair. He was tempted to remove the box from sight. How would Mr Barnett then react when he had cause to need it? Or Colonel Fawkes-William, for that matter. Not that there was any sign of the manager. Still ensconced in his room upstairs? Was this the way to run his branch? Particularly if there were question marks over control downstairs.

But removing the code box would be a mistake. It would destroy any relationship he and Mr Goodhart might have with the staff. And Mr Goodhart would not thank him for that. Trevor had quickly learnt that his boss was a fanatic for doing the right thing; his pedantry with the English language was a case in point. But it also extended to how he always conducted himself. Trevor had never seen him do anything slightly underhand and he would certainly expect likewise from his assistant.

Far better, then, to confront Mr Barnett head on and Trevor picked up the box and marched it across to the sub-manager's desk.

Mr Barnett remained head down, staring at his papers.

Trevor coughed.

"Mr Barnett?"

The sub-manager looked up and raised his eyebrows.

Trevor bit his bottom lip. Was the man still shell-shocked from yesterday?

"Mr Barnett, I've just found your code box on the back desk."

He handed the box over and the sub-manager placed it on the side of his desk.

"Thanks."

Was that all? Thanks?

"Mr Barnett, not only was the code box on the back desk, but it's also unlocked."

The sub-manager put his hand in his trousers' pocket and pulled out a big bunch of keys. He struggled to find the right key for the box, then locked it and placed it in the bottom drawer of his desk. He then dumped his bunch of keys on top of the desk.

Trevor watched this performance in disbelief. Apart from the monosyllabic word of thanks, the sub-manager had remained silent. Not a word of regret, apology or concern. Trevor could not leave it like that.

"Mr Barnett, how could this possibly happen? The code box should be under your sole control – at all times."

The sub-manager shrugged his shoulders and gave a world-weary sigh.

"Him upstairs wanted it. Couldn't come down here and get it himself. No. Muggins had to take it up to him. God knows, sir, I have enough to do down here. What with Grimshawe still not turning up and having to get the bank open again. Never mind taking all the calls from Lamberhurst customers. Do they really believe we should open the sub-branch, so soon after what happened yesterday? No compassion at all. It makes you sick."

He took a deep breath and actually looked relieved at having got so much off his chest. Trevor almost felt sorry for the man. Yet any sub-manager ought to be able to cope with these kind of pressures. And Mr Barnett should certainly not be so overt with his feelings about his manager – whether or not he believed these to be justified.

"But, Mr Barnett, that doesn't explain why the code box was left on the back desk."

"I got distracted – when I came downstairs. And it wasn't me who left it unlocked."

How could the man express such disloyalty to his manager in front of a member of the inspection staff? Was he simply not thinking properly, or was it more sinister than that? Could he be deliberately pointing an accusatory finger at Colonel Fawkes-William?

Yet the blame must be directed at Mr Barnett. He should have checked that the box was locked. As for getting distracted …

No, Mr Barnett had much to answer for. Especially after yesterday's bloomer with the strongroom door.

But that was not all.

Trevor stared at the bunch of keys now sitting on top of Mr Barnett's desk. The bank did not issue key chains to male staff for nothing. Keys must be attached to these chains which must then be fastened to trouser buttons or belt loops. Keys would then be tied to the person at all times.

In no circumstances, should they be dumped on top of a desk.

What if Mr Barnett was suddenly called away from his desk? More than likely, the keys would remain there unattended. Just as the code box had been left unguarded on the back desk.

Mr Goodhart now looked to be spot on with his concern about possible breaches in branch security. And Trevor had only just started his investigations.

It made him think about yesterday's hold-up. Could lapses in security, here in the branch, really have contributed to it?

CHAPTER 13

It would take David about forty minutes to reach Regional Office.

Why these headquarters were domiciled in Haywards Heath, he would never know.

The Region encompassed Kent, Sussex and the southern end of Surrey. Tunbridge Wells was at its heart. Yet Haywards Heath had been chosen.

Just as well. Having Regional Office in his own town? On his own patch? Far too close for comfort.

Especially as he had not always seen eye-to-eye with regional management.

Back in Barnmouth, his regional manager had been called Spattan. There had been times when that name had been despatched through David's lips as if fired into a nearby spittoon.

Yet here, in the south east, the regional manager could not be better.

Reginald Porter was the epitome of a much-respected senior banker. He combined technical expertise with a warmth of personality which put even the most junior of staff at their ease.

There was only one problem associated with Mr Porter: his deputy.

Angus McPhoebe.

David knew they would never get on. Right from their first meeting.

And deportment made a good starting point.

His own days in the RAF had indoctrinated him into standing erect. There was nothing wrong with having the bearing of an old soldier. From what he had heard, it seemed that this certainly applied to Barney Wilson.

But it was one thing to stand tall with head held high. Quite another to have one's cranium permanently tilted backwards, chin pointing forward and with one's nose, apparently, affected by a singularly noxious odour.

Angus McPhoebe to a tee.

McPhoebe also seemed to experience great difficulty in passing the time of day with mere mortals in branches. As for bank inspectors … These unwelcome visitors to his region were bound to make mischief by stirring up potential problems which might be to the detriment of his own planned fast-track promotion.

There was just one mystery surrounding Angus McPhoebe: how did such an excellent man as Mr Porter come to select him as his deputy?

David had received clearance on the telephone to make his visit late in the morning and as he left the outskirts of Tunbridge Wells, he reckoned to be in Haywards Heath by about a quarter to twelve. Mr Porter was out for the day so he would have to see Angus McPhoebe. He only hoped this late-morning meeting with his *bete-noire* would not spoil his lunch.

On his way towards Crowborough, he passed through Eridge, the fishing haunt of Mr Grimshawe, and he wondered, again, what could have happened to this man. He just hoped Mrs Grimshawe would contact him on her return from Northampton. If only she could cast some light on her husband's whereabouts.

Once through Crowborough, he soon reached the A272 which would take him straight to Haywards Heath. On the way, he passed Piltdown Golf Club; this would have made a far more preferable journey's destination.

The Regional Office was situated in a detached Victorian three-storey building with its own adjacent car park. David parked his car alongside a gleaming Rover 90. In the absence of Mr Porter, he imagined this must belong to Angus McPhoebe. This man would definitely not own the only other car in the car park: a rather tatty Morris Minor Traveller.

Once inside the reception area, David was not surprised to be told that McPhoebe was not yet ready to see him. He had never yet started a meeting with him on time. Yet he had never seen anyone leaving McPhoebe's room from a previous appointment. Keeping him waiting must simply be a ploy to make him feel like an underling.

At last. After twenty long minutes, a rather grim-looking secretary said he could now go in.

As usual, McPhoebe remained seated behind his desk. He appeared engrossed in a single piece of paper. He held this in one hand while the other stroked non-existent stubble on his chin. He made it look like a picture of concentration. There were no other papers or files on his desk. This one piece of paper must, then, have held his attention for the last twenty minutes. Did he really expect David to believe that?

He eventually looked up.

"Ah, Goodhart."

David, somehow, maintained his equilibrium. It was like a re-run of his reception yesterday from Colonel Fawkes-William.

McPhoebe waved him to a seat on the other side of the desk and smiled. It was an ingratiating smile; one that failed utterly to reach his eyes. He made no offer of his hand.

Having not been properly greeted or asked any question, David made no response, but sat down obediently.

McPhoebe put his paper down on the desk.

"Ah, Goodhart."

At least the man knew his name.

"I tried to reach you yesterday – at Tenterden."

David nodded.

"Yes, I was out of the branch."

McPhoebe raised his eyebrows. He was clearly seeking elaboration.

"I was in a pub. The Red Lion."

It was just the reply to wipe the smile off McPhoebe's face.

"At that time of the morning?"

"I was doing some research."

McPhoebe now looked apoplectic. It must have been the weakest reason he had ever heard to justify someone going out for a drink in mid-morning. No wonder the man had such a poor opinion of visiting inspectors!

"I think you'd better explain."

David was very happy to do this, but it did seem odd that his visit to a pub was taking precedence over an armed robbery.

"I'm a bit worried about some of the manager's lending."

"Featherstonehaugh's?"

What a long-fangled name that was. No wonder the manager liked to be called Fanshawe. David now had a problem with that: the phonetic link to the missing Mr Grimshawe.

"Yes. He seems to be a little generous with the bank's money."

"You must be joking. He's a good man."

Oh, no. This was definitely like a re-run with the Colonel.

"Well, he's been very generous with the publican. Perhaps Mr Featherstonehaugh likes a tipple or two."

McPhoebe's apoplexy was not diminishing.

"There's nothing wrong with Featherstonehaugh's lending. I selected him for Tenterden myself."

David suppressed a sigh. Well, that's all right, then. Any manager selected by McPhoebe could not possibly go off the rails.

"Be that as it may, and I know it's early days for me in Tenterden, but the amount being lent to this pub seems far too high in relation to its turnover. So, I thought I'd go and see it for myself. And I'm glad I did. If I were its bank manager, I wouldn't lend it a penny."

This stopped McPhoebe in his tracks. David could almost see his mind ticking over. How was it going to affect his own promotion prospects if one of his chosen disciples…?

"Well, we're not here to talk about Tenterden."

Agreed, but David had not been the one to bring this up. He waited for McPhoebe's change of subject.

"Bring me up-to-date with Lamberhurst. Colonel Fawkes-William put me in the picture yesterday – as did the police. I gather they're not getting very far."

"No, it's very worrying. I don't know what the sub-branch

cashier must be going through. At least there's some better news about the guard."

"Oh?"

"Yes, I've just been to the hospital ..."

"The hospital? How come? Colonel Fawkes-William told me it wasn't possible."

"I just popped in."

"Without asking?"

"It seemed the right thing to do. I doubted if I could see him personally. But someone from the bank needed to put in an appearance. Anyway, he's still in Intensive Care, but they think he'll come round soon. If so he's been very lucky."

"But did you tell Colonel Fawkes-William you were going to the hospital?"

"Did I have to?"

"Of course you did. It's his branch. He needs to know what's going on – how his guard's progressing."

"He didn't give me that impression yesterday. He seemed more concerned about Fairweather, his cashier – and the money."

McPhoebe frowned. Was he unsure about what he had just heard?

"The money?"

"Didn't Colonel Fawkes-William tell you?"

McPhoebe slowly shook his head and gave a fair impression of someone not wanting to hear the answer.

"There was over £50,000 in the sub-branch case."

McPhoebe went as white as a crisp new fiver. The significance of the gunman's haul was clearly not lost on him. He could hardly utter his next words.

"How come?"

"That's what I'd like to know."

"But £50,000? That's enough to ..."

McPhoebe's words tailed off and, for the first time, David felt some affinity with the man. Was it possible for this to develop? It would certainly be good to have this man on his side. They might not like each other, but that did not mean they could not work together. This was probably the moment to air his other concerns.

"I think there may be something more going on here than just the armed hold-up. For one thing, the first cashier's disappeared. No one knows where. Nor why. And I think there may be security problems at the branch. I've got my assistant working on this now. As for the manager ..."

"Colonel Fawkes-William? He's one of our best managers. A good man."

David was getting a bit tired of all these good men. To his mind, each of them, apart from the desperately unfortunate Fairweather, seemed to be the subject of a big question mark. Perhaps he was simply not attuned to this good man philosophy. On the other hand, he had to confess to such feelings about Trevor. But Trevor was different. He was good because of his attitude and work ethic. The others were deemed to be good men simply from some form of old-boy syndrome.

"Do you not think he's a touch arrogant?"

David immediately regretted his question. It was taking too much of a liberty. It might be too close to home for McPhoebe. But he was not really surprised by the man's reply.

"He's got plenty to be arrogant about. He's a first-class manager. And what about when he was in the army? He wasn't made a colonel for nothing."

David suppressed another sigh. If McPhoebe had his way, he would probably like to promote Fawkes-William to be a colonel in the bank. But was Fawkes-William really a first-class manager? Did McPhoebe really think that?

"We both went to the same school," McPhoebe added. "Years ahead of me, of course."

So that was it: the old school network.

David never thought of his time at Torquay Grammar in the same light. Perhaps because school days had not been the happiest of his life. And he would not expect anyone from those best-forgotten days to provide him with a McPhoebe-like character reference. He decided to change the subject.

"I'm really concerned about the missing first cashier."

"What's his name?"

"Grimshawe. I went round to his house this morning. There was no sign of him. A neighbour said he was there at the weekend. Apparently he went fishing on Sunday."

"What about his wife?"

"She's away in Northampton. Went on Friday. To see her sick mother."

"He probably followed her up there."

David pursed his lips.

"Perhaps. But the neighbour didn't think so. Anyway, he said she'd probably be back this afternoon. So I left a note for her to contact me."

"Let's hope she does. What about Grimshawe's till? I assume that was in order?"

David knew this was coming. It was something he was getting more anxious about by the hour. If he felt like this himself, McPhoebe was probably about to go ballistic.

"I don't know about the till. We didn't check it yesterday?"

It got the reaction he expected.

"What?" McPhoebe roared.

"There didn't seem a need at the time. There was no reason to believe Mr Grimshawe's till might be linked to the hold-up. I decided to wait until this morning – when he returned to work."

"But he didn't, did he?"

McPhoebe had made no attempt to disguise his sarcasm and now glowered across his desk.

David knew his reaction was fully justified. That made it even worse. And it would do no good now to confirm that he had already decided what to do when he returned to Tunbridge Wells: get the duplicate keys from Lloyds and check Mr Grimshawe's till.

But right now, he could hardly bear the thought of one possible outcome. What if the first cashier's cash box was completely empty? Not to mention his separate safe in the strongroom where he kept the bulk of his cash?

Yet, that thought would not go away. Nor his fear that Mr Grimshawe was now stretched out on a deck chair, basking in the sun on some Caribbean island. Without a care in the world.

McPhoebe was now staring at David with ill-disguised contempt.

"So, Goodhart, let's get this straight. We've got a guard fighting for his life in hospital and a cashier has been abducted with over £50,000. And now there's a missing cashier – with or without the contents of his till."

Yes, that was about it.

Except that there was also a suspect sub-manager who appeared to be at odds with his manager. And although McPhoebe would dispute this, there was a huge question mark over Colonel Fawkes-William. Not only had the manager been reticent in revealing the missing £50,000 to David, but he had compounded this on the telephone yesterday by not mentioning it at all to Angus McPhoebe.

But McPhoebe was not finished.

"I'm not sure you're up to this job, Goodhart. I came to that conclusion when I couldn't reach you in Tenterden. Especially when your assistant didn't know where you were. Now you tell me you were checking out a pub. I ask you. But I have a problem. I've called London. And the chief inspector says there's no one else available. So it's Hobson's choice. I'm stuck with you."

McPhoebe now looked resigned, rather than ballistic. It was not much of an improvement. David could not blame him for such a reaction, but he was anxious as to what was actually said to the Chief. Was his star with the boss now on the wane?

"Anyway," McPhoebe continued, "if I am stuck with you, I want some action. And that doesn't mean faffing about at the hospital and at Grimshawe's house. I need you back at the branch and checking the cash – all of it. And I want you to find out how this state of affairs could ever have happened."

So much for working together.

Five minutes later, David sat in his car and reflected on the ear-bashing he had just received. There was no doubting that, in hindsight, McPhoebe had been correct about Grimshawe's till not having been checked. But, apart from that, David reckoned he and Trevor had achieved a good deal in the last twenty-four hours. Granted there was nothing much specific, but they were getting strong feelings about the branch in Tunbridge Wells, never mind its staff. McPhoebe might not appreciate what they had been doing, but unlike him, they were not automatically taking things at face value. That could only help them to come to the conclusion McPhoebe was seeking.

So, back to the branch post-haste. And David could not wait to hear how Trevor had been getting on with his investigation into branch security.

CHAPTER 14

Trevor stood quietly at the back of the office and surveyed all around him.

Tunbridge Wells branch was little different from any other. As usual, the front door led straight into the banking hall which housed tables and chairs for customers to complete their transactions. The tables were equipped with small trays which accommodated pots of red and black ink, together with steel-nib, wooden-handled pens. Yellow blotting paper, retained in rectangular holders, also adorned each desk. At the end of the day, this paper would be festooned with blotches of ink and inconsequential doodling.

Ballpoint pens were increasing in popularity and Trevor hoped these would soon replace pen and ink. This might not meet with the approval of purist calligraphers, but he knew the move would be popular with bank juniors. When he had held this post in Barnmouth he had managed to get ink all over his hands, never mind the cuffs of his shirt and jacket. The ink pots were tiny in relation to the jars which held the wretched bulk liquid and it was almost impossible to complete the job without spillages.

Running the whole length of the banking hall was a long wooden counter, behind which the cashiers handled the customers' transactions. The counter was similar to the one in Chagford when that gunman had leapfrogged into Trevor's till. Following this experience, Mr Goodhart had written to Head Office to suggest that some form of bandit screening should be installed. Nearly five years later, still nothing had happened.

After what had occurred yesterday, Trevor could well imagine the Tunbridge Wells cashiers feeling particularly vulnerable.

This Tuesday morning, two cashiers occupied the middle two of the four till positions. The missing Mr Grimshawe would normally operate the till closest to the front door, while a relief cashier probably used the fourth till during busy periods, such as lunch hours.

Of the two cashiers, one could be described as a youngster, but the other was in his forties. Why could this older man not have held one of the two strongroom door keys yesterday? Trevor would take this up with Mr Barnett in due course. The sub-manager could provide him with the answer immediately, but he still looked to have the cares of the whole world heaped on his shoulders. Far better, for the moment, to let him get on without further inspectorial interruptions.

Immediately to the rear of the counter, other clerks sat on tall stools behind a high sloping desk which stretched the width of the cashiers' run. Various journals and ledgers of indeterminate size lay on a shelf under the top of the desk. A certain amount of brawn would be needed to heave these heavy tomes on to the desk and one girl, who seemed to be no taller than Mr Goodhart's twelve-year-old son, Mark, was attempting this with some difficulty.

"Here," Trevor said, moving forward from the back of the office, "let me give you a hand."

The girl looked to be in her mid-twenties and she smiled self-consciously, at the same time turning as red as the ink stains on her own piece of blotting paper.

"Thanks."

Two young men working alongside her tried to disguise their apparent disdain at Trevor's offer of assistance. Although commendable *esprit de corps* might well prevail within the branch, it would seem that this did not necessarily extend to acts of chivalry. Having made the move, Trevor decided this girl should be the recipient of his next questioning.

"My name's Trevor Smith. I imagine you know why we're here – Mr Goodhart and myself."

The girl nodded, but said nothing.

"And you are …?"

Trevor left the question hanging in the air. The girl did not look as though she would be very forthcoming, but she eventually replied.

"Miss Simcock."

"Just Miss Simcock?"

The girl looked startled. Then she got the message.

"Daphne."

Trevor smiled. The relationship between branch staff and inspectors was never easy, at least initially. He needed to try and put the girl at her ease.

"We had a Daphne at my last branch. Perhaps it's a National Counties thing."

Daphne reddened even more.

"Sorry," Trevor continued. "It's hardly a time to try and be light-hearted – after yesterday. How could something like that have happened in this part of the world?"

Daphne nodded and her eyes moistened, blurring turquoise irises which, despite the girl's embarrassment, had been directed at Trevor with penetrating acuity.

"I can't stop thinking about poor old Barney. I wonder how he's getting on."

"Mr Goodhart's going up to the hospital this morning."

Trevor again had the girl's full attention and her eyes now shone with alacrity.

"Really? We were told we couldn't go up there. That's what the manager said. How come your inspector can?"

"Our Mr Goodhart's a bit of a free spirit. He thought it was the right thing to do."

The answer seemed to please Daphne

"I'm so glad. Will he let us know how Barney's getting on?"

"I'm sure he will – assuming he gets told something. You all seem to think a lot of Barney. I saw your Get Well card going around yesterday."

Daphne's inhibition had now ebbed away, but she dropped her voice, as if she did not want her colleagues to hear.

"He's lovely. To tell you the truth, he's the nicest man here. He's the last person who should have been attacked."

"Have you been told what actually happened?"

"Not really. But I bet Barney put up a fight. I reckon he got shot because he was protecting Mr Fairweather. How else could it have happened? Who'd want to shoot the guard when Mr Fairweather had the cash? It doesn't make any sense."

Trevor could only agree with her logic.

"Did Barney always go with Mr Fairweather to Lamberhurst?"

Daphne nodded.

"Every day. They were like two peas in a pod. It was like clockwork."

"You mean the routine?"

"Yes. Every morning at twenty past nine Mr Fairweather asked Barney if he was ready. It became quite a joke with us all. Barney was always ready. I'm not sure Mr Fairweather saw the funny side. He doesn't have much sense of humour ..."

Daphne suddenly paused, as if realizing what a predicament Douglas Fairweather must be in right now.

Trevor certainly echoed such a sentiment, but something else was now worrying him.

"You said it was all like clockwork. You mean this was the daily routine?"

"Of course. It had to be. Lamberhurst opens at ten every day. That doesn't give a lot of time to get the cash ready here and then make the journey."

"Did they always use Barney's car?"

"They had to. Mr Fairweather had to sit in the back – with his cash. That way he kept control over it. He couldn't do that if he was driving his own car."

So, at 9.20 every morning, both men stepped out of the bank on to the pavement and got into Barney Wilson's car. Trevor had just one more question.

"And their route to Lamberhurst?"

Daphne looked puzzled.

"Their route?"

"Yes. Which way did they go?"

"Up Frant Road, I suppose. Then past the golf club and Frant railway station. That's the way I go to Lamberhurst."

"And that's the way they went every day?"

"I imagine so."

Trevor groaned inwardly. Same people; same time; same car; and same route.

Just what the raider ordered.

All right, to do otherwise was not necessarily easy. Yet, somehow, routines needed to be changed. And routes certainly needed to be varied. Bank regulations did not stipulate this for fun. It was the same with any procedure which might attract the attention of would-be miscreants.

"You mean Mr Fairweather and Barney didn't vary the route?"

"How could they?"

Trevor would not necessarily expect Daphne to answer that one. But Colonel Fawkes-William and Mr Barnett should have enough nous to seek out varied routes.

Just starting the journey by going up Mount Pleasant, rather than down, would be one option. Making alternative detours around side streets would be another. Anything to break the pattern. And although Trevor had only been in the area for about three months, he knew that Lamberhurst could also be reached from Tunbridge Wells via Pembury and the A21 towards Hastings.

Such a route might take a little longer, but was that not better than making things so easy for villains?

But this was a question to pose to management, rather than Daphne, probably by Mr Goodhart, rather than himself. For now, he decided to change the subject.

"What about the amount of cash yesterday? The sub-branch case must have been crammed to capacity."

Daphne shook her head.

"I don't know anything about that. But there was a bit of a to-do on Friday."

"Oh?"

"I'm not sure I should be telling you this."

Even in his short time 'on the road', as the job of inspection staff was described, Trevor had heard these words before. They could mean something or nothing. And unless the safety of the bank or staff was at risk, he never encouraged junior staff to question where their loyalties lay. He would certainly not expect Daphne to bare her soul to the detriment of her colleagues. Far better, for details of any contretemps to come from the lips of the manager or sub-manager – if they had been aware of what had happened.

But Daphne seemed keen to continue.

"I don't think Mr Fairweather and Mr Grimshawe really got on. In fact, we're all a bit in awe of Mr Fairweather. Well, he's going to be the manager at Lamberhurst, so he told us. And him and the manager upstairs seem to be real buddies. But Mr Grimshawe had set his own heart on being in charge at Lamberhurst – if it was ever going to be upgraded."

"So, was this to-do on Friday about their rivalry?"

"I'm not sure. But Mr Grimshawe always insists the cash in the other tills is kept to a minimum. I know that because I often hold the relief till at the end of the counter. Anyway, after we closed on Friday, I heard them having an argument in the strongroom. Mr Grimshawe wanted the bulk of the cash transferred over to him. But Mr Fairweather refused. He said he needed to have it all ready for Monday, because it was going to be such a busy day."

"That seems fair enough."

"That's what I thought. And it turned out to be the right thing – with Mr Grimshawe not turning up yesterday. What would Mr Fairweather have done if he hadn't stood firm?"

It was a good point. But Trevor could not help thinking it would have meant less cash having been stolen. Yet, it was a strange requirement for Mr Grimshawe to insist on. Cash within tills should always be kept to a minimum on the actual counter – to reduce any loss should a branch be raided. But after the branch had closed for business, provided the cash was properly locked away in the strongroom overnight, did it really matter if it was held under the control of different cashiers? Was Mr Grimshawe being too pernickety? And another thought now crossed Trevor's mind: did this business have any bearing on his disappearance?

"Had Mr Grimshawe not turned up like this before?" he asked Daphne, who now seemed to be quite relaxed about carrying on such a conversation.

She shook her head.

"No. We can't think where he's got to. Mr Barnett thinks he's gone to Northampton with his wife. Her mother's ill up there. But, if that was the case, Mr Grimshawe would have told us, wouldn't he?"

"You'd think so. Mr Goodhart's gone round to his house this morning. To see if he can discover anything. He was going there before visiting the hospital. Perhaps he's found something out."

"I do hope so. Mr Grimshawe's quite a poppet."

A poppet? A relief cashier calling the first cashier a poppet? How would Mr Grimshawe react to that?

Daphne seemed to realize she might have overstepped the mark.

"I shouldn't have said that, should I? You won't tell him, will you?"

Chance would be a fine thing. Trevor had the feeling that far more pertinent things would be said to Mr Grimshawe when he actually turned up.

After giving her the assurance she was seeking, Trevor decided he had taken up too much of Daphne's time. Perhaps a visit upstairs was now warranted.

Trevor had often thought the staff in the securities section of a branch considered themselves to be the elite. Yet, at one time, they had all been accounting clerks and cashiers. Somehow, some of them seemed to try and erase such perceived lowly status from their memories. They had now risen above such tasks. Or so they thought. Here in Tunbridge Wells, these people worked alongside the manager's room. Such an arrangement could only enhance their hierarchic tendencies.

When he entered the section, the first thing Trevor saw was a tin box with its lid wide open. What was it about tin boxes in this branch? This one blatantly contained a stock of travellers' cheques. Once signed by a traveller such cheques were as good as cash. Even before they were issued and signed, they were effectively bearer documents. For this reason, they needed to be kept under lock and key at all times.

And there the box sat proudly on a desk – unattended.

This time, Trevor really was tempted to pick up the box and disappear. Disappear? Mr Grimshawe's name flashed across his mind. With security so lax throughout the branch, had the first cashier done what Trevor was now considering? Had he disappeared with all his cash? With the benefit of hindsight, they really should have checked his till yesterday. Was this thought also now going through Mr Goodhart's mind?

But instead of disappearing with the box, Trevor took it to the man who looked to be in charge of the section.

"I think you'd better have this."

The man looked up.

"Oh, thanks."

Unbelievable! Thanks? Again? Had he and Mr Barnett been on the same training course for good manners? But this time, Trevor could not let the comment go by.

"Is that all you can say?"

The man was probably twice Trevor's age, yet his reply had been so naïve. With inspectors in the branch? Every member of staff should be on full alert to ensure everything was being done by the book.

Instead, no one of any seniority seemed to be bothered.

Was all this laxity down to a form of arrogance? Were they applying that old adage: it can never happen to us?

Yet it had – yesterday.

And rules were still being broken. Mr Goodhart certainly believed the manager to be arrogant. Was that attitude filtering down to his staff?

Trevor stared hard at the man.

"How can you possibly leave travellers' cheques lying around like that?"

"You think I did that?"

"I don't know … Mr …?"

"Chesterton."

"But you're in charge up here, Mr Chesterton?"

Chesterton nodded, albeit reluctantly.

"I can't keep my eye on everything."

Really? Trevor was certainly learning about the best and the worst of people in this branch. Barney Wilson seemed to have what it takes and Daphne had been quite impressive just now. But Messrs Barnett and Chesterton? And they were supposed to be in charge of their respective sections. Yet they certainly left much to be desired.

Trevor watched Chesterton lock the travellers' cheques box before placing it in a cupboard which he also duly locked.

The man certainly looked the part of a senior clerk in the securities section. He wore a charcoal pin-striped suit and he had the air about him of someone in control. Yet the travellers' cheques box had been left unattended and unlocked. Where else was he falling down? What about bearer certificates? Were they being kept locked away under dual control at all times?

Mr Goodhart had always drilled into Trevor that the observance of rules and regulations was especially paramount in the securities section. Apart from housing items of a bearer nature, legal documents abounded – often related to collateral deposited with the bank against loans and overdrafts. These could include deeds of houses, life insurance policies and stocks and shares. All such items had to be dealt with precisely and held under strict conditions of security. In order to handle such legal documentation, Chesterton and his colleagues would have obtained, or would be studying for, their banking qualifications under the aegis of the Institute of Bankers. But no acquired qualification would guarantee the elimination of sheer negligence or carelessness in carrying out their work.

Leaving Mr Chesterton to get on with his duties, Trevor decided, at this stage, not to investigate further possible irregularities in this section. They were unlikely to have any bearing on what had happened at Lamberhurst yesterday. That had been a strictly cash matter. Any control issues relating to cash would be restricted to downstairs.

But if there were also problems of laxity in security measures upstairs – and right outside the manager's room – it was a sure indication of a general malaise in security requirements throughout the branch.

And that could well have had a bearing on what happened yesterday.

CHAPTER 15

They only just made it to the pub in time. David had chosen the one nearest to the branch and, when they walked through the door, the landlord was calling last orders. They might manage to get a drink, but whether he and Trevor would get anything to eat was another matter.

David had collected Trevor from the branch after returning from Haywards Heath. The journey had been uneventful. That was just as well. He needed to put Angus McPhoebe's haranguing behind him and sitting behind the wheel of his Consul, he had been able to plan his major task that afternoon: to check Mr Grimshawe's till.

But before doing this he needed some nourishment. No doubt Trevor felt the same.

"A pint, Trevor?"

Trevor shook his head.

"Twice in twenty-four hours? You know that's not me, sir. No, a lemonade, please."

David smiled and motioned Trevor to a table by the window. He gave the landlord their order and then looked inside a glass cabinet which sat on the end of the bar. It contained a couple of sandwiches whose curled up ends prevented him from identifying the fillings. Ugh! Alongside the sandwiches, two tired-looking sausage rolls appeared a mite more appetizing and he ordered them from the landlord. It was hardly enough to keep them going, but at least Sarah would be cooking something tonight. As for Trevor …

"This enough for you, Trevor?" he asked, when he reached their table with the drinks and food.

Trevor nodded.

"I'm treating myself to fish and chips tonight – with plenty of salt and vinegar."

David could almost smell the mouth-watering aroma. He felt so envious. Then he reflected on what Sarah might provide. It was bound to be even better. He would settle for hot-pot again, but knew Sarah would not serve it up two days on the run. A fry-up would be an enticing alternative.

But before then, there was much to be done and he was anxious to learn how Trevor had got on this morning.

"You're not going to like it," Trevor said, munching into his sausage roll as if it were his last meal. "What I discovered, I mean. I found the code box lying on a desk downstairs – unlocked, would you believe? And upstairs, it was the same with the travellers' cheques box."

It took David a moment to register the enormity of what he had just heard. Strict control over such boxes was sacrosanct. Not only had this always been the case in every branch he had worked, but in his three years on the road, he had not come across a single instance when such a box had been left lying around and unlocked.

Yet, in Tunbridge Wells, it had happened twice in one morning.

"What did they have to say about it?"

Trevor shook his head, dislodging a few crumbs from around his mouth on to his tie.

"Mr Barnett just said thanks when I gave him the code box. And, incredibly, Mr Chesterton – he's in charge of securities upstairs – said exactly the same."

"At least they were polite."

Trevor seemed to appreciate the sarcasm and smiled.

"It was as if I'd handed them one of these sausage rolls."

David shook his head. "They might not thank you for that."

But it was difficult to comprehend such an attitude by senior staff.

"If they're so careless," David added, "with inspectors in the place, what do you think they get up to when we're not here?"

"And that's not all, sir."

David was raising his tankard to his lips, but he quickly put it down. Trevor had a look about him. And his tone of voice radiated real concern. Far better, to let him have his say first. A sup of ale could come later. The last thing David needed was for more outrageous revelations to cause him to splutter into his beer.

"I had a long chat," Trevor continued, "with one of the girls. Her name's Daphne Simcock. She was working on ledgers right behind the cashiers' run. Anyway, I got talking about the routine for Lamberhurst sub-branch. And that's exactly what it is – a strict routine.

David frowned. He could tell what was coming.

"You mean the same every day? Including the route?"

Trevor nodded and pursed his lips.

"It seems they never vary anything."

"What did our Mr Barnett have to say about that?"

"I decided not to tackle him about it. I think it would be better coming from you, sir."

David agreed with that. It might, in fact, be better to raise it first with Colonel Fawkes-William.

"Or the manager?"

"Better still, sir. Especially the way Mr Barnett's looking."

"Oh?"

"When I saw him about the code box, it was as if he didn't care. He just appeared resigned at having put up another black mark. Having said that, he was happy enough to try and put the blame on the manager. But he looks as though he's got the whole world on his shoulders."

"It's all getting too much for him?"

"I reckon so. But I think there's more to it than that. It seems to me something else may have happened."

"Something else?"

As he posed the question, David realized that anything could happen at this particular branch. Such clear flouting of the rules was a recipe for disaster.

"I'm not really sure what," Trevor replied, draining his glass of lemonade. "But there seemed to be an atmosphere around the branch. And not just because I was poking my nose around. It was as if something else had been discovered. And not to do with the raid – or Mr Grimshawe."

"No specific clues?"

Trevor shook his head.

"No, sir. But apart from that, there was something else – about Mr Grimshawe. Something Daphne told me. He had a row with Mr Fairweather. On Friday."

"A row?"

"She actually called it a to-do – in the strongroom, after the branch had closed. She said Mr Grimshawe wanted Mr Fairweather to transfer over his bulk cash. But he refused."

David frowned.

"Why would he refuse?"

"According to Daphne, he said he needed the cash in his till because it was going to be a busy day on Monday. Is that why there was so much in the sub-branch case?"

"Perhaps. But is it possible he had some kind of premonition? That Mr Grimshawe might not turn up on Monday? If he'd passed the bulk over, he'd have been rather stuck on Monday morning – without Mr Grimshawe being there."

"It makes you think, sir."

"But why? Why did Mr Grimshawe want the cash handed over? You said they rowed on Friday after the branch had closed. Why transfer the money over then? Was it part of a plan? Linked to his disappearance?"

The more David thought about it, the more they needed to check Mr Grimshawe's till as soon as possible. He followed Trevor's example and emptied his glass and then rose to leave.

But Trevor raised his hand to stop him.

"Just before we go, sir, how did you get on? This morning?"

"I'll tell you on the way up to the branch. We can't hang around. We must get the duplicate keys out from Lloyds. The sooner we check Mr Grimshawe's till the better."

Chapter 16

David's palms had every reason to be damp. But they were not. Yet he could feel the perspiration elsewhere. Just in case, he wiped his hands surreptitiously on the seat of his trousers.

No one else noticed.

Of the four of them, only Trevor would be feeling as apprehensive as himself. Mr Barnett simply seemed resigned to events which conspired to thwart his normal day's work, while Norman Chilstone, the second cashier, would hardly believe that Mr Grimshawe might have absconded with the contents of his till.

Chilstone was one of the two usual keyholders of the door to the strongroom. He had already clarified yesterday's situation. He had been attending the sub-branch in Rusthall; in his absence one of the juniors had been his designated deputy. With the grille door then having been left wide open, Mr Barnett would certainly be better advised to appoint more senior staff to hold the keys. If they were not available downstairs, what about those in the securities section?

Mr Barnett, himself, was now the deputy for the other key and he and Chilstone unlocked the grille and swung it open.

As they all moved forward into the strongroom, David clasped hold of the duplicate keys for Grimshawe's till. The staff at Lloyds had not been best pleased to be asked to release them in the middle of a busy day. Too bad. David's own concerns far outweighed any sensitivities at that other bank.

He looked around him. The strongroom was similar to most others in branches of National Counties. Apart from racks of shelving which accommodated books and ledgers, inner safes occupied most of the remaining space. A specific section was set aside for items handled by the securities department – deeds, documents, share certificates and customers' valuables held for safe-keeping – while the remaining safes would be reserved for cash.

When not in use on the counter, cashiers' cash boxes would be deposited in individual, lockable safes within the main strongroom. Bags of coin would rest on the floor of each such safe, while surplus notes – too bulky to fit into the actual cash boxes – would be stacked on shelves. Nearly all such notes would normally be held by the first cashier. For this reason, Mr Grimshawe's individual safe was far larger than the others.

The moment had now arrived.

Was David's decision yesterday going to come back to haunt him? Should he have checked all the cash in the branch? Angus McPhoebe certainly thought so. God forbid that David would next have to face this man, suitably shamefaced at having got it wrong.

He could hardly control his fingers as he placed the appropriate key into the lock on the door of Grimshawe's safe. He then glanced at Trevor. The lad did not return the look, preferring to stare steadfastly at the safe. Trevor was almost certainly sharing his own thoughts.

If only they could be as unsuspecting as the other two. As far as Messrs Barnett and Chilstone were concerned, this must simply seem to be an extension of the inspectorial cash check carried out yesterday. They would be far more concerned at having to shelve their other work by being here in the strongroom.

It was all right for them. They did not have Angus McPhoebe on their backs.

David shuddered to think about McPhoebe's reaction should Grimshawe's safe prove to be empty. But was it really feasible for the first cashier to have absconded with all his cash?

Of course it was!

The more David thought about the man's disappearance the more likely Mr Grimshawe had gone off with all the money. And what about Mrs Grimshawe? It was only a neighbour's opinion that she had gone to Northampton to see her sick mother. She could easily be with her husband – all set to bask in riches which could never have been earned from a bank cashier's salary.

David turned the key in the lock and eased the door open.

Relief!

The first thing he saw were a dozen or so brick-like packages. These would be bundles of notes, wrapped and sealed in paper covers. These notes would be surplus to requirements in the branch and were ready for despatch to the bank's regional cash centre.

At least Mr Grimshawe had not taken these with him.

David then cast his eyes down to the floor of the safe. Canvas bags covered almost the entire surface. There were about ten beige-coloured bags for holding silver – half-crowns, florins, shillings and sixpences; four blue bags would contain copper – pennies and ha'pennies; and one green bag would be full of thrupenny bits.

So far so good – provided the packets and bags actually contained their apparent contents.

That just left Mr Grimshawe's cash box. It sat on the bottom shelf of the safe and David momentarily hesitated before lifting it up. What if it felt as light as a down-filled pillow?

Relief again. He needed both hands to lift the box out of the safe and place it on an adjacent table. He selected the most likely-looking key from the bunch in his hand and opened the lid. The box contained as normal-looking contents of a cashier's till box as he could have hoped to see.

His smile of relief matched the expression on Trevor's face.

"I think we can now start counting, Trevor."

Mr Barnett looked at him quizzically.

"Do you need us any longer, sir?"

David looked around the safe. Apart from the table upon which he had placed the cash box, there was another one they could also use to count the cash. Trevor and he would do all the counting, but a member of staff ought also to be present. He would not expect this to be Mr Barnett, nor Norman Chilstone who would be needed on the counter.

"No, Mr Barnett. We'll do all the counting. But we need to have someone with us. A junior, maybe?"

The sub-manager nodded.

"I'll go and find someone."

"And perhaps that person could bring along a set of scales."

Mr Barnett nodded again and left, leaving Chilstone with them until the junior arrived. David glanced at the cashier.

"Have you any idea what might have happened to Mr Grimshawe?"

Chilstone shook his head.

"It's so unlike him, sir. I've only ever known him to be off sick once."

"You reckon he's ill?"

Chilstone frowned.

"What else could have happened?"

David turned his attention back to the cash box and removed bundles of notes for counting. It seemed that Chilstone had no suspicions about Mr Grimshawe's absence. What was more, this must be the case throughout the branch. Any suspicions or conjectures of intrigue would have been avid talking points among all the staff. There would be no way that Chilstone, as Mr Grimshawe's deputy, would have missed out on any resultant speculation. As it was, he clearly thought the first cashier was simply sick.

"What sort of man is he?" David asked, ignoring Chilstone's question. Far better to take the opportunity to establish an opinion of Mr Grimshawe from someone working alongside him. Especially as such a view might not necessarily equate with that of the manager or sub-manager.

Chilstone grinned.

"He's one of the old school. Not like Mr Barnett. Our sub-manager's much older, of course. But Mr Grimshawe's like the old school with his cashiering."

"You mean he's efficient?"

Chilstone actually reddened. Had he perceived the question as an implied rebuke of the standard of cashiering carried out by younger cashiers, such as himself? It was not the first time

David's intended words of humour had been taken literally.

Trevor took it upon himself to come to Chilstone's rescue.

"Don't you remember back in Barnmouth, sir?"

How could David forget? The first cashier down there had been a law unto himself – in more ways than one. But David knew exactly what Chilstone and Trevor meant. The old-school cashier was normally someone who would deal with one transaction in the time a more energetic and younger cashier would handle six. But there could be a consolation. Such precise cashiering usually eliminated differences – and the time taken in resolving them. Was Mr Grimshawe such a cashier? His till was certainly in apple-pie order.

"So he was accurate to a fault?"

Chilstone smiled his thanks at Trevor's intervention.

"Always, sir."

"And do you like him?"

The cashier seemed surprised at the question.

"Of course. Everyone likes him."

The conversation was helping to build up a picture of the man: extremely accurate in his work; diligent in that he rarely took sick leave; and likeable as a man. Yet, according to the neighbour, he preferred to go fishing, rather than accompany his wife on trips to see her unwell mother. Was he a bit selfish? Or did it simply reflect long-standing in-law difficulties, about which the branch might be unaware?

Before David could pursue his questioning, a small girl with long fair hair, tied back into a pigtail, joined them in the strongroom. She was armed with a set of scales and accompanying weights.

Trevor's eyes immediately lit up.

"Hello, again."

The girl smiled and handed over the scales.

"Mr Barnett said you needed these. And he wants me to keep an eye on you."

David raised his eyebrows.

"That doesn't sound like the words he would have used – not for our hearing, anyway."

The girl reacted like Chilstone had just done.

"I'm sorry, sir. They were my words, actually. But I've come to take over from Norman."

Trevor seemed to approve of the change.

"This is Daphne, sir. I told you about her earlier."

Daphne feigned alarm.

"Only good things," Trevor quickly added.

Daphne now displayed mock relief and Chilstone took the opportunity to return to his cashiering.

David could quite understand Trevor's enthusiastic welcome of the girl. Without casting aspersions on Chilstone, Daphne was certainly a more decorative overseer while they counted Mr Grimshawe's cash.

But this was not the time for idle chat and, after shaking the girl's hand, David asked her to take a seat on the solitary upright chair in the strongroom. He and Trevor would do their counting of the cash while standing at the tables.

It took them just under an hour to count all the notes and weigh all the coin. And Mr Grimshawe's till balanced to the penny. So there, Angus McPhoebe!

But this was not about point scoring. The till might have proved to be correct, but Grimshawe was still missing.

At least he had not gone off with all his cash. But what about that in the sub-branch case?

David looked at his watch. Three-fifteen. The branch would now be closed and he needed to see Colonel Fawkes-William. Not only did he want to bring the manager up to date, but he also wanted to tackle him about the lapses in security which Trevor had discovered.

And Mrs Grimshawe might well have returned from Northampton. Would she ring him? A clarifying call about her husband would certainly be most welcome.

With the cash soon locked away, David was ready for his next task: to tackle Colonel Fawkes-William.

CHAPTER 17

Alfie Templeton was ravenous. Neither food nor water had passed his lips for well over thirty-six hours. Even back on Sunday evening he had only nibbled on some biscuits and cheese. He had been too keyed up to have contemplated anything more substantial.

For the same reason, he had then forgone any breakfast on Monday morning. He had been more concerned at getting on the road to Tunbridge Wells. What a bad decision that had been: to shun his normal bacon and eggs.

Now, on Tuesday morning, he was famished.

Almost as bad, he had just stubbed out his last Woodbine. He could not remember when he had gone more that a couple of hours without a fag. Now, he had no idea when he might be able to savour his next one.

No wonder his nerves were still jangling.

Even in his self-imposed incarceration, he could not ignore the irony of it all. There must be over £50,000 in the sub-branch case, with three times that much in the boot of the Oxford. Yet all he now craved was a ham sandwich, a glass of water and a cigarette.

He glanced across the barn to the body which lay prostrate under the only window in the ramshackle building. A sliver of congealed blood was just visible behind the man's right ear. At first, Templeton had feared he had hit him too hard. Now he wished he had finished the job completely.

Fairweather's constant sobbing had increasingly got on his nerves. It had then turned to snivelling. But when this suddenly stopped, to be replaced by scornful vitriol, Templeton could take it no longer.

This was the last thing he needed. His eyes had darted around the barn until he spotted an old pickaxe handle. Its head had been shorn off, otherwise there would be more than just a trace of blood besmirching Fairweather's skull.

But the way Templeton was now feeling, he wished the axe's head had still been attached to the handle.

He now closed his eyes and forced himself to consider his situation. He had to think rationally. But he knew this would be evermore difficult as each hour passed. His growing hunger and cigarette dependency would see to that.

Opening his eyes again, he glanced at his watch. Eleven-thirty. And was it still only Tuesday? He felt he had been cooped up in this barn for at least a week.

He moved over to the double doors through which he had driven the Oxford yesterday morning. Ill-fitting hinges had caused him difficulty in closing the doors behind the car and his best efforts had not been entirely successful. There was a three- inch gap between the doors and he now peered through this to check on the weather.

It was dry outside, but leaden skies threatened imminent rain. Dare he venture out? But how far would he have to go to find some form of nourishment? If only it had been later in the year. The surrounding fields ought then to have yielded something. Potatoes? Beans? Lettuces? And what about fruit? This area was supposed to be the Garden of England.

But now? Towards the end of March he would be lucky to find a petal from a late-flowering daffodil.

No, any chance of finding food would only come from some form of habitation: a farmhouse, cottage or shop. But how far would such properties be from this God-forsaken barn? Suddenly, he realized its sheer isolation was proving to be a liability.

It was then that he saw the rabbit. It sat no more than twenty feet away, nibbling at some undergrowth, apparently without a care in the world. Templeton's eyes narrowed and then widened as two more appeared from the hedge alongside the track which led to the barn.

Was this the answer to his prayers?

He might have a better chance of achieving a direct hit with a shotgun, but all he had was his revolver. But what about the resultant noise? Could he risk taking a pot shot? The barn might well be isolated, but a gun shot would resonate far and wide.

Was it a chance worth taking?

The thought of then skinning and gutting the rabbit was another matter. And how would he cook it? Raw flesh would be inedible, never mind lacking in nourishment. He had, of course, been a boy scout, but that was long ago. Yet he still had a half-full box of Swan Vestas. And looking around the barn, he could see plenty of material with which to build a fire.

Realistically, what other option did he have? He needed to stay in this barn for another day, just to make sure of a trouble-free getaway. By then the police would, surely, have left the area. But that would mean well over two days without food or water. Those rabbits looked to be his only answer and, if the rain did come, it should not be beyond him to collect some water in one form of receptacle or another.

And it was a fact that he was feeling drained of energy and at the end of his nerves. Without food and water how much worse would he be feeling after another twenty-four hours?

But there was another problem: he was not alone. What about Fairweather's needs? Before his coming together with the pickaxe handle, he had been complaining about the lack of food. One rabbit was hardly going to satisfy them both. And Templeton doubted if he would get more than one chance of taking a pot shot.

There was no doubting Fairweather had become an outright liability. If only he had finished off the job earlier. Yet he could not believe such thoughts were going through his mind.

Forty-eight hours ago, he had simply been a petty crook, though about to move up a division after years of careful planning. Since then, he had become an outright killer, with further murderous intent now in prospect. How could it have possibly come to this? But, realistically, another murder rap would make little difference should he ever get caught. And if it enabled him to stay free, the resultant benefits far outweighed the demise of this now-pathetic man. What was more, the longer he was lumbered with Fairweather, the more likely he was to get caught.

Templeton turned his mind back to the rabbits and looked again through the gap between the doors. There were still three of them outside, clearly oblivious of any possible danger. He got out his revolver and checked the chamber. He knew he had only used one bullet on the bank's guard, but it was better to be safe than sorry. Yes, there were still five bullets remaining.

But, because of the noise, he could only really afford the luxury of using one bullet, so which option should he choose? Fairweather or a rabbit?

He looked back and forth between the rabbits and the prostrate body under the window. Clenching his teeth he made his decision and took careful aim.

Chapter 18

There were times when David had no difficulty in hiding his true feelings. He could be as inscrutable as a Chinese mandarin. Now was such a time to draw upon such a facility.

He could not believe what he was seeing and hearing. Having introduced Trevor to Colonel Fawkes-William, he and his assistant now sat on the two chairs across from the manager's desk. And the Colonel was exuding charm personified.

"Good to meet you, young man. My word the bank certainly needs up and coming chaps like you. Got to have good people to replace old-stagers like me, what?"

He leaned back in his chair and positively beamed at Trevor over his pince-nez. But he was not yet finished.

"Of course, I did your job once. My goodness that was many years ago now. Well before the war. Didn't have new-fangled machines in those days. Had to do everything by hand, what? That was when bank clerks really could add up. Had to, of course."

Still beaming he closed his eyes, as if recalling those good old days. But he soon gave Trevor the benefit of his full attention again.

"Expect you've learnt some of our old tricks of the trade. Dreamt them up long ago. Spotting differences I mean. By using transpositions. Like £10 for £100. That nearly always led to the solving of a £90 difference. And how about £54? 6 for 60, what? Good tricks, eh? Could save hours of ticking back. Not so much need for such ruses these days. Not with these new machines of ours."

David stole a glance at Trevor who sat there expressionless. What was the lad thinking? Was he being taken in by all this twaddle? No, he was too wise for that. He was simply mimicking David's own poker face.

But what was Fawkes-William up to? It was still only the day after his guard had nearly been killed and his sub-branch cashier had been abducted with all his cash. Yet, here he was, waxing lyrical about the good old days.

And throughout this exchange – a one-way verbal exchange because Trevor's only contribution had been polite nods of his head – David had been completely ignored. It seemed to be another example of the Colonel wanting to exert some pre-ordained initiative in order to dominate proceedings.

In which case, he was now in for an enormous shock. David had suffered long enough from playing third fiddle.

"Machines of any sort are the last things on our minds," he said, drawing forth a startled reaction from the Colonel. It was as if some interloper had infiltrated himself into his private discussion with Trevor. "I went to visit Barney Wilson this morning. You were right. I wasn't able to see him. But they're pleased with his progress. He should regain consciousness shortly."

It took a couple of seconds for the Colonel to register this abrupt change of subject.

"Wilson? Ah, yes. Good, good. But what about Fairweather?"

What about Fairweather? How could David know anything about Fairweather? It was another instance of Fawkes-William's order of priorities. Simply "good, good" about Barney Wilson, but, more importantly, "what about Fairweather?"

"I've had no news from the police. Have you?"

Colonel Fawkes-William shook his head.

"No. Neither has McPhoebe."

"You've spoken to McPhoebe?"

"Yes, at lunchtime. You'd just left him. He wasn't best pleased."

David started to seethe. These exchanges between McPhoebe and Fawkes-William were looking ever more conspiratorial. But why? Everyone within the bank should be batting on the same side. In this case, the other two seemed to share the same agenda of inspector-bashing. This might simply be a case of neither of them liking him. Or was there something more sinister about their antagonistic attitude towards a visiting inspector?

"In what way?" David asked, attempting to disguise his own antagonism. "What did McPhoebe have to say?"

The Colonel immediately adopted his smug-like pose and leant back in his chair, his hands clasped in front of him, fingers steepled. David now had no doubt that Trevor must share his own opinion of the man.

"Let's just say," the Colonel replied, a smirk touching his lips, "that McPhoebe didn't seem too pleased about your cash check. That you hadn't counted all the cash yesterday."

This time David could not hide his feelings. How dare McPhoebe divulge such information to Fawkes-William! And what else had he chosen to disclose?

"Well it's all counted now! And my judgement yesterday was sound. Mr Grimshawe's till balanced to the penny. So he hasn't done a bunk with all his cash."

This last thought had probably not crossed the Colonel's mind. But why not sow the seeds that this particular investigation might extend beyond the actual armed hold-up in Lamberhurst? Especially as he would soon be hearing about the lapses in security which Trevor had discovered.

The Colonel looked suitably shaken.

"Done a bunk?"

David shrugged his shoulders.

"Had it not crossed your mind?"

"Certainly not! Grimshawe's a good man."

Here we go again.

"But he's disappeared. He hasn't reported in. I went round to his house this morning and he wasn't there. A neighbour said his wife had gone to see her sick mother in Northampton. But she went alone. Mr Grimshawe preferred to go fishing. That was on Sunday morning and he hasn't been seen since. So, the thought certainly crossed my mind – that he'd disappeared with the contents of his till."

"Anyway he hasn't. You've now confirmed that. You just said his till balanced to the penny"

David nodded.

"Yes, thank goodness. But he's still disappeared. I left a note at his house for his wife to contact me – when she returned from Northampton. That should be this afternoon. Maybe, she'll be able to shed some light on her husband's whereabouts."

If only. But what about Mrs Grimshawe, herself? No doubt the Colonel would not deign to mix socially with the likes of the Grimshawes, but he should know something about her. Was she an innocent party in all of this?

"What about Mrs Grimshawe?" David asked. "Do you know her well?"

The Colonel looked wide-eyed.

"Know her? I've met her. Once or twice. But I can hardly say I know her."

Of course not. A first cashier could only be classed as an other rank. Certainly not officer material.

"So, you don't know anything about her lifestyle?"

The Colonel shook his head. But these questions must have got him thinking. He now appeared to be very much in the present. His reminiscences of his early banking years were now long gone.

"I must say, Goodhart, I'm more concerned about what's happened to Grimshawe, himself. It's not in his character. To disappear like this."

It being three years since his previous inspection here, David certainly needed to learn more about Mr Grimshawe and also about the other main players in this terrible scenario – Barnett, Wilson and Fairweather. And what about Colonel Fawkes-William himself? Was he all that he seemed? Could there be factors in his background that needed to come out into the open?

"Tell me something about your first cashier. What makes him tick?"

The Colonel leant back in his chair again, but this time he did not display his previous arrogance or pomposity. From what he had just said, he probably now doubted that Mr Grimshawe's absence was because of sickness. He might even believe it was something to do with what happened yesterday. David was starting to feel this way; why not Colonel Fawkes-William?

"He's been here for nearly thirty years – including the war years. He must be fifty now. Married, as you know. But no children. Always hard up, though. Of course his salary's not great, but …"

"A big spender?"

"No, not that I'm aware of. But someone once told me he likes a bet …"

"A gambler, then?"

"Possibly."

"You mean you don't know?"

David suddenly felt he was getting the upper hand with this man. If Mr Grimshawe was a gambler, the Colonel should certainly know. 'Possibly' was not the answer of someone who was sure of his facts. And a branch manager should certainly know everything that could be known about each member of his staff. It would be particularly pertinent to know whether or not his first cashier was a gambler.

The Colonel now looked unaccustomedly flustered.

"Well … I'm not sure … how would I know, anyway … without hard facts …"

David decided to leave it at that for the moment. It was a snippet of information to store away. But it was likely to come up again when he got round to discussing staff finances generally.

"What about his ambition? Is he management material?"

"Good Lord, no. Could you imagine him doing my job?"

"I don't know. I've never met him."

Trevor now decided to join in the discussion.

"I was told this morning he wanted the Lamberhurst job – if it was made up to sub-manager status."

"What? Grimshawe? No, that's Douglas's job. It's what I've been planning all along."

Trevor raised his eyebrows.

"It's only what I was told. I also understand he had some form of to-do with Mr Fairweather – in the strongroom, late on Friday afternoon. I gather it was about handing the bulk of his cash over to Mr Grimshawe."

"I don't know anything about that. But if Douglas was involved in any kind of dispute, I'd back him all the way. He's got far more about him than Grimshawe."

David frowned. It was only a short time ago the Colonel had called Mr Grimshawe a good man. And David was also feeling concern for Mr Fairweather – and not just because of the ordeal of his abduction. Fawning by a member of staff towards a manager was one thing. But, this time, it seemed to be the other way round. The Colonel appeared to think Mr Fairweather could do no wrong. How did the cashier live up to this star rating? David would have hated it. He wondered if Mr Fairweather felt the same.

As for Mr Grimshawe, he was now hardly getting a ringing endorsement from the Colonel. Perhaps this was the time to return to the subject of the first cashier's finances.

"You said Mr Grimshawe's hard up. Is that reflected in his bank accounts?"

Colonel Fawkes-William fidgeted in his chair.

"His bank accounts? I wouldn't have thought so. But I leave that sort of thing to Barnett."

David was incredulous.

"Leave it to your sub-manager? You leave the examination of staff accounts to your sub-manager? Does that also mean the examination of the actual staff vouchers?"

Colonel Fawkes-William now pulled himself together.

"I think, Goodhart, that you're overlooking the significance of this branch. After all, it is the Royal Tunbridge Wells branch. I need to spend my time looking after the needs of the good people of this most salubrious community. If this means delegating menial tasks to my sub-manager, such as checking staff vouchers, so be it.

Surely you must be a man to understand the not inconsiderable art of delegation?"

What had happened to the staccato sentences? This was nothing short of a lecture. And his pomposity was back with a vengeance. David had never before heard such an excuse from a manager to absolve himself from one of the bank's strictest rules: the examination of staff bank accounts and their respective vouchers could only be delegated in the manager's absence. Such laxity on the Colonel's part could lead to all sorts of misdemeanours arising. And it now seemed clear that his management style and practice might well have led to the lapses in security which Trevor had discovered this morning.

It was also disturbing that if Mr Grimshawe was as hard up as the Colonel believed, close examination of his accounts had not been made by the manager, personally. A first cashier maintains control of many thousands of pounds. As a bank inspector, David was well aware that it was not totally unheard of for such a cashier to succumb to temptation. And, in this particular instance, the first cashier was now missing. At least, this afternoon's till check had established that he had not gone off with all his cash. But could another scenario be lurking around?

"Colonel Fawkes-William, this particular task is not one for delegation. You know as well as I that the examination of staff accounts and their respective vouchers is the personal responsibility of the branch manager."

"And, my dear Goodhart, it is the responsibility of the branch manager to run his branch as best as he sees fit."

"Even if in doing so, it means breaking the bank's rules?"

"The rules are there for guidance, in particular for our more junior colleagues."

"Rules are rules, Colonel Fawkes-William. They've not been laid down to be acted upon indiscriminately. And that includes those specifically relating to managerial tasks."

"Well I treat Barnett as a fully-paid-up member of my

management team. I have complete faith in him. As far as I'm concerned, he is branch management."

David glanced at Trevor and held out his hand, palm uppermost. "I think, Trevor, this is where you come in."

David imagined Trevor had been following this exchange with mounting alarm. And not just because the Colonel had admitted to flouting basic bank regulations. No, never before would Trevor have witnessed such animosity between two bank officials so much senior to himself. And now he, himself, was being thrust on to centre stage.

"Well, sir," Trevor said, addressing himself to the Colonel and failing to disguise a lump in his throat, "while Mr Goodhart was away from the office this morning, my task was to nose around the office to check on matters of security."

Colonel Fawkes-William now looked apoplectic.

"Nose around? Nose around my branch? To check on security? Was this your idea, Goodhart?"

David now wished he had tackled this matter himself. That initial camaraderie by the Colonel towards Trevor was long past. Maybe, Trevor had been indiscreet to talk about nosing around the branch, but he did not deserve such a hostile response.

"It certainly was, Colonel Fawkes-William. It goes back to yesterday afternoon. Trevor found your strongroom door and grille wide open with no one in the vicinity. That was enough in itself to arouse my suspicions that all might not be well generally. You better carry on now, Trevor."

"Yes, sir. Well, the first thing I found this morning was the code box lying on a back desk. Not only was it lying there unattended, but I soon found it was unlocked. I took it to Mr Barnett, but quite frankly he didn't seem too concerned. That made me think it might not have been a one-off incident. And that view seemed to be confirmed when I went upstairs. I then found the travellers' cheques box also lying around unattended and unlocked."

David watched Colonel Fawkes-William carefully for his reaction to what were catastrophic lapses in branch security. His apoplexy had quickly disappeared and he now appeared lost for words. David gave Trevor a nod.

"Carry on, Trevor."

This did bring forth a response from the Colonel.

"You mean there's more?"

Trevor pursed his lips and nodded.

"Yes, sir. I then asked around about the Lamberhurst procedures."

Colonel Fawkes-William frowned.

"Asked around?"

"Yes, I spoke to one of your girls."

"Why not Barnett?"

"I certainly wasn't going behind his back, sir, if that's what you're thinking. I happened to be talking to the girl about poor old Barney Wilson and it developed from there. Anyway, I got the distinct impression the same sub-branch procedure takes place each day. In other words, the same people, the same timings and the same route. I just wonder if this might have contributed to the ambush."

The Colonel now looked furious.

"Damn Barnett! That's all down to him. What did he have to say about it?"

"I didn't actually speak to him, sir. I felt it might be better coming from Mr Goodhart, or you, sir."

David could not have been more pleased with the way Trevor had handled what was a tricky situation. But he was far from impressed by the way the Colonel readily cast the blame in Mr Barnett's direction. And this echoed what Trevor had experienced this morning: Mr Barnett had not been slow to cast blame upstairs. Despite the Colonel's assertion that the two of them were an integral management team, this now looked to be far from the case. As for Colonel Fawkes-William, was there nothing for which he might accept responsibility? Apart from handling the affairs of the dignitaries of Royal Tunbridge Wells?

"So, Colonel Fawkes-William," David said, enunciating his words precisely, " I think you might now agree that it was worthwhile for me to ask Trevor to look into aspects of your branch security. None of this might have anything to do with what happened yesterday, but ..."

He let his words tail off, now satisfied that the Colonel had taken on board all that had been said. But before ending this interview, he needed to obtain information about those other members of the Colonel's staff.

And he was conscious that, with four o'clock approaching, he had still not yet received a call from Mrs Grimshawe.

CHAPTER 19

David pursed his lips and contemplated Colonel Fawkes-William. Trevor's revelations about the lapses in branch security appeared to have sapped the bluster from the manager.

But David had already experienced the Colonel's ability to bounce back from such apparent adversity. Would this be the case now?

"I'd like to know a little more about Barney Wilson," he said, conscious that the Colonel's reaction might contrast markedly with the picture he had already conjured up of the guard.

The Colonel did not let him down. At the mention of Barney Wilson's name, it was as if a film was drawn down over his eyes. And it did not appear to relate to wistful concern for a man lying unconscious in hospital.

Yet, Barney Wilson had been shot down in the line of duty. And according to Daphne Simcock, he would have put up a fight; doing whatever he could to protect Douglas Fairweather.

And what about Mr Barnett's opinion? The sub-manager had apparently shown genuine compassion for the guard's plight. He also told Trevor about Barney's popularity with everyone in the branch – apart from 'him upstairs'. But that snipe about his manager; was it significant? It hardly smacked of a throwaway line. Had he deliberately cast aspersions on Colonel Fawkes-William? If so, why?

David found these different assessments of Barney Wilson puzzling. Perhaps it was simply natural pomposity on the Colonel's part. Did he have some fixation on the comparative merits of officers and men? After all, he had effectively derided Barney Wilson yesterday for being only (?) a batman in the First World War.

The Colonel now focussed his eyes on David.

"Wilson, eh?"

David nodded.

"I'd certainly like to know if he's married."

No one had yet mentioned this. Had any next of kin been told? The Colonel looked bemused.

"No, well … I don't think so. I've never heard him mention a wife."

David could not believe what he was hearing. Did the Colonel really not know whether someone who must be the oldest person on his staff was married or not?

"In which case, I think we'd better look at his file."

The Colonel leant behind him to a single-drawer mahogany filing cabinet. He pulled open the drawer and stretched to the back to retrieve a manila folder marked B Wilson. Without any attempt to open it up himself, he pushed the closed file across the desk to David.

Opening the folder, David soon found it contained the usual contents of a staff file, mainly copies of the annual managerial reports submitted to Head Office. He glanced at the two latest ones and was not surprised to see that Colonel Fawkes-William had eschewed from making full use of his powers of the English language. When required to express his thoughts on the various categories relating to personal qualities and standards of work, the Colonel had restricted himself to one-word opinions, such as, good, satisfactory and adequate. It was evident that he had given no time or forethought to completing what was, for Barney, an important assessment of his contribution to the functioning of the branch.

David was not impressed. Nor surprised.

He then leafed through to the beginning of the file and found the initial letter from the regional staff manager who had appointed Barney to the position of guard. He took up his duties twelve years ago when he was 57, with his retirement expected to be at the age of 65. It would seem that his recent reports, despite their brevity, were sufficiently well-received to justify his continued employment beyond his laid-down retirement age.

His previous employment had been as a night-watchman at a warehouse in the East End and the bank had received impeccable references from his ex-employer. And David then saw what he was looking for: Barney Wilson was a childless widower. Why did the Colonel not know this?

"I see he's a widower," David said, staring intently at the manager, "with no children."

The Colonel frowned and then nodded knowingly.

"Of course. I remember now. He wanted to come down here from London. To start a new life. In that respect he certainly made a good choice. Tunbridge Wells, I mean."

Not Royal Tunbridge Wells? No, that was probably only for dignitaries – not mere batmen.

"So he doesn't have any family? No next of kin?"

The Colonel shook his head.

"Not to my knowledge. He calls everyone here his family. He gets on so well with us all."

Downstairs, maybe. David cast a sideways glance at Trevor. Was that a surreptitious raising of an eyebrow?

Anyway, it seemed there was no family member to be told of what had happened. But assuming Barney was on the road to recovery, he would get plenty of visitors from the branch. It was also more than likely he was popular with customers. It would certainly be good for some of them to visit the hospital. And if Daphne Simcock was correct, one person who would really want to see him would be Douglas Fairweather. But the cashier would first have to escape from the hands of his abductor.

And what about Fairweather's background and family?

Colonel Fawkes-William positively glowed when David mentioned the sub-branch cashier's name, then quickly became stony-faced, as if suddenly recalling the man's current predicament.

"Terrible business. Terrible. What must Douglas be going through?"

David certainly shared that viewpoint and, somehow, he really needed to have some indication as to how the police investigation was proceeding. The only way to do that would be to arrange a meeting with the officer in charge and he decided to do that as soon as this session with the manager was over. He would not expect to be drawn into the actual police operations, but in any investigation such as this, he needed to be kept in the picture about bank staff. In this particular case, any matters relating to Douglas Fairweather and Barney Wilson would be vital. And he was probably as anxious as the police that, once Barney Wilson had regained consciousness, they needed to learn from him exactly what had happened at Lamberhurst.

"I couldn't agree with you more," he replied, conscious that this was probably the only matter upon which he might concur with the Colonel. "But what about his background – and family? You told me he used to work with Grindlays in India, but how did he end up here in Tunbridge Wells?"

The Colonel immediately reverted to his self-satisfied mode, once again leaning back in his chair and fixing David with a look of ill-concealed complacency.

"I'm not one to crow about such things, but I have to confess to playing a major part in this."

"Oh?" How else could David respond to such sham humility?

"Yes, I met him in the Conservative Club. It was about five years ago. Met him quite by chance. He was just passing through the town. I remember thinking later that it was almost pre-ordained. Extraordinary, really. Anyway, we were in the bar, just the two of us. And he approached me for a light. And that one simple act – the way he did it – convinced me he had what it takes."

What was that about not crowing?

"I can sum up people, of course. His whole demeanour spoke volumes. Just our type, I thought. And when we got talking, I soon learnt he was a banker. We were alone in the bar. He and I. And we were both bankers. Quite a coincidence, what?"

David simply nodded. Having asked his original question, he had no option but to hear the Colonel out. And what was Trevor making of it all? If nothing else, he seemed to be enjoying playing a back seat role. He would not have relished his earlier one-to-one with the Colonel who now appeared to be revelling in recounting his original assessment of Douglas Fairweather.

"Anyway that's when he told me he'd been with Grindlays, in India. He'd been a manager – in Calcutta. But he couldn't stand the climate. Made him ill. Probably to do with his fair skin. So he had no option but to return to Blighty."

"And he was looking for a job here?"

"No, no. He was visiting his mother. She lived somewhere in Sussex, not far from here. It was I who brought up his possible return to banking. I could see him fitting in here. Just our sort of man. In the end, I actually recruited him. I told you that yesterday."

"You certainly did. I still don't really see how you got away with it."

"Got away with it?"

"Yes, as far as the regional staff manager was concerned."

"He was no trouble at all. I got such an impeccable reference for Douglas. The RSM had no choice. He had to go along with me."

"And then you decided to groom Mr Fairweather for Lamberhurst?"

The Colonel beamed.

"But that's only a stepping stone. I'm looking for him to take over from me eventually. I retire in three years' time. He'll be ideal to do my job."

"Except that …"

The Colonel now leaned forward, clearly coming back to reality.

"Yes, yes, of course. A terrible situation. Truly terrible."

David shook his head. Douglas Fairweather's current predicament bore no relationship to the background of his recruitment. But what about next of kin? Had anyone been in touch?

"You said his mother lives in Sussex. Is she the next of kin? Or is he married?"

"No, he's not married. And his mother died a couple of years ago."

As opposed to Barney Wilson, the Colonel seemed to know everything about Douglas Fairweather's situation. He had no need to check with the filing cabinet behind him. On the other hand, that was to be expected if he was already working on the planned upgrading of the Lamberhurst sub-branch, with Fairweather in charge.

"So there's no one to inform about his abduction? No children? No girlfriend, even?"

Colonel Fawkes-William shook his head.

"No, it's sad, really. He's a solitary man. Lives for his job. The others downstairs find him rather serious. But I prefer him like that. Dedication to the job is what it's all about."

David could not imagine life without any family around him. It made him realize how lucky he was to have a wife and son. On the other hand, if something terrible should happen to him, he could not bear the thought of what Sarah and Mark would go through. It was strange, though, that neither Barney Wilson, nor Douglas Fairweather had any next of kin. The only spouse he knew about, so far, was Mr Grimshawe's wife. And with her husband missing, God forbid that she might eventually turn out to be the recipient of bad tidings.

But what about Mr Barnett? David needed to learn something about the sub-manager's background. Trevor had certainly formed reservations about the man. Someone, surely, needed to be straightforward in what was proving to be a strangely-staffed branch. Despite nothing untoward having happened to him (yet?), perhaps his own matrimonial situation might be a good place to start.

"Yes," the Colonel said when David posed the question, "he's certainly married. To something of a bombshell, would you believe?"

No, David found that almost impossible to believe. And he noticed Trevor go wide-eyed at the news.

"Much younger than Barnett," the Colonel continued. "In her early thirties, I'd say."

"Really? You do surprise me."

"When they married – a couple of years ago – the gossips had a field day."

"I'm not surprised. Mr Barnett must be nearing retirement."

"And thereby hangs a problem. Rumours abound. About Barnett's forthcoming retirement. The amount of his pension, I mean. How will his drop in earnings finance his wife's lifestyle?"

David was now getting a bit edgy. It was bad enough learning that the first cashier was probably a bit of a gambler, but to have a sub-manager hooked up with a young, extravagant wife …

"What about her lifestyle?"

The Colonel now looked embarrassed. It seemed quite out of character.

"Well … I'm not really sure. But I'm told she puts herself about a bit, if you know what I mean. It's starting to look bad on the branch. That sort of thing shouldn't happen in Royal Tunbridge Wells."

Of course not. David managed to remain serious, but, inside, he was creasing himself over the Colonel's discomfort in discussing such a topic.

"What sort of thing?"

The Colonel started to fiddle with his fingers and surreptitiously gulped before replying.

"I'm told she's a bit of a rocker. But I have to confess, Goodhart, I don't really know what that means."

David was not really surprised and now had difficulty in suppressing a wry smile. He could not imagine the Colonel being a fan of Elvis Presley or Bill Haley. Colonel Fawkes-William rocking around the clock? And this was not the time for Trevor to admit to playing the tenor saxophone.

"How does Mr Barnett fit into all this? He doesn't seem like a raver to me."

"A raver?"

The manager really was unfamiliar with such matters.

"A rocker, then. Does he share his wife's lifestyle?"

Colonel Fawkes-William sighed.

"I simply don't know. All I do know is that there's been a distinct deterioration in his work since he got married. And if this is down to some form of extravagant lifestyle, having to rely solely on his bank pension will put a stop to that."

David's imagination was now working overtime – and not just with fantasizing on what might be going on in the Barnetts' marriage. Putting all of that to one side, David reckoned he was now one step ahead of the Colonel. Over £50,000 had just been stolen from the bank. And he had just heard that two senior members of the branch staff might have financial problems of one sort or another. On the face of it, what happened at Lamberhurst yesterday had no bearing on these two people. But was it possible for there to be some kind of connection? Before he could pursue this line of thinking, the ring of the Colonel's telephone resounded around the room.

"It's for you, Goodhart," the manager said after lifting the receiver. "Mrs Grimshawe wants to speak to you."

Chapter 20

Alfie Templeton sat on the floor of the barn, back against a wall, and held his head in his hands. He felt incarcerated, cold, tired and hungry. And roast rabbit had definitely not featured on his menu.

He had soon discovered that firing a pistol from a distance was no easy task. Back in Lamberhurst, from six inches, it had been child's play, though he still felt distraught at what he had done. But a rabbit? At twenty to thirty feet? As for his aim; at that distance, he would have been lucky to hit this old barn's door.

And he had been right: the loud report from the gun had scared him witless. In no way could he try again. Instead, he had withdrawn into the barn – and then froze. He could hear a bell clanging up on the main road. The wind must have changed direction, because he heard it loud and clear. But was it getting any nearer? Was it coming down the lane to the barn?

That had been four hours ago and he still only had the company of him over there. Clearly, the gunshot had not been heard and the police car had not been after him. But what was his future? How was he going to get out of this mess? Dusk was now falling and, in the short term, he knew he had no option other than to stay another night in the barn. What was worse, it would be another night, at least.

He closed his eyes to think, but must have then nodded off, only for a familiar sound to wake him from his brief slumber. It was so soft at first, but loud enough to put him on full alert. Perhaps he had expected it all along. But he was now rigid, as a car's engine grew louder. A vehicle was clearly approaching the barn.

Templeton broke out of his stupor and raced to the barn's door. And, thank goodness his 'friend' across the barn still appeared to be unconscious, or sleeping. The arrival of a car would have certainly raised his spirits.

Through the gloom, Templeton now saw the vehicle come into sight. It was large and dark and, for one moment, he thought it to be a dreaded police car. But then he could see it was grey, not unlike his own car, and it was either a Morris or an Austin.

The car then stopped, just across from the barn and the engine cut out. Then, nothing. Not a sound. Not a movement. Templeton peered hard to see what was happening in the car, but it was impossible to make out the driver or any possible passenger.

Then he heard, of all things, a giggle and the driver's door opened, followed quickly by the passenger's. Templeton recoiled in horror as he realized what was happening. A young man was soon embracing a girl in front of the car. Only one thing could occur now: they were bound to make for the barn to continue their canoodling.

What was he to do? Withdraw his gun, for a start. But the horror of the resultant outcome appalled him. What had he got himself into? All because he wanted just one shot at the big-time.

But he was soon closing his eyes in relief. Instead of making for the barn, the driver, with increased giggling from the girl, opened the offside rear door and they squeezed into the back of the car.

Yet, would Templeton's relief be only short-lived? Would this courting couple eventually decide that the barn would be a far more agreeable place to carry out their coupling?

CHAPTER 21

It was such a cheerless room.

Having sat in it alone for over ten minutes, David decided that this police interview room had not been designed to put malefactors or suspects at their ease. Not that he was such a person; he was there at his own request. But in his solitary state, he could imagine harbouring feelings of guilt.

The room must be to blame for this. For a start, it was windowless, with one solitary, unshaded , centrally-hung light bulb which cast hostile shadows against the grey emulsioned walls. The furniture was restricted to an antiquated wooden desk and three accompanying upright chairs. Their unapologetic starkness did not aim to encourage miscreants to feel any vestige of comfort. David might be able to accept this overall unforgiving ambience, but not the two pictures which hung on the wall behind where the interviewing officer would sit. These black and white prints depicted two of the most godforsaken buildings that had ever been built: the forbidding prisons at Princetown on Dartmoor and Parkhurst on the Isle of Wight. What kind of message did this convey to interviewees?

David glanced at his watch; just after half past four.

On his arrival at the police station, the duty front desk officer had immediately shown him into this room and he had been pleased and a little surprised that the detective in charge of the case had agreed to see him so quickly. The police station was just around the corner from the bank and it was only twenty minutes ago that he and Trevor had been sitting in Colonel Fawkes-William's room.

It was just a pity he was now being kept waiting in this dismal room.

David had decided to come to the police station on his own, leaving Trevor to nose around again in the branch, though making sure this expression had not been used in front of the Colonel. Mrs Grimshawe's telephone call had emphasised his need to liaise with the police as soon as possible. She was at her wit's end, not knowing where her husband might be. He had certainly not followed her to Northampton and all she understood about his plans was that he would go fishing on Sunday, as usual. She clearly needed to report her missing husband to the police, but, instead, readily accepted David's offer to do this for her, provided he was able to arrange an immediate interview, himself.

When he telephoned, he had been fortunate to be able to speak to the officer in charge of the case. Chief Inspector Maxie had agreed to see him straightaway. The development concerning Mr Grimshawe had clearly disturbed the policeman.

David was now becoming increasingly worried that there was probably more to yesterday's robbery than was at first apparent. He also reckoned his input could be vital for the police investigation. It was not just because there was now a possible question mark over two senior members of the branch staff, one of whom was missing, but he was feeling distinctly uneasy about what was said in this afternoon's meeting with Colonel Fawkes-William. He could not put his finger on what was troubling him, but something was rather odd. It made him feel that he needed to know much more about the manager. In doing so, he would have to force to one side his natural antagonism towards the man. Somehow, he needed to keep an open mind if he was to come to any satisfactory conclusions.

Yet, from where would he be able to glean some meaningful information on the man? It was easy enough with members of the staff; the Colonel, himself, ought to be able to tell him all he knew – with a little help from his filing cabinet. But David could hardly grill the Colonel about himself. The most obvious person to help would be Angus McPhoebe, but after this morning's meeting with the regional manager's deputy, it was unlikely he would offer much insight, apart from the Colonel being a 'good man'.

Perhaps David should go over McPhoebe's head and speak to Mr Porter, but that could be tricky – approaching the regional manager direct. No, for the moment, he would have to mull this one over, but, one way or another, he needed to know more about the Colonel's background and personal circumstances.

At that, he heard the door open behind him.

He turned in his chair and was somewhat shocked at what he saw. Could this possibly be Chief Inspector Maxie?

David did not necessarily expect the man to be in uniform, but a suit and collar and tie ought to be obligatory. Instead, the man wore an open-neck shirt and he carried a sports jacket over his shoulder, the first finger on his right hand clasping the hook on the inside of the jacket's collar. His other hand held a black document case.

The Chief Inspector was surprisingly short in stature. Too short to be a policeman? Obviously not. Perhaps his wide girth made him appear less tall than the minimum requirement. David guessed that he was in his early forties, but he showed signs of being much older. Unruly dark hair, thining on top, and deep furrows on his brow made him appear careworn, but when their eyes met, David knew that first impressions could be deceptive. This man's steel-blue eyes radiated resolute determination and not a little wisdom. David could only hope that this augured well with the investigation.

The Chief Inspector smiled as he extended his arm.

"Mr Goodhart? Peter Maxie."

David had risen from his chair and was impressed with the Chief Inspector's firm grip.

"Pleased to meet you. And thank you for seeing me so quickly."

The Chief Inspector waved David to sit down again and took the other chair on the same side of the desk. At least, this meant David would not have to face those inhospitable prisons.

"Many thanks for phoning," Peter Maxie said, placing his document case on the desk where he left it unopened. "This missing man's a bit worrying."

David was pleased they were getting down to business quickly. There might be times for initial small talk, but as far as he was concerned, this was not one of them. Yet, what was this? Was the

Chief Inspector having second thoughts on such trivia?

"First of all, though," Peter Maxie said, draping his jacket on the back of his chair, "I must apologize. Not only for having kept you waiting, but also for my appearance."

He now looked rueful, as he patted his ample stomach.

"And I don't mean this. I'm talking about my attire. I can assure you I normally wear my jacket and tie, but I have a problem. I've just contracted shingles."

David could now see the Chief Inspector's neck was covered in angry blotches and he suppressed a wince, knowing how painful this complaint could be.

"I'm so sorry …"

Peter Maxie put up his hand.

"No, there's no need for that. And don't worry. I'm told it's not catching. But I can't bear anything touching my neck. I gather shingles can be caused by stress. And that can certainly be par for the course as far as my job's concerned. Especially after yesterday. I'm just hoping your visit might lead to some respite – working together on the case, I mean."

That was music to David's ears – working together. It had been like that when he had experienced all his problems back in Barnmouth branch. At that time, he had dealt with Inspector Hopkins and when everything had been solved, the man had been promoted to Chief Inspector. Perhaps David's contribution this time would lead to promotion for Peter Maxie.

"That's the main reason why I rang. I'm hoping we'll be able to share our findings. I certainly don't expect to get involved in your chase for the gunman, but I'd like to hear any news you might gain about our bank staff. And I'm coming across things in our branch which could have a bearing on the case. Our missing first cashier's a case in point."

"And his name is?"

"Grimshawe."

Chief Inspector Maxie now opened his document case and withdrew a notebook and pen.

"When did he go missing?"

"As far as the branch was concerned, yesterday morning."

"First thing? Before the hold-up?"

David nodded.

"Yes. He usually arrives at the branch by eight-thirty, but he didn't turn up. The manager assumed he was sick, but they couldn't reach him at home. His wife wasn't there, either."

"Where do they live?"

"In Tonbridge. And, this morning, I went round to their house. It was empty, but nothing seemed untoward. It had a proper lived-in feel to it. A neighbour then came across the road and said Mrs Grimshawe had gone to Northampton – to visit her sick mother."

"Alone?"

"Yes. Apparently, Mr Grimshawe doesn't see eye to eye with his mother-in-law. So he stayed at home. The neighbour saw him on Saturday, though not after that. But he said Mr Grimshawe probably went fishing the next day. It seems he does this every Sunday."

The Chief Inspector was writing studiously in his notebook and then looked up.

"Do you know where?"

"Not exactly, but somewhere around Eridge."

"I know where that'll be. I think I'd better get a team over there to have a look round."

"I was hoping Mrs Grimshawe would be able to help when she returned from Northampton. She rang me just before I spoke to you. But she has no idea where her husband might be. She's now distraught. It's clearly a police job, but as I hoped to see you quickly, I suggested I'd make the initial report for her."

The Chief Inspector pursed his lips.

"Do you have her address?"

David told him and explained that Cardinal Close was on the south side of Tonbridge. The Chief Inspector wrote it down and then frowned.

"Do you think it's a coincidence – that Mr Grimshawe

disappeared on the morning of the hold-up?"

David shrugged.

"I simply don't know. But I don't really believe in coincidences."

Peter Maxie smiled.

"You sound just like a policeman."

David was certainly warming to this man and now felt they could definitely work together.

"I suppose my job's similar to yours – being a bank inspector. Apart from all the blood and gore."

"We certainly had some of that yesterday."

David did not need reminding of that. He could still see that chalk outline in the road and the dark stain encompassed within it.

"And thank goodness Barney Wilson wasn't killed."

The Chief Inspector now scowled. Surely he could not disagree with such a sentiment?

"I've already instigated an internal enquiry into that. Our chaps actually believed he was dead. How could they get it so wrong? Thank God one of them eventually came to his senses."

So there was incompetence. David wondered if Barney Wilson would ever find out – assuming he made a full recovery.

"I went to the hospital this morning," he said. "Couldn't see him, of course. But they seemed confident he'd soon regain consciousness."

The Chief Inspector now appeared more relaxed.

"He actually came round this afternoon. But he's still in a bad way. I just hope he'll make a full recovery. But he might not remember anything. It all depends on what sort of brain injury he's sustained."

It was an assessment which David had no difficulty in accepting. He had come to learn a great deal about brain injuries in Barnmouth. It was not so much that his father had experienced such an horrendous car crash, but that it had taken years for him to be diagnosed as having a permanent head injury. Physically, he had seemed all right. After the crash, he was only adjudged to have been suffering from mild concussion. But as time went by, his behavioural patterns became more and more irrational. And the general assumption that this was down to senility was only eventually quashed by a clued-up consultant at Torbay Hospital in Torquay. What was more, the consultant said that full recovery from a serious brain injury was nigh on impossible.

That assessment had certainly turned out to be the case with Dad, but he still managed to achieve some quality of life until his sudden death from heart failure two years ago.

So, things did not look at all good for poor old Barney Wilson, if he had suffered brain damage.

"Was he shot at point-blank range?" David asked. If so, it was a miracle he had survived.

"We think he must have been. Yet the bullet only took a glancing blow to the head. It was still nearly fatal and he lost a lot of blood. Either the gunman panicked, or was distracted. Maybe, Wilson was aware of the danger and somehow shifted his head – to offset the full impact of the bullet. If that was the case, he was certainly on the ball – and very brave."

This was certainly fitting in with the opinions of those at the branch – downstairs, anyway.

"I've been hearing good things about him at the branch. In fact one of the girls actually said she'd expect Barney to put up a fight. Perhaps she was spot on."

"Could be. Anyway I've now got a man at his bedside. And if I hear he's able to talk and put us more in the picture, I'll go up there straightaway."

"What about the gunman? And our abducted cashier – Douglas Fairweather? Needless to say we're worried sick about him."

The Chief Inspector now closed his notebook and laid his pen on the table. It was an ominous sign that he might have little to say on the matter.

"As you probably know, the gunman got clean away. And because everything happened so quickly there were no witnesses in Lamberhurst. Not one. Quite extraordinary, really."

"So he could be anywhere?"

"Possibly, but we don't think so. We had a slice of luck – in Horsmonden. There'd been a serious accident on the A21 which blocked the road. So, we had a car with two officers in that village. They were directing traffic away from the accident. Anyway, a grey Morris Oxford approached from the A21 and one of our men spoke to the driver. He said he'd just picked up a friend from London Airport. Our officer could see this man was asleep on the back seat."

David was now wide-eyed.

"It must have been them."

"Almost certainly. Unfortunately, our man then waved the car through. The driver said they were going to Ashford."

"But if they'd come from London Airport, they'd have used the A21. Yet you said this road was blocked. Didn't your man twig this?"

The Chief Inspector now looked annoyed and shook his head.

"As a force, we didn't cover ourselves with glory yesterday. But in mitigation the officer had been urgently called back to his car. His colleague had just picked up a radio message about the hold-up in Lamberhurst. But by then it was too late. All they could do was watch the Morris Oxford disappearing up the road."

David was now getting excited. It was as if he had been caught up in the thrill of the chase.

"And did your chaps go after the car?"

The Chief Inspector shook his head.

"No. They decided to carry on re-directing traffic. That was the job they'd been given to do."

This was crazy. Where was their initiative? The Chief Inspector appeared to recognise from David's expression how his mind might be working and he held up his hand.

"But they radioed other vehicles in the area and gave a good description of the car and its occupants. Within minutes, road blocks would have been set up."

"Covering all those country lanes? The gunman would hardly use the main roads."

"Agreed. But we're still pretty sure he wouldn't have got far. We reckon he's holed up somewhere – until things have died down."

"For how long would that be?"

The Chief Inspector shrugged.

"Perhaps not long. The gunman couldn't have planned for this happening. What would he do for food and water?"

"Plenty of village shops."

"But he wouldn't want to show his face. Don't forget, he'd just been eyeballed by a policeman. He'd know his description – and that of the car – must be ingrained on the minds of every policeman in the area."

By the second, David was getting more hopeful of a successful outcome. And he still had one piece of information about which the Chief Inspector was probably unaware.

"Do you know how much money was actually stolen?"

Peter Maxie shook his head.

"I was at your branch yesterday morning, but the manager didn't know'"

"Well he knows now. There was over £50,000 in the sub-branch case."

The Chief Inspector let out a low whistle.

"Was that normal?"

"Not at all. The case would normally only contain their daily requirements. I don't know how much that would be exactly, but it'd be nothing like £50,000."

The Chief Inspector's steel-blue eyes now came into their own, locking on David like a searchlight picking out an enemy bomber.

"Are you implying the gunman managed to select the very day when the case was crammed full?"

David held the policeman's rather disconcerting gaze and nodded.

"For that reason it doesn't sound like an opportunistic robbery to me. You were critical of your own men just now and I've already discovered flaws in our own systems."

"Oh?"

"For one thing, the daily Lamberhurst operation was never varied. Same people, same time, same route, same everything."

"So if our gunman kept his eyes open …"

David was pleased they were on the same wavelength.

"He could have been casing our branch for weeks."

"But what about the amount? That was different – yesterday."

"He could have had inside information."

As he said this, David prayed that this would not be the case. But in twenty-four hours, he and Trevor had discovered so many things awry in the branch. And that included question marks over those two senior members of staff – one of whom was missing. Added to this he had been palpably disconcerted by some of the things he had been told by Colonel Fawkes-William.

The Chief Inspector continued to stare at him.

"It seems there may be more to this case than meets the eye. And apart from finding the gunman and your Mr Fairweather, we need to get on looking for Mr Grimshawe."

Yes, they were certainly on the same wavelength, but what were the realistic chances of success? And David now thought back to what might be happening in the branch. Was it possible that Trevor could be discovering further misdemeanours?

CHAPTER 22

After Mr Goodhart had gone off to the police station, Trevor started to look around the general office. But he was immediately distracted.

By Daphne Simcock.

The girl was making him feel decidedly unnerved. He had experienced the same symptoms when he had first contemplated dating his long-time girlfriend, Katie, back at Barnmouth branch. Was it Daphne's physical attraction which so distracted him? Although small, she was still a mite taller than Katie, and just like his girlfriend, she could match the looks of any Hollywood starlet. He had only spoken to her twice, but she also seemed to share Katie's quirkiness of character. And he sensed she had the same ability to tease, without causing the slightest offence.

He watched from behind her as she filed vouchers into the pedestal drawers beneath her desk. Not a little shamefaced at his thoughts, he tried to look away, but was immediately drawn back to her. Could this be because Katie was over two hundred miles away in Barnmouth? And what might she be getting up to down there, with his being so far away? Was she being distracted by someone else?

Just as he was now? He could hardly take his eyes off Daphne Simcock.

The girl was now on her knees as she started to file her vouchers into the bottom drawer of her pedestal. Trevor could imagine her praying like this in church. But in church she would have the benefit of a hassock. In the office here, her bare knees were likely to suffer. The wooden floorboards did not even have a linoleum covering to ease her discomfort.

But though her back was to him, Trevor sensed that something was troubling her.

It was in the way she paused when placing the cheques and

credit slips in between the cards which separated one customer's space from another. Because of the tedium of the task, staff got on with it as quickly as possible. Yet Daphne was taking her time, as if her mind were on other things.

As Trevor continued to watch her, she suddenly turned her head, making her ponytail swing to and fro. Perhaps she sensed being observed. On finding this to be the case, she quickly returned her attention to her drawer and Trevor immediately saw that the back of her neck had reddened. He could have kicked himself for having embarrassed the girl.

But Daphne then stood up and beckoned him over. She still looked flushed, but it was the deep furrows on her brow which disconcerted him more. He must have really offended her by his overt staring.

"I'm so glad you're here," she said, immediately easing his conscience. "I've been wondering what to do. I'm not sure I should be speaking to you about it, but …"

Her words tailed off and it was now Trevor's turn to frown.

"Speak to me about what?"

Daphne pursed her lips and looked around to see if anyone else was listening. Two young men – the ones who had looked questionably at Trevor yesterday when he had helped Daphne with her ledger – were working on an adjacent desk. Although their heads were down, they would certainly be able to eavesdrop on any conversation.

"I don't want anyone else to hear," Daphne whispered. "But I'm ever so worried about something."

Trevor now looked around him. The general office was hardly the place to have a confidential discussion. The obvious place would be the small room which Mr Barnett had allocated to them, but he was a little loath to be seen heading off in that direction with Daphne in tow. On the other hand, there really was no alternative.

"You better come along to our room," he said, beckoning Daphne to follow him. He was relieved to see that the others in the vicinity were taking no notice.

They passed by the strongroom, its grille door well and truly locked, and Trevor then got out his keys and selected the one to open the door of their room. Once inside, he asked Daphne to sit down on one of the two upright chairs which flanked the small table and he took the other one, not a little perturbed at his close proximity to the girl. Why did she have such an effect on him? What would Katie think? He only hoped his own embarrassment would not be too apparent.

"What's actually troubling you?" he asked, praying that it would be only of a minor nature.

Daphne continued to look anxious and glanced around the small room. It was as if this were the last place she should be with a young man such as Trevor.

"I'm not sure that …"

Trevor tried to look comforting. It was not easy. He was too disconcerted about what this might be all about. Only this morning he had the feeling that something else had happened within the branch. Was he about to learn the answer to that?

"It was you who raised the subject, Daphne … whatever it might be."

Daphne nodded, but still looked unsure of herself.

"I know. And I must get it off my chest. I'm worried about one of our customers."

"Oh?" Trevor was now feeling rather uneasy – not helped by the girl's mention of her upper regions.

"Yes, it's one of our wealthiest customers – General Kettleman."

"An army man?" Possibly a pal of Colonel Fawkes-William?

"I suppose so. But that would have been a long time ago. He must be in his eighties now."

"How wealthy?"

"I'm not really sure. But he always has huge balances on his accounts."

"Deposit accounts?"

"And his current account. I think the manager's tried to get him to switch his money from current to deposit. But he seems reluctant to do that. It's as though he's not bothered about earning interest on his balances."

"He must be wealthy then. But why are you worried about him?" Daphne now looked really concerned.

"It was when I was filing his cheques."

"What was?"

"When I saw all the cheques he's just cashed."

Trevor now felt distinctly uneasy. But why should that be? If customers needed cash, they cashed their cheques.

"Go on."

"He'd cashed five separate cheques for £5,000 – all on Friday."

Now this really did sound serious. Why would such an elderly person need £25,000 cash? And why would he get it by cashing five separate cheques? And which cashier might have cashed these cheques? Surely not Mr Grimshawe?

"Go on."

"I first asked Norman Chilstone about it."

"Why Norman?"

"Because he cancelled the cheques."

"So he actually cashed them?"

"No, he just cancelled them."

That was odd. If the cheques had been cashed, the cashier would have done the cancelling. He would have struck his initial across the customer's signature when he cashed the cheque. In doing this, he would be authenticating the correct completion of the cheque, the validity of the customer's signature and that there were sufficient funds on the account.

"I'm not with you," Trevor replied, frowning.

"Norman cancelled the cheques when they arrived in this morning's clearing."

Now it was making more sense to Trevor. Cheques processed through other banking branches would be sent by them to their head offices who would then despatch them to the account holding branches in what was known as the morning clearing. So, cheques arriving this Tuesday morning would have been processed elsewhere last Friday. That would be the day when General Kettleman must have cashed his cheques, not here, but at other branches.

So, that seemed to let Mr Grimshawe off the hook.

"And for some reason," Daphne continued, " General Kettleman went to five separate branches to cash his cheques."

"All on the same day?"

Daphne nodded.

"I asked Norman about that. But when he cancelled the cheques, he didn't notice where they were cashed. He just made sure the cheques were technically correct and that there was sufficient money on the account. Then he cancelled them."

"You mean he never wondered why ...?"

"No. So I then went to see Mr Barnett."

"And?"

"And he just said if the General wanted to cash these cheques, it was up to him. Mr Barnett then told me to let it be. He said he had more problems on his plate than having to worry about the General's cash requirements. But I know the General. He simply wouldn't do something like this. And I don't think he's well enough to go traipsing round the countryside cashing cheques."

Trevor frowned. This really was looking decidedly odd.

"So did you go and see Colonel Fawkes-William?"

"The manager? I wouldn't dare go and see him after what Mr Barnett had just said."

Was the manager that unapproachable? It was a far cry from how the Barnmouth branch had been run by Mr Goodhart. Trevor had felt able to approach him about anything. But that was then; now he needed to know more about these encashments.

"Where were the cheques cashed?"

That would have been easy for Daphne to establish. Each banking branch had an identifying rubber stamp which would be impressed across the front of all cheques drawn by customers of other banks. In addition, if such a cheque had been cashed, the cashier's till stamp would be imprinted on the cheque.

"They were all cashed at our own branches. One was at Tenterden and another was cashed at Hawkhurst. But I can't remember the other branches. I can get the cheques out of the drawer."

Tenterden? The rest of what Daphne said was just a blur. Tenterden? Mr Goodhart had a feeling that things were not quite right at Tenterden. Surely, these strange cheque encashments could have nothing to do with his disquiet?

"Yes, you better get the cheques out," Trevor replied, wishing Mr Goodhart was with him to hear about Daphne's concerns first-hand. "I think they might bear extra scrutiny – over and above what Norman did when he cancelled them."

Daphne made a move to leave the room, but Trevor called her back.

"Just a second, Daphne. If cheques for £5,000 were to be cashed at other branches, someone here must have first authorized the encashments."

Daphne now gave him her full attention. In other circumstances, he would have found it quite disconcerting. Or rewarding?

"That's what's been worrying me. Neither Norman, nor Mr Barnett, seemed concerned about that."

"But to cash cheques at those other branches, the General would either have to make the arrangements here first, or the branches would have to telephone for authorization."

Daphne now looked really bothered before answering.

"And the only people to give such authorization would be the manager or Mr Barnett. They'd have to calculate the codes. They're the only two who hold keys to the code box."

CHAPTER 23

"This General did what?"

It was enough to make David splutter into his beer. And Harvey's best bitter deserved better than that. As with last night, he and Trevor were enjoying their pints, sitting at the same table, in the same pub and at the same time. The connotation with the standard Lamberhurst procedure was not lost on him. But the only risk attached to their own routine might be to have one pint too many.

Yet now, on top of everything else, it seemed that Trevor had discovered further potential problems at the branch.

"I think you heard me the first time, sir."

At least Trevor's grin offset any hint of impertinency.

"All right, all right, Trevor. But from what you've said, I don't believe it. Customers don't go cashing multiple cheques like that. Especially at £5,000 a time."

"The cheques certainly looked genuine, sir."

"Including the signatures?"

Trevor nodded, but did not seem totally convinced.

"They looked okay, but I suppose they could have been forged."

"If the General's above board, he'd be able to confirm whether or not that's the case. Have you tried to make contact with him?"

"Yes, sir. Daphne tried to phone him, but there was no answer."

"Daphne?"

Trevor now looked a little contrite. And was he blushing?

"It was Daphne who brought it all to my attention. She's a smart girl. Clearly goes around with her eyes open. And she knows the General. Says he wouldn't do such a thing. And she doesn't think he's fit enough to travel around our branches to cash his cheques."

"So, she thinks they're forgeries?"

"That's been going through both our minds. Anyway I felt it was best for her to try and phone him – rather than me do it."

That was fair enough. The customer would be far more receptive to a call from his branch, rather than from a stranger.

"But you say there was no answer, Trevor. I hope we haven't got another disappearance on our hands."

It would certainly be embarrassing to have to report a second missing person to Chief Inspector Maxie. Or to Angus McPhoebe, for that matter. By the look on his face, it seemed Trevor agreed.

"That's why I was glad when Daphne offered to call at the General's house on her way home. She said it wouldn't be much out of her way. If he's not there, a neighbour might be able to help."

David could now see this turning into a re-run of what happened to him this morning in Cardinal Close.

"If so, I hope she doesn't get told this General has gone fishing."

The irony of his rather flippant remark did not get lost on Trevor.

"In that respect, sir, what about Mr Grimshawe? Did the police have any positive thoughts?"

David shook his head. If only they did have. But at least he had confidence in the Chief Inspector.

"I'm afraid not. But I had a good meeting. It was with the man in charge of the case – Chief Inspector Maxie. He certainly shared my concern – especially with Mrs Grimshawe not knowing where her husband might be."

"Do you think she's playing it straight, sir?"

The boldness of the question shook David. Mrs Grimshawe had been so anguished on the telephone. In no way had he thought she was putting on an act. Yet could that have been the case?

"I'm surprised to hear you being so cynical, Trevor. But you're right – to think like that. Perhaps we shouldn't take anything at face value."

Trevor appeared pleased at the compliment. He took a sip of his beer and then raised his eyebrows.

"So what's the next step, sir?"

"The police are going to investigate Mr Grimshawe's fishing haunt. In case anything comes up, I've given Chief Inspector Maxie my home phone number. If they discover anything, I'd like to know about it as soon as possible."

Trevor frowned and put his tankard down on the table.

"Do you reckon it's a popular place to fish?"

David shrugged.

"I don't know. But the Chief Inspector reckoned he knew exactly where the spot was. That rather indicates it's well-known."

"If it is that popular, other fishermen might have seen Mr Grimshawe. They could have been fishing with him. If he goes there every Sunday, he might be a member of a club."

This was good thinking on Trevor's part, but if Mr Grimshawe had, in fact, gone fishing, it was more than likely his disappearance had arisen subsequently. In which case, his fellow fishermen might not be able to be of any assistance.

But this discussion about the first cashier was something of a distraction over the latest matter in hand – the General's cheque encashments. From what Trevor had said, it really did seem as though these might be fraudulent, despite the cheques having apparently been drawn correctly.

David followed Trevor's example and raised his glass to his lips, but rather than just taking a sip, he drained half its contents.

"Ah, that's better," he said, wiping his lips with the back of his index finger. "But getting back to the General's cheques, how have you left it with your Daphne?"

Trevor looked shocked.

"My Daphne, sir?"

In other circumstances, David might have smiled at Trevor's discomfort, but there was a serious element to this. What about Katie?

Back in Barnmouth, David's secretary and Trevor had been inseparable. Until Trevor's promotion. Yet, it had been Katie who had urged the lad to further his career around London, rather than in the backwaters of South Devon. She was probably right about this. But not if his feelings for her were now waning.

David could only hope this was not the case as he elaborated.

"Well, you seem to have struck up a good rapport with her. Is she going to let you know the result of her visit to the General's house? Tonight, I mean."

Now, Trevor was definitely reddening.

"I didn't think to ask her to do that, sir. I was just going to find out from her in the morning."

So no liaison between them tonight. David was glad about that. Quite apart from the situation with Katie, it was not unheard of for inspector's assistants to seek out the company of female members of branch staff. But within twenty-four hours of the start of an inspection? And this was not a normal inspection where minds could wander off towards other things, simply because of the sheer routine of it all. Here in Tunbridge Wells, it was a specific investigation, as opposed to a standard branch inspection. Full concentration on the job in hand was vital, without outside distractions coming into play.

But was David reading too much into Trevor's reaction whenever Daphne's name was mentioned?

As for those cheque encashments, he was now imagining all kinds of scenarios. One of these was whether they had anything to do with Mr Grimshawe's disappearance. But first he needed to know where the cheques had been cashed.

"One was at Tenterden," Trevor replied, in answer to his question.

David lowered his eyelids and sighed audibly. Yet, it was not as if Trevor's reply had surprised him. Bearing in mind his misgivings about what might be happening there, he would have been surprised if one of the cheques had not been cashed at Tenterden. It now looked as if they might be returning to that branch post-haste.

"And the others?"

"Hawkhurst, Marden, Cranbrook and Wadhurst."

"And there'd be no telling in which order?"

Trevor shook his head.

"The times wouldn't be recorded anywhere. But we could ring the branches up. They'd have a pretty good idea from when the withdrawals were entered on the cashiers' counter sheets."

"And they should certainly remember carrying out the transaction. They'd be unlikely to have any other £5,000 withdrawals by a customer from Tunbridge Wells."

Trevor nodded enthusiastically.

"And each one would have to be de-coded by the manager. He's bound to remember when he did it."

David agreed, but that would not necessarily give them the time when the General – or whoever – actually went into the branch. The authorization from Tunbridge Wells could have been made at any time – by telephone, or post. In which case, the manager at the receiving branch would de-code it immediately on its receipt. The arrival of the customer would then occur later. But would the timing of the authorization's receipt and the transaction itself be significant?

"I think we might be looking at this from the wrong angle. The timing probably isn't pertinent. It's the authorization process that's important. Who actually did this at Tunbridge Wells?"

"It must have been the manager or Mr Barnett."

Normally yes. But Trevor might have overlooked something significant.

"Think back to yesterday, Trevor."

Trevor frowned and then looked incredulous.

"Are you thinking what I'm now thinking, sir?"

David nodded, pleased that Trevor was getting attuned to this inspection business.

"You're the one who found the code box unlocked and unattended."

David could imagine that when Trevor had been appointed as an inspector's assistant, he might have expected his main task would be to check that branch staff were obeying the bank's stringent rules and regulations. He would then either tick the appropriate boxes, or give the staff and the branch a black mark when they had fallen down on procedures. As far as Trevor was likely to be concerned, it would be a theoretical exercise, part of the bank's normal auditing function. It was now beginning to look as if his discovery yesterday was going to turn out to be anything but a simple theoretical procedure.

"But, sir …"

"Anyone could have made those authorizations."

"I agree, sir, but … but if someone happened to find the code box unlocked, it would take that person time to work out how the system operated. The whole thing is far too complicated to do it quickly."

Trevor was correct in that respect. Someone who, on impulse, opened the lid of an unlocked code box would be immediately baffled by the system the bank had put in place. But impulse might not have been a factor. Far more likely, it would have been a planned operation. If through laxity within the branch someone had ready, unauthorized access to the code box, the instructions could be learnt over a period of time. Or the actual code cards could even have been copied.

The code system used throughout the bank was a numeric one, taking into account the date, the amount of the transaction and the sorting code number of the receiving branch. From time to time, the bank would change the configuration process, but David was not aware of this happening in recent weeks. This meant that someone who had recently become familiar with the current procedure, could be confident about calculating a code correctly.

"It's all about planning, Trevor. Given an appropriate amount of time and being aware of the general laxity over the control of the code box …"

"So, if some shenanigans have been going on, it's probably down to someone other than the management? Does that mean it lets Colonel Fawkes-William and Mr Barnett off the hook?"

"Good Lord, no. But it does mean that anyone in the branch, including the manager and the sub-manager, could have authorized these withdrawals, whether or not they're fraudulent."

David emptied his glass and was pleased to see Trevor was making a better fist of his than he had done last night.

"Another one, Trevor?"

Trevor looked at his glass and smiled.

"You know, sir, I'm getting to like this local ale."

"Good man. That's just as well, because we might be in for a long evening."

Trevor now looked alarmed. Was that because of the prospect of having to down more than two pints, or that he had something else on his agenda?

"Don't forget, sir, you might be getting a call tonight. Shouldn't you be getting home?."

David grimaced. He had momentarily forgotten about Peter Maxie. After his next drink, he really should make the move home – just in case a call came through. In any event, he would not want Sarah's latest offering to get dried up in the oven – for one very good reason. The last time it happened, Sarah had threatened to down tools completely on the culinary stakes. Not even a couple of extra pints of beer would be recompense for something as critical as that.

"Just one more, then."

David rose to get the drinks and decided that if Trevor was, indeed, taking a liking for Harvey's, he might even let the lad stand a forthcoming round – whenever that might be. All the time Trevor indulged himself with lemonade, it was hardly right for him to share the financing of David's thirst for something stronger. But if their drinking was to be on the same footing …

"What we need to do first thing tomorrow," he said, when he returned with their two foaming pints of nectar, "is to confront the manager and Mr Barnett with what's happened. Who knows, they might be able to confirm the withdrawals are okay. But if not …"

"Especially if Daphne comes up with something. I mean, if she's been able to meet the General and he says they're forgeries. I'd better then ring round the other branches."

David nodded and then frowned.

"It's strange that all five branches are within a relatively small circle of each other. That, in itself, makes it look as though the withdrawals are fraudulent. And they're all small branches – in small towns or villages."

"Do you think that's significant, sir?"

"It could be. Any wrongdoer might think they're manned by less experienced staff. A sort of soft touch."

In reality, David knew this should not be so, but outsiders might think differently.

"And one other thing," he added. "if these withdrawals are fraudulent, could it have anything to do with Mr Grimshawe's disappearance?"

"How could it, sir? He was here in Tunbridge Wells on Friday. He couldn't have impersonated the General and cashed the cheques at the other branches."

"Unless he had an accomplice?"

"You must be joking, sir."

"I don't think this is turning out to be a joking matter, Trevor. But I agree, it does sound far too fanciful. Yet where is Mr Grimshawe? That's what I'd really like to know."

Chapter 24

"Your Mr Grimshawe's turned up."

David clasped the handset to his ear, hardly able to believe what he had just heard. He stared at himself in the mirror that adorned the wall behind the telephone table in the hall. He saw the smile of satisfaction slowly emerge around his lips and then reach up into his eyes. Not even the revered sounds from Ben Webster's tenor saxophone could hold a candle to the sweetness of those five little words.

David had only been in the house for five minutes, the aroma of Sarah's Irish stew immediately making up for those spurned extra pints. But before he could even think of an appropriate aperitif, Peter Maxie's call had come through. It was as if David's decision to leave the pub early had been predestined. And if the Chief Inspector had not been on the end of the telephone line, David would have hugged him. The bearer of such good news deserved nothing less.

"Thank God for that. Where's he been?"

His question went unanswered and, for one moment, David thought the line had gone dead. Then he heard the policeman clear his throat.

"I'm afraid it's not quite like that. He's not been anywhere."

Chief Inspector Maxie paused and David heard him clear his throat again.

"We found him at the bottom of the lake – drowned."

David sank on to the upright chair which nestled next to the telephone table. His initial euphoria immediately vanished. It was the last thing he had wanted, or expected, to hear.

"But … but how …?"

"We're not really sure. But it seems he slipped down the bank into the water. There were clear slide marks. His fishing gear was still there. It was on the bank above where he slipped. We know it was his. His name was stitched inside his tackle satchel."

David was dumbstruck. Was it still less than thirty-six hours since Angus McPhoebe's phone call had come through at Tenterden? That pathetic man had referred to an incident having occurred at Lamberhurst. Only last night, as he lay restlessly in bed, David had thought back to that call. In his wildest dreams, he could not have imagined McPhoebe's innocuous choice of word to have resulted in an attempted murder and an abduction – and now a fatal accident.

Yet, as the recipient of this latest piece of bad news, David was only a relative outsider. How would Mrs Grimshawe react to it? And what about the staff at the branch? How would they be able to handle this additional trauma? There were only about twenty people manning the branch, yet three of them had now been put out of action, one of them, at least, permanently. There may well be a case for the temporary closure of the branch. It was hardly fair for the staff to suffer such grief, yet still be required to carry on working as normal.

David needed to talk to Colonel Fawkes-William about this as soon as possible. He would try to reach him on the telephone tonight – right after he had finished speaking to Peter Maxie.

"Have you spoken to Mrs Grimshawe yet?" he asked, anxious to know how she had taken the news. Having no children, and with her mother being miles away in Northampton, it seemed she would be devoid of any immediate family support.

"Yes," the Chief Inspector replied. "I went round straightaway to see her myself. I took a WPC with me. I've left her there with Mrs Grimshawe. She's going to stay as long as she's needed. If necessary, overnight."

That was good news. And David's high opinion of the Chief Inspector went up another notch.

"And? And how is she?"

"Much as you'd expect. Totally distraught. Yet … let me put it this way, it was almost as if she'd anticipated something like this happening."

David immediately stiffened. In the light of everything else, the Chief Inspector's words sounded distinctly ominous. The thought of suicide crossed David's mind.

"In what way, Chief Inspector?"

There was a pause on the other end of the line. It was only slight, but long enough for David to agonize over the eventual reply. It certainly gave him time to recall the apparent disagreement on Friday afternoon between Mr Grimshawe and Douglas Fairweather. Had this been a one-off spat? Or had there been a continuing problem between the two men? Had it, even, been deep rooted? But, even so, this would hardly lead to possible suicide.

Had Mr Grimshawe been disturbed in any other way? By his financial position? Colonel Fawkes-William had said he was hard up – with gambling being a possible factor? And there was another thing: Daphne had said he was seeking promotion. He was keen to get the Lamberhurst job when that branch was upgraded. Yet Douglas Fairweather was the Colonel's only choice for that position. Could Mr Grimshawe's disappointment at not being in the running have been playing on his mind?

The Chief Inspector then broke into David's thoughts.

"Mrs Grimshawe only went fishing with her husband once. When he first caught the bug – a couple of years ago. But it worried her straightaway. She felt the bank was unsafe. On one of the times he cast his line, his feet actually slipped. He simply laughed it off. He said it was just his inexperience. He compared it to when he first played golf. He'd thrashed his club at the ball, rather than swinging it smoothly. He'd soon learn to cast his line properly."

This certainly made sense to David. He was still conscious about his own golf swing. It was far too quick – despite his concentrating hard to slow it down.

"But Mrs Grimshawe never forgot that slip," the Chief Inspector continued. "Since then, she always urged her husband to be careful – every time he went fishing. So, you might imagine her reaction when I told her what had happened. And what's more, she's consumed with guilt. She feels she could have stopped it happening – if she'd been firmer with him. It's illogical, I know, but …"

His words drifted off and David nodded to himself, knowing exactly what the Chief Inspector meant. But this explanation did now seem to rule out possible suicide. Thank goodness for that. Losing the life of a loved one by way of an accident was bad enough. But for the person to do it deliberately did not bear thinking about.

"I can certainly understand her feelings of guilt," he said, greatly moved by Mrs Grimshawe's plight. "Having had a premonition like that …"

"But that's the power of hindsight. What more could she have done? Realistically? Each time he went fishing, she implored him to be careful. Anything more and he would have pooh-poohed her for mollycoddling him."

David could certainly relate to that. He had experienced something similar with Sarah. In his footballing days, he had liked to think of himself as a fearsome tackler. When Sarah had first watched him, she was horrified. Serious injury was inevitable. He had done his best to explain: that it was far more likely to happen if he went into a tackle half-heartedly. Needless to say, she did not believe him. Now he played golf.

"Those thoughts aren't going to help her now."

"That's one reason I've left my WPC with her. She's a good girl. She'll be able to empathise with her. She's also sensible and realistic. Just the person to help ease Mrs Grimshawe's mind."

David certainly hoped this would be the case. Thank heaven for good old British coppers. What would the country do without them? Long live the Dixons of Dock Green. On the other hand, those policemen in Lamberhurst and Horsmonden had hardly covered themselves in glory.

But another matter needed clarification: what about the timing of the accident?

"I presume Mr Grimshawe drowned on Sunday afternoon?"

"We're not sure yet. It's possible, but other anglers would have been there in the afternoon. If so, someone should have seen something. So we think he might have stayed on into the early evening. Before it got dark"

David bit his lower lip and nodded.

"That figures. His wife was away in Northampton. There was no reason for him to get home early."

"Anyway, the post-mortem will tell us. It's already underway. That'll give us a pretty good estimate of the time of death. Not that it'll mean much. The timing's hardly going to be significant."

David agreed with that. Sunday afternoon? Sunday evening? It had to be one or the other. Otherwise, Mr Grimshawe would have turned up for work yesterday. Now, he would never turn up. Absolutely shocking. And the sooner Colonel Fawkes-William knew what had happened to his first cashier, the better.

"Have you spoken to his manager yet?"

"No. Only to Mrs Grimshawe and yourself. I thought I'd leave any other contact with the bank in your hands."

David agreed with that and he would try and reach the Colonel straightaway. He would then deal with the other staff in the morning.

"Yes, I'll do that. Is there anything else I should know?"

"No. But I'll call you when I get the result of the post-mortem. To keep you in the picture. That should be some time tomorrow."

With that, David finished the call and replaced the handset into its cradle. Sarah immediately joined him in the hall.

"That all sounded rather ominous."

David nodded and wrapped an arm around her shoulder. He gave her a peck on the cheek and led her into the sitting room. He then briefly described what had happened.

"That's absolutely dreadful," Sarah said, cuddling up to him on their trusty Grieves and Thomas settee. They had bought this piece of furniture when they had married – could it really be over fourteen years ago? It was still their favourite haven for heart-to-heart discussions. "What are you going to do?"

For a start, David knew he would have to delay tucking into Sarah's

Irish stew. His call to the Colonel must take precedence over that.

"I must ring the manager," he answered, kissing her and then wresting himself from her grasp. He rose from the settee and returned to the hall. The telephone table had one narrow drawer under its work surface and he opened it to withdraw the directory. Opening it up, he pondered on whether the Colonel would be listed under F or W. He plumped for F and then realized he did not know the man's first name. But would there be any other Fawkes-William listed? In any case, the Colonel would have stipulated his title being included in full.

Sure enough, although there was another Fawkes-William in the book, only one bore the title of Colonel. The address was Nevill Park, one of the most salubrious private roads in Tunbridge Wells. That certainly fitted.

David looked at his watch. It was only approaching nine o'clock, but even if it had been much later, the call was far too important not to be made. He immediately dialled the number.

After four rings, the receiver was picked up at the other end.

"Colonel Fawkes-William's residence."

David could hardly believe his ears. What a way for a private line to be answered. It was a woman's voice, displaying all the timidity of a browbeaten servant. A servant? A maid, even? Yet if anyone in Tunbridge Wells (Royal Tunbridge Wells?) should consider employing such a person in 1960, it was bound to be someone such as Colonel Fawkes-William. And if it had been a man who had answered the telephone? A batman, no doubt.

"May I please speak to the Colonel?"

"The Colonel?"

David sighed. It was as if the manager did not normally take calls at this hour.

"Please."

"Whom shall I say is calling?"

Whom?

"Just say it's David Goodhart."

"Does he know you, sir?"

David sighed again.

"He does. May I now speak to him, please?"

"I'll just see if he's available."

David heard the telephone drop on to a hard surface and waited, wondering if the Colonel would deign to speak to him.

After what was probably only half a minute, but seemed much longer, David heard the handset being picked up.

"Goodhart?"

The tone of voice, never mind its brusqueness, made it clear the Colonel was not pleased to be giving an evening audience to a bank inspector.

"Colonel?"

The salutation clearly increased the man's level of irritation.

"My wife says you want to speak to me," he snapped.

His wife? So what was that about it being the Colonel's residence? Was his wife not a member of the family household? And why had she called David 'sir'? If ever there was a case of a downtrodden wife, this must be it.

"Yes. I'm afraid I've got some bad news."

"Oh? Can't it wait until the morning?"

"Not as far as I'm concerned, Colonel. Mr Grimshawe's been found. And it's not good news. I'm afraid he's been found dead."

"What? Has he topped himself?"

David was taken aback. Why should the Colonel immediately think of suicide?

"It doesn't look like it. But the police are bound to keep an open mind. It looks more like an accident. You know he went fishing on Sunday. It seems he slipped down the bank into the water. He was found drowned."

There was silence at the other end. All David heard was a slight sound of breathing which might have been a sigh.

"Why did you think it might have been suicide, Colonel?"

Now, there was a definite sigh.

171

"Oh, I don't know, Goodhart. Just a hunch, I suppose. What with his finances. You know I said they appeared stretched. And he was probably banking on getting the Lamberhurst job – when the sub-branch gets upgraded."

David frowned. There was something not quite right here. This afternoon, Trevor had recounted Mr Grimshawe's apparent interest in that job. Yet this had come as a surprise to the Colonel; he had only considered Douglas Fairweather for the position. Yet, now, the manager was implying that the first cashier's finances would be further stretched by his not getting a job which he had never been in line for. And this might have made him suicidal?

"But, Colonel Fawkes-William, you had never considered Mr Grimshawe for the job of sub-manager at Lamberhurst. And you certainly told me he wasn't management material. Why are you now saying he was probably banking on getting the job?"

"Oh, Goodhart, I don't know. But promotion would certainly have helped his finances."

"A promotion he could in no way have expected?"

Again, there was a silence at the other end. But this was not the time to pursue the matter further. David was more concerned about the practical aspects of operating the branch tomorrow.

"Anyway," he continued, before the Colonel chose to break his silence, if there was, indeed, anything he could say by way of further explanation, "what about the staffing of the branch tomorrow? Everyone's going to be shell-shocked when they hear the news. I seriously doubt if they'll be able to cope with even the day-to-day work."

There was no reply from the other end and all David could hear was a faint pitter-patter, as if the Colonel was drumming his fingers on a hard surface. Perhaps after his initial response – one that had not rung with any compassion – the Colonel was becoming aware of the significance of what had occurred.

"Yes, Goodhart," he eventually replied, "you're right. With everything else that's happened …"

"We need to come up with a plan of campaign," David said, somewhat surprised by the Colonel's apparent agreement. "And quickly. We could meet up tonight. Shall I come round?"

The Colonel almost choked into the telephone.

"No ... no, Goodhart. I don't think that's going to be necessary. It's far too late. And I want to get my head round this one first. You might imagine, Goodhart, how distraught I am at hearing such shocking news. I need to be thinking straight before we meet. But I certainly think your idea about a plan is a good one. Two heads better than one, what?"

David shook his head and was glad the Colonel could not see the look on his face. The Colonel distraught? That was the last impression the man had given. And it was David who was now feeling doubly distraught – not only because of Mr Grimshawe's sudden death, but also because the Tunbridge Wells branch of National Counties Bank was being managed by such a supercilious man. He now decided this was not the time for any prevarication and he would take the initiative by immediately laying down some operating rules to be brought into effect in the morning.

"Right, Colonel, if we're not going to meet tonight, this is what I think we should do. And I want you to consider all these points between now and the morning. Agreed?"

The Colonel grunted a form of acknowledgement and David hoped this was accompanied by a nod of acceptance, even if this was with some reluctance.

"So," David continued, "we'll delay opening the branch, if necessary for the whole day. We'll have an early meeting with all the staff to put them fully in the picture. Some will be more upset than others and we'll allow any of them to return home, if that'll be of help. We'll have someone on the front door to tell customers what's happened. And we'll make arrangements with Lloyds to take in our customers' credits and to cash their cheques. All right, so far?"

"Cash their cheques? Without formal arrangements?"

"Correct."

"But what if that results in fraudulent withdrawals?"

"I'll take responsibility for that. Should it happen."

David very much doubted that, in the circumstances, they would run into such problems and he certainly did not share the Colonel's scepticism. He decided to carry on regardless of that.

"We'll then talk to staff individually. We must listen to their concerns. You, Trevor and I will do this. We'll listen carefully to any views they might express. No one will be forced to do anything which might distress them further. If necessary, we'll get relief staff in. Such people won't have the same personal involvement. And, that way, we can re-open the branch on Thursday, at the latest."

"I don't want any Tom, Dick or Harry working in my branch."

David suppressed a sigh.

"I'm talking about qualified bank staff. That's hardly Tom, Dick or Harry."

"You know what I mean, Goodhart."

David was not sure he did. But he pressed on.

"I'll let Angus McPhoebe know exactly what we're doing and I'll also ring the bank's chief inspector in London. Mr Grimshawe's till will then have to be taken over by someone. As to who will depend on the reaction we get from the other staff."

David then got the Colonel's agreement that, in the morning, they would both get to the branch before anyone else – by eight, at the latest. And he forewarned the manager that there would be another major item on their agenda: the possible fraudulent encashments on General Kettleman's account.

Shrugging off the consternation that this further potential difficulty caused at the end of the telephone, David ended the call. And with all these problems on his mind, it would certainly now be a relief to get his teeth into Sarah's Irish stew.

CHAPTER 25

Alfie Templeton lay still with his eyes closed. He was in that transient state between dream and reality. Yet where did one end and the other begin? And why did he have the gut feeling that the nightmare from which he had just awakened was only the start of something much worse?

He could not believe this had been only his second night in this frightful barn. It felt like months. It had been a miracle he had been able to get any shut-eye on this apology for a bed. People in films might frolic around on heaps of straw. Directors would try to make it look romantic. Perhaps the presence of the likes of Jane Russell helped. But here? Romantic? What he was lying on was rough and smelly. It also played havoc with his sinuses. He normally only suffered asthmatically in the summer months, recently-mown grass being the main culprit. To this end, he had concreted over his front and back gardens. Yet, now, his asthma had resurrected itself in, of all places, this dilapidated barn. And it was still only March.

As if on cue, he sneezed and then immediately again – and again.

At least, he had not had to share his 'bedroom' with that courting couple. After about half an hour in the back seat of their car, they had moved on, much to Templeton's relief. But that was not the end of his problems.

In the last two days and nights, he had discovered that bats did not just occupy belfries. They were here in droves. Yet he had still not actually seen one. But at night-time he could certainly feel their presence. Guided unerringly by their inbuilt radar, they swooped and soared throughout the barn. He might not be able to see them, but he could definitely sense them eyeing him up as a potential target. And the sonar of one bat must have gone on the blink last night; it had brushed his cheek while he lay in a fitful sleep, shaking him wide awake. For one moment, he had wondered if that particular bat had been part of his nightmare, where it had metamorphosed into a blood-thirsty vampire. But this bat had been real enough. It had left behind its calling card. As had many others. Their minute black droppings lay all over his Morris Oxford.

Templeton might not have specifically seen the bats, but that could not be said of the multitude of infectious rats which inhabited the barn. Yet, simply seeing them was his least unnerving sense; when leaving their nests at dusk, they actually seemed inhibited by a human presence. But it was another matter when he had lain down and attempted to get some much-needed sleep. Even now he could still hear his piercing scream when one had scampered over his face. And the constant rustling in the straw was driving him mad. No wonder he had been experiencing such frightful nightmares.

He now lay there, eyes half open, and tried to rid his mind of the sheer repugnance of the night. Light was now appearing through the cracks in the barn's walls and roof, so it must be at least seven o'clock. Yet it was ghostly quiet. He was not thinking about outside where a chirruping bird was attempting to extend the dawn chorus. No, it was inside the barn which was abnormally silent. What had happened to Fairweather's constant wheezing? It had driven him to distraction since the man recovered consciousness.

Templeton drew himself up from his makeshift palliasse and looked across the barn. Fairweather should have been lying on his own heap of straw. But there was no sign of him. Templeton sat bolt upright and took in the whole barn. Where had the man gone? It was as if he had vanished into thin air.

Panic now gripped Templeton. He had clearly made the wrong decision yesterday. He should have eliminated Fairweather, not the rabbit. Especially as he had failed dismally to slay the rabbit. Getting rid of Fairweather would have been a far better option. The man had become a real liability, quite apart from the fact that he was the only witness to all that had happened. And now, not only was he still alive, but he had vamoosed.

Templeton sneezed again and pondered on what to do. And he was still so hungry. Not only was this sapping his physical strength, but, mentally, he seemed to be stuck in first gear. Or was it simply his desperate circumstances which were preventing him from thinking straight. And how he could do with another fag.

Yet, what about Fairweather? He must be just as hungry. Perhaps he had simply gone outside to forage for some food. But as soon as that thought crossed Templeton's mind, he dismissed it with contempt. He had already discovered that the vicinity of the barn was deprived of any form of food. So, why would Fairweather be anywhere nearby? He could go wherever he wanted to seek out food – if that was what he was doing. Much more likely, he had other ideas in mind. And all because of Templeton's own stupidity.

He cursed himself for being so brainless. Why had he not kept Fairweather chained up? The chain was still there, attached to the case. Why had he taken pity on the man? Why had he been so complacent?

He had simply succumbed to Fairweather's constant wimpering. And Fairweather had clearly become a broken man. Seeing that stupid driver being gunned down must have been the last straw. And he must have feared for his own life – having been on the receiving end of that pickaxe handle. For that reason, Templeton had hardly expected him to make a break for it. Yet, on reflection, that particular experience could have triggered his desire to escape.

Templeton could not contain his fury.

He lashed out at his palliasse, scattering straw high into the air. His impulsive action may have relieved something of his tension, but it did nothing for his sinuses and he sneezed four times in rapid succession. He leaned back against the wall of the barn and thought back to that old doctrine of his. The one which he had always practised religiously: planning, planning and planning. How had it all gone so horribly wrong this time? But what he did now appreciate was that he needed to think fast. And there was only one thing for him to do: get away from this barn as quickly as possible.

He moved across the floor to where the sub-branch case lay. He needed to get it into the Oxford, but he soon realized there was no way it would fit into the boot. With all that other cash stashed in there? Yet the back seat was no place for the case. Visible to all and sundry? Should he be stopped, it would be a right giveaway. And that would be that.

He went to the boot of the car and lifted its lid. How much space was still available for the sub-branch cash? There was clearly insufficient room for the actual case, but he could remove its contents. He should then be able to stuff the individual bundles of notes into what free space remained.

Returning to the case, he unlocked it, thankful to have had the foresight to take the key from Fairweather when they had arrived at the barn on Monday. Opening the case, he was relieved to see bundles of notes staring up at him, most of them in paper packets of £500. It lay to rest the end of his nightmare when he had opened the case only to find it crammed full of bricks.

Hauling the case across the floor, he then threw the packets of banknotes into the car's boot, jamming them into every possible nook and cranny. There was just sufficient space and he slammed the lid shut. All in all there must be getting on for £200,000 hidden from view. He could not resist licking his lips. But all that did was to make him realize how much he craved another Woodbine. It was over twenty-four hours since he stubbed out his last one on the floor of the barn.

But his greater priority now was to make for the open road.

Before flinging open the doors to the barn, he needed to make sure all was clear outside. He peeked out and found it as quiet as when they had arrived on Monday morning. And there was no sign of Fairweather. Not that he had expected to see him there. That thought had only briefly crossed his mind. Fairweather was probably miles away by now. But doing what? Could it really be possible he was now spilling the beans to someone? Whatever, it was a prime reason why Templeton must get away as soon as possible.

With everything all clear outside, he heaved back the doors to the barn and went back inside to start up the Oxford. But before getting into the car, he scanned the floor area. Was he leaving behind any evidence of their stay? The sub-branch case was the only item of any note, but what did it matter if it was discovered? It could not be linked to himself. It was Fairweather's case, not his. Provided he cleared it of possible fingerprints, he might as well leave it where it lay.

After wiping it clean, he was ready to get under way. A sense of relief flooded through him as he got behind the wheel of the car and turned the engine over. But all the starter motor did was to emit a tired whirring noise. He tried again. And again. Still no joy. He frantically attempted to bring the engine to life, but this simply weakened the whirring to virtually no sound at all.

The battery was as flat as one of the white fivers in the boot of his car.

In sheer frustration, he hammered the steering wheel with his clenched fists and shouted obscenities at the car. It had never let him down before. Why now, for God's sake?

He eventually slumped back in his seat, aware that his actions had been as impotent as the cells inside the car's battery. Then he remembered the starting handle. It had been with the rest of the tools in the boot when he had stowed them in the rear footwells to make room for the cash. He leapt out of his seat and, within seconds, had inserted the handle into its slot in the front grille. With all the effort he could muster, he swung the handle over and over again. Still nothing. He finally gave up and wanted to weep in his exhaustion. But, despite all his efforts, he still found the strength to hurl the iron starting handle across the width of the barn.

He then sank to his knees and any interloper would have assumed he was praying. But he had not been inside a church for years. He had always believed that prayers were only said by those good people who really had no need to pray. He reckoned they only used prayer as a form of insurance. If they should subsequently encounter a crisis, they believed their past praying would then provide them with a good return on their investment.

But this was not for him. Praying would not get him out of this predicament. Somehow he had to get a grip on himself and think this thing through.

Yet, realistically, what the hell could he possibly do?

CHAPTER 26

David awoke early on Wednesday morning. Sarah lay by his side, gently snoring. It really was ironic. He was the one who was always blamed for snoring; always the one who allegedly prevented the other from enjoying a good night's sleep. Yet, who was now disturbing the peace alongside him?

Not that it mattered. The last thing he now needed was to sleep. He had so much to think about. For a start, he could not get over last night's call to Colonel Fawkes-William. Did the Colonel really treat his wife as a servant? But was that of any relevance? Should his domestic arrangements have any bearing on how he managed his branch? Probably not. But it certainly broadened the picture David had been painting of the man.

And it was another example of an apparent lack of compassion – a disturbing omission in any manager's make-up. Or was this just an impression he had been giving? Was there more to it than that? There had been times when he had seemed unsurprised at some of the dreadful events which had occurred under his watch. Or was this simply a case of his being nonplussed as to how to deal with the happenings of the last two days?

One thing certainly did come out of last night's call: it would be David's plan of action which would be put to the test this morning. Yet, it was odd how the Colonel had been so complicit about this. He was not the sort of man who would normally want to play second fiddle.

David was also concerned about how the staff would react to Mr Grimshawe's fatal accident. Daphne Simcock, for one, appeared to have had a soft spot for the first cashier, as she also had for Barney Wilson. Now, one of them was dead and the other might not recover in hospital. And goodness knows what was happening to Douglas

Fairweather. Would Daphne, and the other staff, now experience a 'who's next' scenario? It was certainly something going through David's own mind.

And why were all these murky goings-on related to National Counties? Why not Lloyds? Or Barclays? And why Tunbridge Wells, for that matter? To David's mind, it was the least likely town to bear witness to such appalling events.

On the other hand 'least likely' was the recipe concocted by the most plausible con men. Or bank robbers? David firmly believed that obvious miscreants were the least likely to succeed. Some could be spotted a mile off. But the credible confidence trickster was quite another matter. Such a person would ensure that he was the least likely person to be under suspicion. In his early days as an inspector, David had come across one of these in the bank. This particular clerk had oozed charm and personality. But even as a raw inspector, David had a gut feeling and it eventually turned out to be one of his success stories. He had not ignored his sixth sense and he had discovered that, for several years, the man had been fleecing elderly lady customers left, right and centre. It might have been of little comfort to those customers afterwards, but the clerk had subsequently become a long-term guest of her majesty.

And now, here in Tunbridge Wells, his gut feelings were being put well and truly to the test.

As arranged, he reached the branch at eight o'clock and was pleased to see the Colonel had already arrived and was waiting to let him in.

"Ah, Goodhart, on time, eh?"

Was that meant to be an expression of surprise? Did he not expect David to be on time? Or was he simply trying to lighten the mood with a sense of jocularity? In which case, David felt it was a serious misjudgement on the Colonel's part.

"We have a lot to do."

The Colonel nodded.

"Better come up to my room and we can sort out our plan of campaign."

Our plan? That would only be the case if the Colonel was in compliance with all of David's proposals.

Once in the room, David opened his briefcase and took out a foolscap notepad, setting it down on his side of the manager's desk. He then withdrew his favourite Parker fountain pen from his inside jacket pocket and looked the Colonel in the eye.

"Right, let's set down what we need to do. First of all, do you agree to keeping the branch closed? For the time being, anyway?"

The Colonel nodded.

"I don't think we have any other option."

"In which case, we need someone on the door – outside. A notice pinned to the door won't do. Customers deserve some form of personal explanation. Who would you suggest?"

The manager frowned.

"I could do it myself?"

The answer surprised David. He had not considered the manager. But it would certainly give weight to the decision not to open the branch at the right hour. Customers who felt it inconvenient were less likely to express their wrath to the manager, himself. And there were two hours to go before normal opening at ten o'clock. It would give plenty of time before then for the manager to be involved in the personal discussions with the staff.

"I think that's a very good idea – to start with, anyway. Provided we can cover all the other things by ten. Remember, I also want to talk to you about General Kettleman. But we must deal with everything else first."

"I've been thinking about the General …"

"Later, Colonel. The staff will be arriving shortly. Let's first decide how we should deal with them."

In the next fifteen minutes, they worked out their strategy. As members of the staff arrived, Colonel Fawkes-William would greet them at the front door and simply ask them to congregate in the general office. He would simply say there had been an accident and the branch would not be opening until at least later in the morning.

The opening of the safes and drawers, together with dealing with the morning's post and cheque clearings would be delayed for the time being. Once everyone had been told collectively about Mr Grimshawe, the manager, David and Trevor would see them individually to discuss any possible concerns they might have. The subsequent opening of the branch and the manning of the tills would be dependent on the reactions expressed by the staff.

It would then be down to Trevor to organize the transfer in of any required relief staff, while Colonel Fawkes-William would liaise with Lloyds about cashing arrangements for his customers. David would contact Regional Office – if possible Mr Porter, rather than Angus McPhoebe – and the bank's chief inspector in London.

By half past nine, all this had been done, except for the drafting in of any relief staff. They were not required. The response from the staff had been exceptional. No one wanted time off and all would carry on with their duties as best they could. Daphne even volunteered to take over Mr Grimshawe's till. She would normally be too junior for such a position, but her attitude was exemplary. David felt more than encouraged to support her. And he could not help but notice that Trevor appeared to be particularly pleased about her positive response. Last night, they had retained hold of the duplicate keys from Lloyds which would enable Daphne to take over the till right away. In due course, they would need to obtain the original keys from Mrs Grimshawe.

David could only admire the maturity and sense of duty being displayed by the staff.

There was only one exception: Mr Barnett.

The sub-manager wandered around in a trance. David watched him carefully. His face had drained of colour when he had heard about the first cashier's death. But it seemed to David that it was not so much that the man had died, but in the manner of it and the way he had been found. Perhaps his reaction was simply an accumulation of all that had happened in the last two days. Perhaps it was the fact, even, that only older members of the branch staff had come to some harm. Could he, himself, be feeling vulnerable? But that was hardly feasible. How could Mr Grimshawe's accident be linked to the hold-up and the abduction of Douglas Fairweather?

There could, of course, be something else bothering Mr Barnett. Maybe it was linked with his home life and that young and extravagant wife of his. The last thing David liked to see was a member of staff with potential money problems. In an exclusively financial working environment? Succumbing to temptation was certainly not unheard of. And, in this particular instance, £50,000 was missing.

David shook his head. There was a danger of his becoming too fanciful and he had to move on. He needed to see Colonel Fawkes-William about those withdrawals on General Kettleman's account.

But he stopped in his tracks as he started to make his way to the manager's room. First he needed to see Daphne Simcock. In all that had gone on this morning, he had completely overlooked Daphne's visit last night to the General's house.

Had she discovered anything?

He turned round and scanned the office. Daphne was nowhere to be seen. She must still be in the strongroom, taking over Mr Grimshawe's till. David walked across the office to get to it and, yes, Daphne was there, counting the cash.

With Trevor.

"Just about finished, sir."

As he said this, Trevor heaved a £5 bag of copper into Daphne's cash safe and then stood back as the girl first locked the safe and then the cash box which she would eventually use on the counter.

"All present and correct, sir."

David would have been aghast if it had been otherwise, having only checked the contents of the till with Trevor yesterday. Because of this, it might have seemed a waste of time for Daphne to have to count all the cash again. But, as a cashier, she would know that whenever a till is handed over, the receiving cashier must be personally satisfied that all the cash was there as stated. And in a case such as this, with the current holder not there, the checking must take place in the presence of another person. Hence Trevor being in the cash safe alone with Daphne.

David felt a little contrite that another motive had previously crossed his mind.

"Now Daphne," he said, searching the girl's face to try and gauge her true feelings about what she had learnt this morning, "you're sure you're all right … to take over this till. It's not going to be easy for you … with customers, I mean. They're clearly going to be curious …"

The girl gave a wistful smile and nodded.

"I really want to do it for him, sir. Mr Grimshawe was such a sweetie …"

She broke off and looked away, as if struggling to hold back tears. David decided this was a good moment to change the subject.

"That's good, Daphne. But on another matter, how did you get on with General Kettleman last night?"

Daphne turned back to him, now wide-eyed, her eyes darting between him and Trevor.

"I'm sorry, sir, but with all that's been going on this morning … it just slipped my mind."

That was understandable enough. But her expression was now making David feel anxious.

"And?"

"And there's definitely a big problem with those cheques."

"Oh?"

"Yes, sir. The General couldn't have possibly cashed them himself. He wasn't there last night. But I spoke to a neighbour. He said the General went into a nursing home last Wednesday. He's been there ever since. Yet all the cheques were cashed on Friday."

So, they were definitely fraudulent encashments. He and Trevor had virtually come to that conclusion in the pub last night. Now it must be unequivocal. And last night he had also questioned whether there might be a link with Mr Grimshawe's disappearance. Although the cashier could not have cashed the cheques himself, he could most certainly have had an accomplice to do it for him. Yet Mr Grimshawe was now dead. Was it just an unfortunate accident? Or could it really have been suicide? If he had been involved in something underhand, could he have had a sudden fit of conscience?

But was he becoming too fanciful again? Apart from possible questions over his finances and whether or not he was a hardened gambler, Mr Grimshawe had always been a fine cashier. Although the possibility of gambling had been raised, there had been no previous misgivings about his integrity. And Daphne, for one, held him in high regard; she had called him a sweetie. So, he was probably the least likely person to get involved in any wrongdoing.

David closed his eyes and pursed his lips. The least likely?

CHAPTER 27

It took Alfie Templeton twenty minutes to come up with any sort of plan. Of those first ten minutes, he had done nothing. He had simply held his head in his hands, leaning down heavily on the Oxford's steering wheel, which now bore the full weight of his misery.

Despair engulfed him.

Stashed away in the boot of his car, there was more money than he could ever have imagined; yet he might as well be a pauper. What was the good of any of it, if he was stuck here in this wretched barn, unable to get away?

When he finally came out of his self-imposed trance, his first thought had been to bury the cash. And then return for it later. He had read about this being done by real villains, not just in fiction. But buried treasure? Here in the heart of Kent? It hardly sounded feasible. But what else could he do?

Yet, if he were to do this, there was at least one positive aspect: this place was so isolated. Its insularity had been the attraction when he had holed up here on Monday morning. A good start was its being half a mile from the main road, while the overgrown track to the barn had appeared not to have seen a vehicle in years – until last night. But apart from that courting couple, the only other form of life these last couple of days had been birds, bats, rats and the occasional rabbit.

So why not bury the cash around here – or simply hide it?

But would he have time to do this? And what about Fairweather? That clown could be spilling the beans right now. If so, time must be running out. For this reason alone, Templeton must get away – and fast. And his gut was also telling him to get going. He was so hungry. And he was starting to reek. Even in his war service, he had never gone three days without any washing or changing. Getting home would solve all this. Yet, his car was kaput.

How the hell would he get there?

On foot was a non-starter; it must be over thirty miles to the Holmesdale Road. Hitch-hiking? Not a chance; he needed to keep well away from the open road. The railway, then? But where was the nearest station? And he would again be putting himself in the public eye. Could he possibly take that risk?

The more he thought about it, the more the plan appeared to be fraught with difficulty – and danger. Even if he made it home, he would eventually have to get back to the barn to recover the loot – if it was still around.

All the time he was away from the barn, the Oxford would be cocooned here – just waiting for the arrival of the fuzz. And despite the barn's isolation, it would be just his luck that, apart from the police, someone else might nose around, see the car and raise the alarm. In no time at all, with or without Fairweather's doing, the place would be crawling with coppers. And even the most plodding of them would soon discover his hiding place for his precious horde of bank notes.

No, it was not on. This whole plan was crazy.

But what else could he do?

Then it struck him. The track had led down to the barn. Down to the barn! It had been downhill all the way and the track did not end at the barn; it carried on, to some eventual destination. To some out-of-the-way fields? Or to a farmhouse? Yet either case seemed unlikely. Otherwise, there would be some evidence of the track having been used. On the other hand, if there was a farmhouse around, it might be more easily accessible from a different direction.

But this was all speculation. As far as Templeton was concerned, the main factor was that the track continued downhill after the barn. If he was able to push the Oxford outside and steer it in that direction, he might be able to bump-start the car to get it going.

Yet, there could be a downside. If he failed to start the car, it would then lie abandoned – right out in the open. At least, at present, it was hidden away in the barn. And he had no idea how far the track extended past the barn. He knew from past experience that bump-starting a car did not necessarily work at the first attempt. On one occasion, he had run out of road and got well and truly stuck.

So, was it worth the risk?

His instinct told him yes. But before doing anything, he needed to reconnoitre the area. If the track petered out quickly, trying to bump-start the car was not on. The same would apply if there was a nearby building. And he was still worried should bump-starting fail. He would then have to abandon the car, with the boot stuffed with all that dosh. How would he get out of that one?

But he was now in a more positive frame of mind. He sat upright in his seat, drumming his fingers on the steering wheel as he decided what to do. This plan must, surely, be worth exploring, as must the area around the barn. And he needed to do something soon. He had already spent twenty minutes getting nowhere and he must now spring into action. Time had to be running out.

Making sure his revolver was still in place, he climbed out of the car and opened the barn's double doors, then immediately closing them behind him. He did not want the Oxford to be in any way visible while he was exploring down the track. Although he was confident no one would be in the vicinity, he moved as quietly as possible and was thankful his recent fit of sneezing had not recurred.

His heart started to beat faster as he made his way down the track. This soon became narrower and even more overgrown. It remained wide enough to take a vehicle, but, in places, he had to stay in its middle to prevent his clothes being snagged by out-of-control brambles and offshoots from the hawthorn hedges which lined the sides. But this only confirmed the track must have been abandoned long ago. And it was also extending far enough away from the barn to give him several chances to bump-start the car. His plan was now looking distinctly feasible.

He carried on for about three hundred yards and found no sign of any building. The hedges were too high for him to see what lay further ahead, but he now felt confident the track did not lead to anything significant in the near vicinity. But there would be no hiding place should he fail to start the car. What would he then do?

Leave the car out here abandoned? Stuck in the open, with the boot crammed with so much money? And with the place about to be invaded by the police? At the very least, he would have to get a replacement vehicle. That would normally be no problem; he had spent a good part of his life nicking cars. But how long would that take? There was no way he would have enough time.

Yet, all this would only happen if he failed to start the Oxford. If he succeeded in bump-starting the car, all his problems would be over.

He turned tail and ran back to the barn. Opening the doors wide, he stared at his car and shook his head. Why had he chosen such a tank of a vehicle? He had bought it on holiday in Devon and it had seemed a good idea at the time. But the Oxford must weigh well over a ton. Would he have the strength to move it, especially as there was a slight incline between where it was parked and the doors of the barn?

He bit his lips hard. He had never been the strongest of men. Brain, not brawn, had always been his philosophy. Not that he had been proud of his acumen over these last two days. But it was not just the weight of the actual car that was troubling him: added to this was the content of the boot. Paper, in itself, might not weigh much, but in bulk? He well remembered how heavy the sub-branch case had been when he heaved it across the barn's floor.

On Monday, he had driven the Oxford straight into the barn and he now went to the front of the car to try and push it back towards the doors. He placed both hands on the bonnet and put his full weight – all ten stone of him – into moving the car backwards. Nothing. His efforts were to no avail. The car would not budge an inch.

In sheer frustration, he leant back from the car and swore viciously. What was he to do? Then he thumped his forehead with the palm of his right hand. What an idiot! He really was losing it; not thinking straight. The handbrake! He had not thought to release it.

Once he had done just that, he soon had the car moving. But only so very slowly and he now cursed the slight incline. Not only did he now fear this would defeat him, but also that his exertions would bring on an asthma attack. But once he had the car properly rolling, the momentum gradually inched the car towards the doors and then into the open air.

He reached a level area outside the barn and decided to take a breather. Although the air was cool, he was sweating profusely and he got out his handkerchief to wipe his brow. His shirt was sticking to his back and he could smell the perspiration, but there was nothing he could do about that. It was just one more reason why he yearned to get into a change of clothing.

But he could not hang around for long. Time was now the essence and he quite expected to hear police cars pounding down the track. With the Oxford out in the open, he moved round to the driver's side and opened the door. He leaned inside to switch on the ignition and then got the car rolling forward. Before it picked up any speed, he jumped into the car, depressed the clutch pedal and selected top gear. As the car increased its speed, he slowly let up the clutch and the car jerked in response. But there was no sign of life from the engine. He let the car's speed increase and tried again. This time he released the clutch sharply and – joy of joy – the engine swung into life. To prevent the car careering forward, he slammed his left foot hard down on the clutch pedal and his right foot on to the brake. He then blipped the accelerator. The last thing he needed was for the engine to stall.

And that was that. He pressed back into his seat and took a deep breath. He had never been a man of prayer, but he did roll his eyes up to the heavens. The sound of the running engine was music to his ears.

His next task was to reverse the car up the track. It would not be easy. The route was narrow and winding, with little leeway on either side of the car. And, at all costs, he must avoid stalling. The battery would still be too flat to turn over the engine and he would then have to go through the whole bump-start routine again.

He slipped the gear lever into reverse and the car edged slowly backwards. He kept the engine revs high, despite his concern about causing undue noise. He had to reverse about two hundred yards to reach the barn and, when he got there, he found the level patch outside was just wide enough for him to turn the car around.

Taking another deep breath and letting out a rapturous holler, he started the car up the track and made for the open road.

CHAPTER 28

David knew in his bones that things had, perhaps, gone too smoothly this morning. Colonel Fawkes-William's total co-operation had been a good start. The commendable attitude of all the staff had then enabled the branch to open at eleven, just one hour later than the scheduled opening hour. Even Mr Barnett had got a grip of himself. Perhaps that had been through the influence of the other staff.

David had subsequently received full support for his actions from the bank's chief inspector in London. And Angus McPhoebe had been no problem, simply because he had been away from his desk and could not take his call. David was told that either Mr Porter or McPhoebe would ring back.

All this enabled him to concentrate on the fraudulent withdrawals from General Kettleman's account.

He had already decided to visit the branches where the cheques had been cashed and Tenterden would be his first destination. He hoped he would be able to establish exactly how the branches had received authorization for the encashments and, with any amount of luck, the cashiers would recall the person who actually made the withdrawals.

Yes, everything had gone as well as could have been expected.

Until now.

"I can't believe you allowed the branch to remain closed until eleven o'clock," Angus McPhoebe snapped.

The returned call. Why could it not have come from Mr Porter? Where was the regional manager when he was most needed? Instead, it had been left for David to brief his deputy on what had happened that morning.

"In your role, Goodhart," McPhoebe continued, not attempting to disguise his animosity, "it might not be of concern to you, but, at branch level, we aim to provide our customers with top quality service. And we can't do that if we keep the front door closed. You mean to tell me, Goodhart, that you took this decision because a member of staff had an accident over the weekend? You must know that I'm the last person to be insensitive to such a thing and I fully accept the tragedy of the man's drowning. But really! You actually decided this gave you sufficient reason to delay opening the branch?"

David eased the handset away from his ear to lessen the impact of McPhoebe's ranting. His action also moved the phone away from his mouth. That was just as well, for he had no intention of responding. Such an outburst did not deserve the courtesy of any reply. Could it be that McPhoebe was espousing such views simply because of his antagonism towards David? Or was he really indifferent to how this third calamity to members of the branch staff might adversely affect the remainder of their colleagues? As for McPhoebe professing not to be insensitive; he was now making Colonel Fawkes-William appear to be a paragon of sensitivity.

"Goodhart?"

David remained silent.

He could not think of anyone else to whom he would react in this way. And he knew he was acting childishly. But he found it immensely satisfying that McPhoebe might be feeling a little disconcerted at the lack of any response from the other end of the line.

"Goodhart? Are you still there?"

David coughed quietly, just to let McPhoebe know the line had not gone dead.

"Ah, good. For one moment, I thought there was a problem with the line. So, what made you take such a decision?"

David decided the time had come to reply.

"It wasn't just my decision. Colonel Fawkes-William agreed with it. We both thought it was the right thing to do."

It was now McPhoebe's turn to take stock. As a firm champion of the Colonel, he probably did not appeciate hearing such an answer.

"Oh … well …"

"And Colonel Fawkes-William did more than that. He personally made arrangements with Lloyds – for cashing cheques and taking in credits. He even stood outside on the pavement to tell his customers what he'd done. So, they got the top-quality service you're talking about – even with the front door closed."

David paused. Perhaps he should have resisted being sarcastic. But it probably went over McPhoebe's head, anyway.

"As it turned out," he continued, "the arrangement was only needed for an hour. The Colonel would have been prepared to stay closed for the whole day. But the commendable attitude of the staff made that unnecessary."

David did not need to be a psychologist to know how McPhoebe would react to this. After the man's initial outburst, he was now aware of the manager's involvement – a manager for whom he seemed to have such a high regard. David had dealt McPhoebe a 'Get out of Jail – Free' card and this sad man now felt duly obliged to use it.

"That doesn't surprise me at all. Colonel Fawkes-William has always been a good motivator. He can get the most out of his staff. Man-management they call it, Goodhart."

David gritted his teeth. He was glad he was on the end of a telephone line and not sitting opposite this unctuous man. How had McPhoebe turned out this way? He would not have been like it when he joined the bank. As with David, he was probably a sixteen-year-old recruit, maybe eighteen if he had been bright enough to stay on at school. So, when had he developed this superior air? This fawning over people he deemed to be 'good men'? This arrogance which set him apart from lesser mortals – such as David?

"Be that as it may," David replied, "the branch is now up and running again. But apart from all that's happened these last two days, there's another problem."

"Oh?"

"Several cheques appear to have been drawn fraudulently on a customer's account – a General Kettleman."

"General Kettleman?"

Oh, no. David might have known it. Generals, as well as Colonels, must fall neatly together in McPhoebe's coterie of supposed good men.

"That's the man.".

"He's a good friend of the bank," McPhoebe said. David immediately imagined him leaning back in his chair, smug satisfaction gracing his face. "We've entertained him here at Regional Office several times. Board lunches, you know. But what do you mean? Fraudulent withdrawals?"

David would have preferred not to raise this matter with McPhoebe. But he felt duty-bound to do so – simply because his gut instinct told him that it was, somehow, linked to the other goings-on at the branch. But he had no intention of sharing any speculation of what that might be. And he did not want to be dictated to by McPhoebe as to how he should carry out his investigations.

"Cheques have been cashed at local branches – quite inconsistent with any pattern on the General's account. And we now have good reason to believe he didn't cash the cheques himself."

"Oh? Why's that, Goodhart?"

"Let me come back to you when I've got the full story."

"You're working on it, then?"

"Of course."

"What are you …?"

David decided to put a stop to this right away. It would be bad enough facing an inquisition when he had all the answers, never mind now. And he did not want McPhoebe dictating his every move. Whatever else, David needed to maintain his independence on how he was to proceed.

"I'll keep you informed, of course. But I must now get on."

Within ten minutes, David had dismissed McPhoebe from his mind and he sat behind the wheel of his car, with Trevor at his side. They had only been away from Tenterden for forty-eight hours, yet, with all that had since happened, it seemed more like a month. They would visit all five branches where General Kettleman's cheques had been cashed and he felt Tenterden was the best place to start.

He decided to make his way via Lamberhurst, effectively reversing the route he had chosen on Monday. The sub-branch was still closed and he was anxious to gauge the reaction of one or two customers. Maybe he was thinking along the lines of Angus McPhoebe: not being able to provide a top quality service if the front door remained closed. But he hoped customers would be understanding, especially as it should be possible to re-open shortly.

Stopping the car outside the branch, he decided the village general store would be as good a place to start as any. Another good option would be the pub opposite. Putting temptation to one side, especially as the pub was about to open, he asked Trevor to have words with the landlord, while he made for the shop.

When they returned to the car, they both had the same story: customers were, indeed, most understanding. Their main concern was for the welfare of Douglas Fairweather and Barney Wilson, not to mention their dismay that such a dreadful crime should have taken place in their peaceful village. As far as everyone was concerned, their banking requirements could be delayed until the branch re-opened. In any case, they took the view that it was not far to Tunbridge Wells to carry out any urgent transactions.

This reaction was just what David had hoped to hear and it was with a glow in his heart for mankind when he re-started the car, now able to concentrate on his next task.

Before leaving the branch in Tunbridge Wells, Trevor had gathered up a batch of General Kettleman's cheques and he now held these in his hands. They included the five cheques cashed at other branches – each for £5,000 – and some recent cheques which the General had clearly drawn himself.

David glanced across at him and then back to the road to avoid a close encounter with the nearside hedge.

"Have another look at the signatures. Could they all be genuine?"

Trevor turned the cheques over in his hands and then held two of them up in front of him. He placed the others in his lap.

"I'm not sure about the signatures, but these two cheques certainly look different."

"Which ones?" David asked, resisting the temptation to look across at them.

Trevor indicated the one in his left hand.

"This one must be genuine. It was made out to Boots the Chemist, three weeks ago. That figures – bearing in mind the General's not well. This other one's the £5,000 he cashed at Tenterden – allegedly."

"And?"

"There are definite slight differences. For a start – although it might not mean anything – the £5,000 cheque isn't written with the same pen."

Trevor now examined the other cheques in his lap.

"And this different pen was used for the other cashed cheques. It's a biro."

"And the others?"

"All of them a fountain pen, sir."

That figured. David could imagine an elderly General eschewing modern-day biros in favour of a trusty fountain pen. He even felt the same way himself.

"What about the actual writing? Not just the signatures, but the words and figures on the cheques?"

Trevor turned each cheque over in turn.

"The actual signatures could be the same. Some slight differences, but that can be the case with anyone. But ..."

"Well?"

Trevor now became excited.

"There's definitely a difference here, sir. Look ..."

"Trevor! You know you're never happy with my driving at the best of times. You really want me to take a gander?"

Trevor chuckled.

"Point taken, sir. But one actual letter is written totally differently. His Fs. On the cashed cheques, the F in Five is printed like a capital letter, but on the others it's always written the other way round. They call that script, don't they?"

David nodded, Although he had occasionally used both styles himself, most people would use one or the other. The cashed cheques now looked to be forgeries – especially if there were other discrepancies in the handwriting.

"Can you see any other variations? The same thing could happen with the letter A."

Trevor again scrutinized the cheques.

"No, sir. No As. But, I wonder … Yes, sir. The M in March. All the cheques were made out in March and the cashed ones are all written like a typed M. The others are all in script."

That made it definite, then. It was certainly good to have some tangible evidence, such as this. The question now was who actually made out the cheques and cashed them? And why did the branches feel authorized to allow the encashments?

"I think that settles it, Trevor. Now it's a matter of who and how."

They had now reached Goudhurst and David had to ram down hard on the brake pedal as he came face-to-face with a Massey-Ferguson tractor. What on earth was it doing, breaching the narrow hairpin exit out of the village? But he had to suppress a smile as Trevor grabbed hold of his seat with both hands.

"The branches must have been given the go-ahead by Tunbridge Wells," the lad replied, apparently undaunted by the emergency stop. "Do you think it was done by phone?"

"That's certainly possible. But I doubt it. Whoever might make such a call could be asked some awkward questions – such as about identification. It wouldn't be worth the risk. I reckon it was done by post, using our standard form 69. If the form included a specimen signature of the General and the amount was properly coded, the other branches wouldn't seek any other identification or authorization. They'd just await the arrival of the General and make sure he signs the cheque in front of them. If the signatures compare, there's no reason why they shouldn't pay out the money – unless they have specific grounds for suspicion."

"Sounds so easy, sir."

David nodded. Yes, indeed. Given the correct authorization and faced by a plausible impersonation of the customer, it would be difficult to fault the actions of the branches. Perhaps the emphasis was on plausible. An army general, even if retired, was likely to have some basic characteristics. Anyone impersonating such a person would need to get those right in order to avert any suspicion by the bank cashiers. But another thing was now troubling him: it went back to one of the problems he faced when he was the manager at Barnmouth.

"What about the cheque numbers, Trevor?"

Trevor let out a grunt and it was clear he was also thinking back to Barnmouth. He rummaged through all the cheques in his lap.

"You're right, sir. All the cashed cheques are from a different cheque book."

David's eyes narrowed.

"And I bet it's one he's never been issued with."

It was a fair assumption. This whole business now had the hallmarks of an inside job. From his experience, David was only too aware of how easy it was for a member of the staff to purloin a cheque book from the branch library. These books were simply kept in sequential order and it would be far better if they were personalized with customers' names. Perhaps, one day, the bank would get round to such a system.

"When we get back to Tunbridge Wells, the first thing I'd like you to do is examine the register – to identify which book has been used. With luck these five cheques from that book will be the only ones to have been cashed. We'll just have to hope more haven't been cashed on other customers' accounts."

"Wouldn't we have known that by now?"

"Possibly."

But David was not convinced. He had a feeling there was more to come. It would probably come to light when they got back to Tunbridge Wells.

"Anyway," he added, as they approached the junction in the centre of Sissinghurst which would take them towards Tenterden, "who's actually been cashing these cheques? And whom do we have to worry about in the branch?"

Trevor remained silent. Either he was pondering on possible miscreants, or he was concerned that David had almost missed the turn, forcing the car to swing round sharply and making Trevor cling on to his seat again.

Once on the open road, it seemed that Trevor was confident enough to reply, but, as it turned out, not to David's question.

"Look over there, sir," he said, pointing to a sign against a farm entrance. "Even I know that's got to be wrong."

David was going slowly enough to glance at the sign which displayed produce for sale: Potato's, Carrot's and Turnip's.

"The dreaded greengrocer's apostrophe, Trevor."

The lad grinned.

"You see, I'm learning, sir. But getting back to these encashments, do you think they're related to everything else?"

It was a question which had been exercising David's mind for some time. He had considered various options, but each one seemed inconceivable. Yet, one particular possibility was now starting to trouble him.

"I just don't know. But let's just think about the code system. Who had actually calculated the codes and inserted them on to the forms 69?"

"We know who should have done it – Colonel Fawkes-William or Mr Barnett. But we also know how lax they've been over the code box."

David nodded.

"Which means that anyone else – someone with the required will and inclination – could have obtained details from the code cards to calculate the fraudulent codes."

Trevor frowned.

"And that person," he said, "could have delved into the code box days or, even, weeks ago. The person could have worked out the codes when an opportunity arose."

David shook his head in despair. This was why strict rules were in place. But if they were disregarded?

"More likely, the information on the code cards could have been copied. The person could then bide his time until the codes were needed. Then the forms 69 could be completed and dispatched, together with a pretty fair forgery of General Kettleman's signature."

Trevor appeared shocked at such a scenario.

"That's it in a nutshell, then. Someone in the branch is definitely the perpetrator of the withdrawals."

"Or a party to them."

"You mean more than one person's definitely involved?"

David could see it no other way.

"I'm sure that's the case."

"But who, sir?"

David mulled over the question, his mind now also concentrating on a lorry and trailer which had been ahead of them for a couple of miles. It was laden with logs and slowed to a crawl whenever it reached any form of incline. He was tempted to overtake it, but immediately felt the tension next to him and decided that caution was the better option.

"Theoretically it could be anyone – bearing in mind the code box has been left lying around and unlocked."

"But realistically, sir?"

David felt like counting off the possible perpetrators on the fingers of his hand, but resisted the temptation and kept both hands on the steering wheel – especially as he still hoped for an opportunity to overtake the lorry.

"We certainly can't discount the manager and sub-manager. Irrespective of their failings over control of the code box, they're the most likely ones to have issued the codes. Perhaps unwittingly, of course. Otherwise? Mr Grimshawe? Or the fellow in charge of securities? Your Daphne, even?"

David stole a look at Trevor and saw him immediately redden. An apology was clearly needed.

"Sorry, Trevor. That was uncalled for. But what about Mr Grimshawe? The poor man might be dead, but was it really an accident? If he'd been involved with these cheques – along with the person who cashed them – could there have been a falling out? Or did he then have pangs of conscience? Could that have driven him to taking his own life?"

David sensed that Trevor had accepted his apology and it was also clear that Mr Grimshawe's possible suicide had shocked him. And no wonder. Such a death, following on from Barney Wilson's near demise – not to mention what might have happened to Douglas Fairweather – was enough to shock anyone. And neither Trevor, nor David, had experienced anything like this happening to a banking colleague.

Trevor now looked across at him.

"I'm sorry, sir, but I can't get my head round all of this. I'm actually glad I never met Mr Grimshawe. That would have made it even worse. And it seems he was such a good person. In which case, how could he have possibly been involved in anything like this?"

David shook his head.

"I simply don't know. But someone was. Irrespective of who actually cashed the cheques, someone in the branch must have been involved. As to our prime suspect? Who knows?"

The lorry had now turned off the road and they were fast approaching the outskirts of Tenterden. David hoped that one piece of the jigsaw would soon be put in place: a description of the person who had actually cashed the cheque at the branch. And the way in which the encashment had been authorized should also be revealed. But another matter was now bothering him: his previous feeling that something was not quite right at Tenterden. Was it just a coincidence that one of General Kettleman's cheques had been cashed at this, of all branches? Or was there a specific link at Tenterden to all that had been happening at Tunbridge Wells?

CHAPTER 29

Having asked Trevor to make some general enquiries in the general office, even to nose around, David now sat opposite the manager in his room. At least David was senior to Charles Featherstonehaugh. The Tenterden manager was unlikely to have the temerity to give him a McPhoebe-like reception. And thank goodness the man called himself Fanshawe; it made the pronunciation of his name far less of a mouthful.

But today, Featherstonehaugh did have a McPhoebe-inspired air about him. Was it an in-built form of arrogance? It showed up in his facial expression, rather than by way of his bearing. He was about David's height of just under six foot, but as they sat opposite each other in the manager's room, he seemed much shorter. Perhaps he was simply slumped in his chair. Yet that seemed unlikely. With a bank inspector sitting opposite? He should be alert, or at least giving the impression of being bright-eyed and bushy-tailed.

More likely, his height related to long-leggedness. It made David recall two of his old girlfriends – way before he had met Sarah. They were both about the same height, but one had long legs to die for; the charms of the other lay mainly above the waist. Featherstonehaugh was probably akin to the former – though his own legs would hardly make the same impression on David as those of the girl.

Featherstonehaugh looked at him quizzically.

"I didn't expect you back so soon."

"Nor did I."

"Not after what happened at Lamberhurst. What a dreadful thing."

David nodded. News of the hold-up must have spread throughout the region. But he wondered how many branches would be aware of the true facts. Most would have heard about what happened through hearsay, or gossip – every titbit being embellished as it passed from person to person. He wondered if Featherstonehaugh was angling for some inside information. If so, he was to be disappointed.

"Awful," David replied, shaking his head. "Everyone's in shock. And there's so much for Trevor and me to look into. That's why we're here now."

Featherstonehaugh raised his eyebrows and looked puzzled.

"So, you're not here to carry on with your inspection."

"If only …"

"But why? Why then come back?"

"Something else has come up. Not to do with the hold-up. Well, not directly."

The manager now looked anxious, rather than puzzled.

"But to do with us? Surely not?"

David pursed his lips and now wished Trevor was sitting next to him with the General's cheques.

"There's a problem with a Tunbridge Wells customer. Several cheques have been cashed on his account. They appear to be fraudulent."

"So, what's that got to do with us?"

"There were five different cheques. Each for £5,000. All cashed last Friday. One of them was cashed here."

Featherstonehaugh visibly bridled.

"You mean we've done something wrong?"

"No, no, no. Well I wouldn't have thought so. No, it looks to be some kind of organized scam. You probably had every reason to cash the cheque."

Featherstonehaugh frowned and stroked his chin with his right forefinger and thumb.

"On Friday, you say? For £5,000?"

David nodded.

"It was coded, then."

David nodded again and then saw the dawn breaking over the manager.

"General Kettleman!"

"The very man."

"I've had to decipher several codes recently, but his was the only one for £5,000. And I'd remembered him well. I'd met him only recently."

This was interesting.

"Really?"

"Yes, I had lunch with him – three months ago. At Regional Office. At one of their board lunches. He'd been taken there by Colonel Fawkes-William."

David managed to remain expressionless. So there was a link. A triangular one between Tenterden, Tunbridge Wells and Regional Office in Haywards Heath. Yet, on the face of it, this was only a lunch party. Was it really a tangible link? Hardly. These Regional Office luncheons were mainly social occasions, for managers and their selected customers. They gave the regional management an opportunity to meet influential customers in their region. Colonel Fawkes-William clearly thought highly enough of the General to be his choice of customer – perhaps simply through military connections. And it would seem that, even in Tenterden, there must be at least one bigwig deserving of such entertaining. David only hoped that Featherstonehaugh's choice had not been the landlord of the Red Lion.

It did seem strange, though, that the managers of Tunbridge Wells and Tenterden just happened to have been invited by Regional Office to the same lunch. Unless there was already a connection between the Colonel and Featherstonehaugh, never mind Angus McPhoebe.

Whatever, this did mean that Featherstonehaugh had already met the General. In which case, it was more than likely he would have made a point of renewing their acquaintance on Friday. If so, how could anyone, other than the General himself, have cashed the cheque? Yet, it appeared that this had patently happened.

David looked enquiringly at the manager.

"You saw him then? On Friday?"

Featherstonehaugh now looked disappointed.

"No. He came in between one and two. I'd popped out for a pub lunch."

The Red Lion, no doubt. Checking that his investment – the bank's investment – was safe?

"But you'd already checked the code? It was okay?"

"Yes, as soon as we received the form 69 from Tunbridge Wells. It came in at the beginning of last week."

"And General Kettleman's signature was in order?"

Featherstonehaugh looked confused at the question. And with good reason. It had been a stupid question. How could he know if the signature was all right. The General was not his own customer.

"I assume it was."

"But what about the form 69 itself? Who actually signed it – at Tunbridge Wells?"

Featherstonehaugh now looked relieved to hear a question he could answer.

"It was Mr Barnett – Colonel Fawkes-William's sub-manager. I was actually glad to see his name. It reminded me I hadn't been in contact with him for such a long time."

"You know him, then?"

"Yes, I know him well. I was at Tunbridge Wells before him. He took over from me – when I got promoted to this job."

So that was the link! Probably why he and the Colonel were invited to the same Regional Office lunch. But apart from that, could this be the reason for David's previous disquiet about this branch? The gut feeling he had that something was awry? It might have nothing to do with the lending to the Red Lion. Nor to any other customer, for that matter.

No, if Featherstonehaugh had been Colonel Fawkes-William's sub-manager – probably for several years – the Colonel's management style must have been a considerable influence on him. And it was a style with which David had no truck. In his view, the Colonel was the least appropriate role model for Featherstonehaugh to have had as a grounding for his first managerial appointment.

No wonder such an arrogant air had traversed the manager's desk at the start of this meeting. At the time, David had felt it to be McPhoebe-like, but Fawkes-William-like was even more fitting. Before he had been called to the hold-up at Lamberhurst, David must have been getting subliminal messages about the man. But he would have expected any such feelings to be linked to his banking acumen. The Colonel's influence could not have possibly come into his reckoning.

But all this had little to do with David's current brief. He might be posing question marks over Featherstonehaugh's management style, but did that really matter in respect of what happened on Friday? He now needed some specific information about the encashment of the General's cheque.

"Do you know which cashier actually cashed the cheque?"

The manager shook his head.

"No, but I can soon find out. And ..."

A light tap on the door interrupted him.

"Enter," Featherstonehaugh bellowed, in sharp contrast to the timidity of the tap.

The door opened and Trevor came in, followed by a young man who looked frightened to death. Was this because of something he had done? Or simply because Trevor was wheeling him in to see his manager? Or a bank inspector?

"Excuse me, sir," Trevor said to the manager. He then glanced across the table and specifically addressed David. "We definitely have a problem, sir"

Featherstonehaugh looked alarmed.

"Why's that, young man?"

Trevor seemed unsure about whether to answer the manager directly. David decided to help him out.

"Just carry on, Trevor. We're both listening."

"Well, sir, this is Mr Bridgeford. He cashed the General's cheque on Friday."

Featherstonehaugh switched his gaze from Trevor and glared at the cashier.

"Go on, Bridgeford. Explain yourself."

David was not impressed. The manager was making no attempt to put the lad at his ease in front of a visiting inspector. Why bark at him? Was this why young Mr Bridgeford had appeared so alarmed when he came into the room? Was it the normal reception he would expect to receive from Mr Featherstonehaugh?

The young man visibly gulped before replying.

"I'm sorry, sir, but ... but everything seemed to be all right ..."

His words tailed off and his head dropped, as if he were unable to hold his manager's gaze. Featherstonehaugh was clearly not impressed.

"Go on, then. Get it out, man."

Having been bailed out by his boss in the Colonel's room yesterday, Trevor apparently decided to do likewise and come to the youngster's assistance.

"Mr Bridgeford did all he should have done – with the signature, I mean. He made sure the cheque was signed in front of him and he compared the signature with the specimen on the form 69. They appeared to be identical. But the man in front of him was far younger than General Kettleman."

Featherstonehaugh now rose from his chair, his eyes blazing at the cashier.

"Then why did you cash the cheque?"

David could only feel sorry for young Mr Bridgeford. Did Featherstonehaugh really think this to be effective man-management? David had come across such aggressive tactics in the Forces. It had been particularly so during his square-bashing days in the RAF. It was probably far worse in the army. Had Featherstonehaugh been an army man – in the war? In which case, he might have developed his methods at that time, rather than under the wing of Colonel Fawkes-William. Bullying tactics by NCOs had appalled David and he was not entirely convinced by the argument that they led to unquestioned obedience in times of warfare. But this was Civvy Street. Banking. David saw no reason for employing such tactics anywhere in the bank, never mind here in Tenterden branch.

Yet?

Yet, had such training been behind Barney Wilson's valiant reaction in Lamberhurst? Or was he simply an innately brave man? Whatever the case, David could not forget that Barney was now fighting for his life in the Kent and Sussex.

Despite David feeling sorry for the cashier, it seemed that the manager's blatant accusation was now giving the lad some self-belief.

"I didn't know how old the customer was supposed to be."

"But he's a general, for God's sake. You know … the sort of people who won the war for us. How could he have been a much younger man?"

David groaned inwardly. Bridgeford was hardly old enough to remember the war, never mind know who might have helped to win it. He was probably not even old enough to have done National Service.

"Can you describe the man for us?" he asked quietly, attempting to reduce the charged atmosphere inside the room. It seemed to have the desired effect: the manager took his seat again.

"He was probably in his forties," Bridgeford said, looking pleased to be able to direct his attention to David. "He was short and a bit weedy, sir – if you know what I mean."

Featherstonehaugh snorted.

David was encouraged.

"Go on."

"He didn't say much. Just that he'd made an arrangement to cash the cheque. He signed it in front of me. It was exactly like the specimen, honest it was …"

Many questions were now flying around David's mind. An exact replica of the specimen signature? The specimen of which had been attached to the form 69 – signed by Mr Barnett? And the sub-manager's predecessor had been Featherstonehaugh – now the manager of the branch where General Kettleman's cheque had been cashed?

Yet, four other of the General's cheques had been cashed elsewhere. Had the staff of those branches also been duped by Mr Bridgeford's short and weedy man? A man who could not have possibly accomplished such skulduggery on his own? And did these other branches also have a link with Tunbridge Wells?

"I need to see the form 69," David said, addressing the manager. "You're sure you deciphered the code correctly?"

Featherstonehaugh looked indignant. It was probably not just because he deemed David to be questioning his ability. More than likely he was personally affronted that a cheque had been cashed at his branch for the wrong person. He turned his wrath on the cashier.

"Off you go, then, Bridgeford. Dig out that form 69. And while you're at it, bring in the code box."

David winced at the snapped order. He had now placed a serious question mark over the manager. Was he up to managing this branch? David had always reckoned that incompetent managers tended to show themselves up in poor light. Those who felt overwhelmed by their responsibilities would be the ones to lash out at their subordinates. It was their way of tempering their own shortcomings. And the more they realized these shortcomings, the more aggressive they became, leading to quite unacceptable bullying. Did Featherstonehaugh fit into this category?

Once Mr Bridgeford had left them, an uncomfortable silence embraced the room. David had no intention of lifting it by way of conversation. And Trevor would not have the nerve to say anything. As for Featherstonehaugh, he appeared to be seething. Did he feel himself under fire? That David believed he had erred with the code? Or was he now realizing that he had shown himself up in front of a visiting inspector – especially as this particular inspector would be reporting on him at the end of the normal branch inspection?

He certainly looked relieved when the cashier returned to the room. David held out his hand for the form 69, while Mr Bridgeford gave the code box to the manager. Featherstonehaugh immediately unlocked the box and withdrew the code cards.

Without checking the details from the form, he calculated the code from the cards, based on his apparent knowledge of the amount, the branch's sorting code number and the date. He then looked up at David, as if about to challenge him.

"7184."

But David had no qualms about the code number. He was sure it had been calculated correctly on the form in the first place. It was just a question of who had done it.

Yet, he now had an inkling as to the possible perpetrator. The first seeds of this had come to him yesterday in the Colonel's room and then again while lying in bed this morning, waiting for the alarm clock to ring out. For the moment, he would keep his thoughts to himself. He needed to carry out some further checking, especially at Head Office. After that, he would share his speculation with Trevor – should it still stack up. In the meantime, Featherstonehaugh was clearly seeking his response.

"Good," David replied and then turned his attention to the cashier.

"Now, Mr Bridgeford, when you leave this room, I want you to put pen to paper."

The lad frowned in puzzlement.

"I want you to write down everything you can remember about the man who cashed the cheque."

"But I …"

"Everything you've already told us and anything more you can think of. If this business ends up in court …"

The cashier now looked aghast.

"In court? You mean …"

David smiled to try and put the boy at ease.

"You could be the star witness. A time for you to make a name for yourself."

His attempt to provide some solace did not work. The lad looked even more alarmed.

"Don't worry," David said, " it might not come to that. But the matter of identification could be vital. I know several days have gone by since Friday. And it would certainly have been better for you to have done this then. But still write down everything you can remember. Such as the man's appearance. Something more than that he was short and a bit weedy. Did he have any distinguishing marks? The colour of his hair? And what did he actually say – and in what accent? Was he right or left-handed? And is it possible there was someone with him – in the background. In other words, write down everything you can think of."

The cashier nodded and David excused him from the room, indicating Trevor to go with him. David then turned to Featherstonehaugh, but before he could say anything, the telephone rang.

The manager stretched across his desk and picked up the handset, listened and then passed it across to David.

"It's for you."

David frowned. What had happened now? He put the phone to his ear.

"Goodhart here."

"Ah, good. I was told I'd get you at Tenterden."

David immediately recognized Peter Maxie's voice.

"Oh?"

"Yes, I wanted you to know straight away. And I need to see you when you get back to Tunbridge Wells."

David had that sinking feeling.

"Oh?"

"Yes. We've just received the result of the postmortem. It wasn't an accident. It seems that Mr Grimshawe was murdered."

CHAPTER 30

The news had shaken Trevor rigid. Murder? Everything else that had happened to members of the staff had been bad enough. But now? The first cashier murdered?

No wonder his own early-morning good news was now an unmitigated anticlimax. The envelope was still burning a hole in his jacket pocket. Not literally. But, for someone like himself, its content was as hot as it got. The coveted letter had landed on the doormat of his digs just after breakfast – about seven hours ago. On reading it, he had wanted to shout the news from the rooftops. Or at least tell Mr Goodhart.

It had been a moment worth years.

But that had been seven hours ago.

And the letter still remained in his pocket.

Yet how could he have extracted it – with everything else that had been going on? Mr Goodhart's single-mindedness over the events throughout the day had seen to that. And the revelation of Mr Grimshawe's murder had been the main topic of conversation during their return journey to Tunbridge Wells. There had been no opportunity at all to share what was, seven hours ago, such momentous news – that he had been invited to play at Ronnie Scott's.

Invited?

Is that really how it normally happened? More likely, would-be performers would have to beg on hands and knees to play there. But he had been invited! The letter actually asked if he could make himself available to play at the Club the weekend after next.

How could he refuse?

There was only one snag: the weekend gig also included Friday night – the early-evening warm-up set before the main performance. So, he would have to leave work early. Especially as a group rehearsal would be needed. How would Mr Goodhart react to that? With all that was going on around them? Investigating fraudulent cheque encashments was bad enough. Never mind an armed hold-up. But now they were embroiled in a murder enquiry.

Trevor clenched his teeth. It hardly seemed feasible for all this to be sorted out by the end of next week.

They had returned to Tunbridge Wells at about three-thirty, Mr Goodhart immediately making his way to the police station to meet Chief Inspector Maxie. Trevor's brief was to try and establish how the encashment of General Kettleman's cheques could have possibly been authorized.

After leaving Tenterden, they had visited the other four branches that had also cashed the General's cheques. These all confirmed what young Mr Bridgeford had said at Tenterden: the General's impersonator had been a short and weedy man. In each case, standard cashing requirements had apparently been followed, particularly in checking the accuracy of the codes and comparison of the signatures. But these were technical points. Not one branch had used much-needed initiative. Not one cashier had thought it appropriate to judge whether the man at the counter might be a general in the British Army. A short and weedy-looking general?

Now, back in Tunbridge Wells, Trevor needed to confront Mr Barnett with the forms 69, all of which he had retrieved from the five branches. How would the sub-manager explain the presence of his authorizing signature on each of these forms?

But as soon as Trevor entered the branch, Daphne made a point of catching his eye.

In other circumstances, he would have welcomed such attention, but, right now, he needed to see the sub-manager.

Daphne drew alongside him.

"Trevor."

She had never before used his first name.

"Later, Daphne."

"But Trevor …"

Her eyes pleaded for his attention. He did not surprise himself by wilting.

"All right, then."

She glanced over her shoulder, as if anxious not to be seen talking to him.

"I shouldn't be telling you this."

Trevor tried to remain expressionless. But his mind was racing. This had the makings of something conspiratorial. In which case, he wanted nothing to do with it.

"But you're about to?"

Daphne looked distraught. Trevor immediately felt contrite. She did not deserve such a sharp response. She had taken him into her confidence before. Was she trying to do the same again?

"I'm sorry," he quickly added. "It's just that … put it this way, we've had quite an afternoon."

"General Kettleman?"

Trevor nodded. He would restrict his comments to the General. It was not the time to divulge Mr Grimshawe's murder.

"His cheques were definitely cashed by someone else."

Although her composure started to return, Daphne now looked even more concerned.

"And it doesn't end there," she said, her voice actually breaking.

"You mean more of his cheques have turned up?"

Trevor's mind was now working overtime. The cheques cashed last Friday had turned up here in Tunbridge Wells in yesterday morning's clearing. The procedure always took two working days, the cheques received from other banks and branches having been remitted via those banks' head offices in London. That meant any cheques received in this morning's clearing would have been cashed elsewhere on Monday.

Yet, Mr Goodhart reckoned there was probably a link between the fraudulent encashments and the armed hold-up. But the hold-up took place first thing on Monday morning – before any encashments could have been made on that day. So, how could there be a connection?

Daphne's unease was not lessening. She shook her head and, once again, her pigtail swung from side to side, like an out-of-control pendulum.

"No," she answered, her eyes failing to disguise her disquiet. "A lot more cheques have come in. But not drawn on the General's account. They've all been cashed on other accounts."

Trevor frowned. On other accounts?

"How many cheques are you talking about?"

"At least a dozen."

"And all cashed on different accounts?"

Daphne nodded.

"And for £5,000 again?"

"No. This time they're for £10,000. Each one of them."

Trevor winced. This was big money. And Mr Goodhart needed to know about it at once. Yet there was something odd about this. Why was Daphne approaching him so covertly.

"Why did you say you shouldn't be telling me this?"

Daphne now looked towards the stairs and kept her voice low.

"I think the manager wanted to see Mr Goodhart first. But you've come back on your own. I thought you should know – in case you wanted to go up and see the manager yourself."

Trevor grimaced. It was not what he would have chosen. But Mr Goodhart could be some time.

"I might just have to do that. Mr Goodhart's gone to the police station. I don't know how long he'll be."

Daphne raised her eyebrows.

"Sorry, Daphne. It's Mum's the word. For the moment, anyway. But there's been a dreadful development. You'll know about it soon enough."

"What on earth's going on, Trevor? I mean everything. All that's been happening here?"

"I only wish I knew, Daphne. But I'd better go upstairs. I doubt if the manager will be best pleased. But Mr Goodhart might be ages."

The thought of a one-to-one with Colonel Fawkes-William

219

appalled Trevor. It had been bad enough last time – even with Mr Goodhart in the same room. But with the Colonel? On his own?

Yet, he had no choice.

Seeing Mr Barnett would clearly have to wait and he made his way up the stairs to the manager's room. As before, the Colonel's door was wide open. Trevor certainly liked that. It was far less intimidating if a manager operated an open-door policy.

Colonel Fawkes-William sat behind his imposing desk, his head down as he pored over a bundle of cheques – presumably the problematic ones.

Trevor tapped lightly on the door.

The Colonel looked up and immediately put the cheques inside a folder.

"Ah, you're back. I need to see Mr Goodhart straightaway."

Trevor stood in the doorway and wondered if, somewhere within this gambit, there was an implied invitation for him to step into the room. He made his decision and moved inside, closing the door behind him. He did not want the securities staff in the nearby section to overhear what was said.

The Colonel frowned, as if affronted that Trevor should have had the temerity to close the door, but he then motioned him to sit down.

"I'm afraid Mr Goodhart's not here, sir. He's at the police station."

"What? Why?"

Trevor tried to hold his nerve.

"Something terrible's happened."

"When? How? Where?"

Just like that. The five basic questions.

"He's gone there to get the full story. So far, we've only been given the bare facts …"

"Come on, lad. Get on with it."

Trevor gulped and tried to compose himself. Mr Goodhart, himself, had wanted to let the Colonel know about Mr Grimshawe

– once he had the full facts from the police. But Trevor now had no option but to tell the manager what he knew. He only hoped Mr Goodhart would understand.

"It's about Mr Grimshawe, sir. It seems his drowning wasn't an accident. The police now think he was murdered."

Trevor expected the Colonel to be stunned by the news. Instead, he simply sat there, looking straight ahead. It was as if the manager had always known this might be the outcome. Yet, how could that be so? On the other hand, he might simply have had a premonition that something like this could have happened.

"Are they certain?" the manager eventually asked.

"I don't know, sir. Mr Goodhart should be finding that out right now. And, because of that, I don't think the staff should be told yet. Not until Mr Goodhart gets back."

Trevor was relieved to get a nod of acceptance and Colonel Fawkes-William then rose from his chair and started pacing the room. Trevor was not sure whether he should also stand or remain seated. The Colonel quickly came to his rescue by sitting down again and opening the folder.

"Murdered," he muttered. "It makes this lot pale into insignificance."

Trevor raised his eyebrows, but remained silent.

"I was waiting for Mr Goodhart to come back," the Colonel continued, scrutinizing Trevor, as if considering whether or not to take him into his confidence. "Something else has come up. As your boss isn't here, I suppose I'd better put you in the picture."

Trevor was uncertain whether to feel pleased or annoyed. The manager's apparent reluctance to confide in him was offset by the fact that it seemed, nevertheless, that he intended to do so. At least, this meant Trevor would not now be privy to knowledge of these further encashments simply by way of what Daphne had told him.

The Colonel passed the cheques across the desk.

"What do you make of these?"

Even though Trevor was aware of what this was all about, he

was wide-eyed when he saw the actual cheques. Each one was for £10,000 and the lot had clearly been cashed at a range of other branches. Such a thing would normally be quite unheard of. A dozen or so cheques for £10,000, all cashed on the same day? For customers of the same branch? And following on from the encashments on General Kettleman's account, these further cheques were almost certainly bogus. He looked up at the Colonel.

"All in this morning's clearing?"

The Colonel nodded, but chose not to elaborate.

"So they were cashed two days ago? On Monday?"

The Colonel now shook his head.

"No. Look at the dates and the cashiers' stamps."

Trevor re-examined the cheques. The manager was right. They had all been cashed on Saturday. They had taken an extra day to arrive here because Saturday's work, being that for only half a day, was always amalgamated with the business transacted on the following Monday. The items for the combined days were then remitted that evening. Trevor now twigged what this meant. The cheques had actually been cashed before the hold-up on Monday morning. There could, then, still be a connection between the encashments and the hold-up.

Trevor glanced up at the Colonel.

"All cashed on Saturday."

"Yes. And on different accounts and at different branches."

Trevor looked back at the cheques. This was certainly a different tactic from that on Friday, when only General Kettleman's account was used. And, this time, the cheques had not been cashed at branches close to Tunbridge Wells. If this was still the work of the short and weedy man, he had chosen a range of branches in and around Surrey. And if it was down to just one man, he would have had to get his skates on to visit so many branches on a Saturday morning.

"What about the signatures, sir? Are they all forged?"

The Colonel nodded.

"They're nothing like the true ones. There's been no attempt to copy the customers' signatures."

Trevor frowned. That was certainly different from the cheques cashed on General Kettleman's account. Those had been excellent attempts at forgery. It was almost as if the perpetrator of Saturday's encashments had become blasé. Because the cheques would not be presented until the following Wednesday? When he had long fled the scene? But there was something else.

"There's one thing I don't understand, sir. If the signatures were clearly forged, why weren't the cheques returned this morning?"

Colonel Fawkes-William would be well aware that the signature on a cheque was the customer's authorization for it to be debited to the account. If the signature was clearly forged, that authorization was not valid. The cheque must then be returned to the bank which accepted it. That bank would then suffer any loss which arose from its negligence. So why were these twelve cheques not returned to the banks which cashed them?

The Colonel now looked rather sheepish.

"The cheques had clearly been cashed by our branches. No other bank was involved. Only National Counties. The money was now gone. What was the point in returning them? It wouldn't get the money back."

Trevor could hardly believe the reply. The bank, overall, might well have lost the money, but why should the Colonel and his Tunbridge Wells branch suffer the loss, if they had done nothing wrong? On the other hand …

"What about the forms 69, sir? These must have included specimen signatures. The other branches would have compared these with the ones on the cheques. And who actually signed the forms 69 – here in the branch? And who coded them?"

Colonel Fawkes-William appeared stunned. All that bonhomie of his at their first meeting had well and truly disappeared. Could it be that he was the one responsible? On the other hand, it had been Mr Barnett who had signed the forms 69 covering General Kettleman's withdrawals.

"I don't know," the manager replied and then looked indignant. "How could I know? The forms are at those other branches. Anyway, young man, I hope you're not thinking it was anything to do with me."

Trevor looked down at his lap and deliberately let the question hang in the air. He surreptitiously checked his wrist watch, sheltered from the manager by the desk. It was now about six hours since the cheques must have been brought to the manager's attention. Surely, during that time, someone, even if it was not the Colonel, must have made contact with the other branches? Someone must have tried to establish what had been going on.

"Could it have been Mr Barnett, sir? We've discovered he was the one who signed the forms 69 for General Kettleman's encashments."

"What? And did he code them?"

Trevor shrugged. It seemed a fair assumption.

"In which case," the Colonel exclaimed, leaping from his chair, "he must have done the same with all these other cheques. Come on, young man. Downstairs. Let's see what he's got to say for himself."

Trevor rose to follow him, a little disconcerted at such a dramatic response. Something did not seem quite right. But at least it meant the manager would be interrogating the sub-manager, rather than himself.

As he followed the Colonel to the stairs, his hand brushed the side of his jacket. The action momentarily switched his mind to another matter. That momentous letter was still there, burning a hole in his pocket.

CHAPTER 31

David came out of the police station and looked up at the sky. There was moisture in the air. And he was not wearing a top coat. At least the clouds were high. They did not seem that ominous, but he would step out smartly, just in case.

He certainly welcomed the fresh air on his face. Chief Inspector Maxie's interview room had been confined and stuffy. And the content of their meeting had made him hot under the collar. Yet there was one piece of good news: Barney Wilson was now fully conscious. He was still not able to talk, but his consultant was confident he soon would. Also that, in time, he should make a full recovery.

Which was more than could be said for poor Mr Grimshawe. How could he have been murdered? What possible motive could have been behind such an heinous act? The police had their thoughts on this and were in no doubt about how it had happened. The post-mortem revealed that Mr Grimshawe had suffered a sharp blow on the back of his head from a blunt object. It might not have killed him, but the police were certain he had then been pushed down the bank into the water to simulate death by drowning.

Thank heavens for the skills of the pathologist.

The murder hunt was now on, the first around Tunbridge Wells for some years. Police leave had been cancelled and the county was now swarming with officers – all searching for a grey Morris Oxford.

And that was extraordinary.

Back in Barnmouth, some five years ago, David's first car had been a grey Morris Oxford. Thank goodness he now owned a Ford Consul; otherwise he might be the target of zealous traffic policemen.

At least, he was as one with Chief Inspector Maxie. They both now believed there must be a connection between all these crimes involving the bank. The policeman had been particularly interested to hear about the man who had cashed General Kettleman's cheques. His description aptly fitted that of the driver of the Oxford which had been stopped by the police in Horsmonden. Those officers had also noted the car's number plate: RTA 841.

Another coincidence: a Devonian registration.

David had got to know such registration numbers well; on journeys with Mark, they had often indulged themselves in number-spotting. TA, TT, and DV were the most prevalent final two-letter prefixes in Devon and he was mightily relieved that this registration plate had not been that of his old car. Yet he was curious as to why an Oxford from Devon was now in this area. The only other Devonian car he had seen in Kent had been an Austin A30, registered TTT 959. Sarah had said "how sad was that?" – at his remembering such a number.

Chief Inspector Maxie had now become convinced that the armed gunman and the cheque fraudster were one and the same person. Which then led him to speculate on the killer of Mr Grimshawe. Was it possible he had been hit on the head by this same man's revolver?

But what possible connection could there be between Mr Grimshawe and the gunman?

Yet …?

Yet, this fitted in with the view that the gunman had an accomplice. Mr Grimshawe? Peter Maxie certainly thought so. Had there been, for whatever reason, a dramatic falling out?

One good thing had come out of the meeting: despite a clear link between the crimes, Chief Inspector Maxie had wanted to concentrate his resources on the murder enquiry, leaving David to investigate the banking misdemeanours. That suited him fine. He would much prefer the bank's branches to be free of police officers who might not be fully cognisant with banking operations. Far better, at this stage anyway, to leave such delving around to himself and Trevor.

David now hurried down towards the cinema and then turned into Mount Pleasant. He glanced at his watch and was amazed to see the time was almost six o'clock. In case he was this late, he had arranged to meet Trevor at the Kentish Yeoman, rather than in the branch. The staff would hardly welcome the arrival of an inspector at such a late hour – should they still be working. In any case, by this time, he knew he would be dying of thirst.

It was just as well he had made this arrangement. When he reached the branch, there appeared to be no sign of life inside. So, he carried on down to the bottom of the road and then made his way up to the pub.

But when he stepped inside the bar, there was no sign of Trevor. That was strange. He ordered himself a pint of Harvey's and chose a table in a corner where there was less chance of anyone eavesdropping on their conversation – once Trevor turned up.

The first pint hardly touched the sides and he ordered another. But where was Trevor? He glanced at his watch again; it was now nearing six-thirty. Then the door swung open and Trevor came in, breathing hard.

David rose from his chair and caught the landlord's eye to order another pint.

"Where've you been, Trevor? The branch looked empty when I passed by."

Trevor slumped in his seat, still out of breath, and loosened his tie. David could now see he was also perspiring.

"I'm sorry, sir," Trevor gasped. "I've run all the way here."

All the way? It was only about three hundred yards from the branch. David was even confident he could have managed that distance without generating too much sweat.

The landlord brought over the pint of Harvey's and Trevor took a long swig, then placed the tankard on the table and leant back in his chair.

"Even I needed that one," he said, his ill-concealed irony eased by a wry smile. "I've just run all the way from the hospital."

"The hospital? The Kent and Sussex?"

Trevor nodded.

No wonder he was perspiring. The hospital must be well over half a mile away. But why the hospital? David now had another feeling of foreboding.

"I think you'd better explain, Trevor."

The lad took another gulp from his tankard and now looked a little more composed. But the smile had gone and he looked uncommonly serious. The ambience of the pub was clearly not relaxing him – nor the quality of the ale.

"I've just had to take Colonel Fawkes-William to the hospital. I got a taxi there, but had to run back."

"I need that explanation, Trevor."

"Yes .. of course. Sorry, sir. He had a badly gashed lip. It needed several stitches."

"Trevor! You're dangling me in the air."

The lad smiled and now seemed ready to deliver the punch line: one that soon turned out to be literally correct.

"Mr Barnett hit him."

Of all the things David might have imagined had happened, this would never have even made it on to his list. A punch-up in the branch? That was unprecedented. And if he had ever come to predict such an occurrence, the least likely pugilist would have been Mr Barnett. David forced himself to react calmly.

"Go on, Trevor."

"First of all, sir, I need to backtrack a bit."

Trevor loosened his tie still further and, in the manner of an American crooner, undid the top button of his shirt. He then explained how Daphne had tipped him off about the further cheque encashments and what had transpired in his subsequent meeting with Colonel Fawkes-William. It had culminated in the manager dragging him downstairs to confront Mr Barnett about the coding of the forms 69.

"It was then really embarrassing, sir. Colonel Fawkes-William was so aggressive – not physically, but verbally. He didn't give Mr Barnett a chance to say anything. He virtually accused him of setting the whole thing up – the fraudulent withdrawals, I mean. And it was all in front of the other staff. Anyway, at that stage, Mr Barnett took it without batting an eyelid. He didn't say a word. It made me think there might be something in it. But then …"

His words tailed off, as if he were reluctant to carry on.

"Go on, Trevor."

"Then something snapped in Mr Barnett. He had been getting redder and redder, but he then turned away, as if he couldn't take any more. Then he swung around and thumped the manager in the face. It was Freddie Mills-like, sir. And the ring on his finger must have gashed the manager's lip. There was blood everywhere."

David could hardly believe what he was hearing. This really was unprecedented. There was simply no excuse for doing such a thing. Yet, he was ashamed to feel some admiration for the sub-manager. Many a time, he, himself, had felt like administering such retribution when he had been on the receiving end of Angus McPhoebe's diatribes. Fortunately, he had resisted such temptation. Otherwise, he would have faced a banking-type court martial which Mr Barnett would now surely undergo. And it could prove worse for the sub-manager – should the Colonel invoke the involvement of the police.

"What happened then?"

Trevor's intensity now actually lightened and he even smiled.

"It was extraordinary, sir. Peace descended on the place. All the other staff were agog. They seemed too stunned to do anything. Then Daphne stepped forward to give the manager a hand and I managed to get an arm around Mr Barnett to drag him away. But the manager waved everyone back. And you'd never guess what, sir."

Oh, Trevor. David hated being kept on a string like this. It was like being involved in some parlour game. His annoyance must have shown through, because Trevor quickly continued.

"Sorry, sir. But Colonel Fawkes-William actually apologized. He had almost been knocked out by his sub-manager and it was he who was apologizing. And he didn't just apologize. He actually put his arm around Mr Barnett and said he'd deserved all he got. And what's more, he said he wouldn't take matters any further."

Extraordinary! Colonel Fawkes-William apologizing? And eating humble pie? It was simply not in his make-up. But even if he had chosen to make light of what had happened, could David ignore it? Insubordination within a branch must always be of inspectorial concern, but especially by way of a sub-manager thumping his manager in front of all the staff.

"It seems to show the Colonel in a different light," Trevor added, intruding into David's thoughts. "Who would have thought he'd have played down such an incident?"

David frowned. It certainly sounded as though the manager might have a soft centre under his brusque and arrogant exterior. Or was there another reason to play down what had occurred?

"What happened next?"

"I ordered a taxi to take Colonel Fawkes-William to hospital. We were able to stem the blood with tissues. But it was a deep cut and clearly needed stitches."

"And Mr Barnett?"

"He was shell-shocked. It was just as well it was the end of the day. He couldn't put his hand to anything. The manager told him to go home and forget what had happened. Not that such a thing would ever go out of his mind. But can you believe the manager saying that?"

David shook his head. No, it was all unbelievable. But had this incident made them lose sight of what had caused the rumpus.

"But what about all those cashed cheques? And the forms 69? And who'd actually coded them?"

"Colonel Fawkes-William said that would have to wait until the morning."

David now glowered at Trevor.

"But we're talking about big money here. £120,000. For God's sake, it's not like a £5 till difference. And you went along with him?"

Trevor visibly bristled at the unsubtle admonition.

"But what could I do, sir? Force the manager to stay in the branch? Let him bleed to death?"

And with that, he drained his glass and stormed towards the bar. Without stopping, he then glanced over his shoulder.

"I suppose you'll want another one … sir?"

David slumped back in his chair. Another case of insubordination? But had he been too hard on the lad? In Trevor's place, what would he have done? Yet that was not a fair question. Being the inspector in charge of the investigation, he had far more clout than a humble inspector's assistant. It would have been asking a lot for Trevor to have opposed the manager's decision.

Trevor was clearly still smarting when he returned to the table and he set the tankards down sharply enough for the beer to slop over the rims. David chose not to inflame the situation further and refrained from expressing his displeasure. He would have to put up with Sarah's subsequent carping about beer stains on his tie. Here in the pub, it was far more important to get things back on an even keel.

"Thanks, Trevor. I think we both need these. Life'll certainly seem dull when we get back to that routine inspection in Tenterden."

Trevor looked at him quizzically and then smiled. Back to his normal self?

"Aren't you forgetting Mr Featherstonehaugh?"

"Even with him there. He'd hardly be able to conjure up what we've encountered here. Can you believe what's happened in just over two days?"

Trevor lifted his tankard, but then stopped before it reached his lips.

"I'm sorry, sir. I've been so engrossed with what's just gone on at the branch. But what happened with you at the police station?"

The change of subject would be good for them both. They could return to those further cheque encashments later.

"It seems Mr Grimshawe was hit on the back of the head with a metal object. I reckon it was the butt of a revolver."

Trevor raised his hand to his mouth.

"But he'd drowned, hadn't he?"

"Probably. After he'd been hit, it must have been easy to push him down the bank into the water."

"And his killer was the Lamberhurst gunman?"

David nodded.

"I reckon so. And so do the police. What's more, we believe it's the same man who cashed General Kettleman's cheques."

Trevor grimaced.

"Not someone you'd want to come up against. But what about his accomplice? You're still sure he has one?"

"Must have. Chief Inspector Maxie thinks it was Mr Grimshawe. And he was killed after some kind of falling out. That sounds logical enough."

Trevor looked puzzled.

"But what about the forms 69? I don't know about the latest ones, but those for General Kettleman were signed by Mr Barnett. And it seems likely he coded them, as well."

David did not necessarily agree. But one way or the other, they needed to find the answer to that in the morning.

"That's for you to sleep on Trevor – and then establish the facts tomorrow. I've got another matter to get on with. Something's been nibbling away at the back of my mind. And it won't go away. I hope to get an answer in the morning."

He now looked at his watch. It was well past seven and he had not warned Sarah he would be late. Another pint and he would be really in the doghouse. Three pints were enough, anyway; he had a very early start planned for tomorrow.

"Come on Trevor. Home James."

David drained his glass and rose to leave, but Trevor raised his hand.

"Before we go, sir, I've just had a thought."

David stopped, but remained standing.

"Go on, then."

"It's about Mr Barnett. He was genuinely affronted when the Colonel challenged him so aggressively. I'm sure it wasn't an act. But why would the manager treat him like that? Do you think it's possible he was trying to deflect suspicion from himself?"

"That's certainly possible."

"Yet I can't believe the manager could be involved. He's so well-to-do. But if we eliminate him and Mr Barnett, that only leaves Mr Grimshawe. And he's been murdered. So how will the police be able to prove it was him?"

"Catching the gunman would help. But as I just said, sleep on it, Trevor. Think about all possible angles – however unlikely. And then we'll put our heads together. But it won't be until late in the morning. You'll be on your own first thing. And I want you to speak to all those other branches who cashed the cheques. Talk to the managers, particularly about the codes and the specimen signatures on the forms 69. And get descriptions. Try and speak to the cashiers. If you get the answers I expect, we probably won't have to pay them any visits."

Trevor now looked bewildered.

"But where will you be, sir?"

"I'm off to London. By train. As early as possible. I'm going to Head Office. That thing that's been bothering me. I need to look through staff records. But it shouldn't take long. So I'll be back before lunch. Now, Trevor, I must be off."

Trevor walked with him to the door and then put his hand in his jacket pocket.

"Just before we go, sir, there's something I'd like to show you."

"About what we've been talking about?"

"No, sir, but ..."

"In the morning, then, Trevor. I really must be on my way."

Trevor shrugged, but could not disguise his disappointment. As they made their way to the pavement, David could not help feeling he had offended the lad again.

Chapter 32

Alfie Templeton approached the top of the lane with extreme caution. He had just spent forty-eight hours cooped up in the barn and the heat should now be off. But better to be safe than sorry.

There was one problem: which way to go?

He thought he had acquired a good knowledge of the area, but he now felt disorientated. He grimaced. What should he do? Left or right?

Then he remembered. On Monday, he had turned left into the lane, so returning that way was a non-starter. Back towards Lamberhurst? That could be the equivalent of writing a suicide note. So, it had to be the other way. But where would that go to?

He would have to rely on his sense of direction – especially as he would get no help from the sun. Leaden skies saw to that. But that should not be a problem. He was normally like a homing pigeon when he came to making it back to SE25. Particularly when Palace were playing at home.

He reached the junction and made sure he kept the engine revs high. Stalling now would be a nightmare. The short drive up from the barn had been no distance to re-charge the battery and the last thing he needed was for the engine to die on him.

Looking left and right, he was relieved to find the main road clear of other traffic. He glanced at his wrist watch; it was now approaching eleven-thirty. Traffic was unlikely to be heavy at this hour, but that could prove to be a snag. He would not have the advantage of mingling with other vehicles. Instead, he might stand out like an away supporter at Selhurst Park.

But should that be a worry? As far as he was aware, no one had witnessed his Oxford at Lamberhurst. Nobody should be looking out for his type of car.

Then his heart almost missed a beat: that policeman in Horsmonden. Not only had that bobby checked out the car, but he had also seen and talked to yours truly. And his colleague had been on his walkie-talkie. About the raid? Almost certainly. In which case, the whole force in Kent would most definitely now be looking out for a grey Morris Oxford.

But the encounter with those policemen had been over forty-eight hours ago. Forty-eight hours? His gut-wrenching hunger and general dishevelment screamed out that it was far longer than that. Anyway, the police would assume he was miles away by now. There might still be road checks around the ports, but in this area? Surely not.

Yet, there was another possible pitfall: Fairweather.

Where was he? What was he doing?

It must be five or six hours since he vamoosed from the barn. Would he have raised the alarm by now? Or would he have holed up again? Self-preservation might have dictated this latter option. He had been scared witless at how that stupid guard had been gunned down. Goodness knows how his mind might now be working. He had become a nervous wreck. More than likely, Fairweather had been expecting to hear the click of a trigger every step of his way from the barn. But he was not to know that his captor's only priority was to escape with all the cash.

Templeton gritted his ill-preserved teeth and winced as a nerve-end protested painfully. He may be wrong, but was there anything immediately to fear from Fairweather? In time, maybe, but by then, Templeton would be safe and secure – with all that cash safely removed from the boot of the car.

With this in mind, he turned left into the main road and hoped he would soon reach a signposted junction which would guide him in the right direction.

The road was still devoid of other vehicles and, for one moment, he feared it had been closed off in the search for his car. Then an Austin Cambridge came towards him, followed by a Morris Minor Traveller. He glanced in his rear-view mirror, something he would need to do frequently. A motorcyclist appeared and soon overtook him at great speed, even though the rider's machine was only a BSA Bantam. Then the road was quiet again and he breathed more easily.

And alone in the car he felt more in control. It was as it always had been – working alone. Had it been a mistake taking on a partner this time? Of course not. He would not, otherwise, have a boot crammed full with cash. If he had not been concentrating so hard on his driving, he would have rubbed his hands together in glee. All that loot was now his. He no longer needed to share it out fifty-fifty. This really would be his very last job. Retirement beckoned. All he had to do was make it home safely.

But at what cost? He would now be looking over his shoulder for the rest of his life. And all because of his blasted gun. Why had he used it down at that damned lake? Could he not have handled that situation better? No wonder it had contributed to his panic at Lamberhurst. He had never been a man of violence, yet he had thumped one man with the butt of his revolver and had killed another by actually firing the weapon. Yet, the gun had only been there as a form of insurance. Could he not have resolved both matters without using it? Of course, he could. But on each occasion, he had simply panicked – fair and square. If only he could wind the clock back and start all over again.

Just thinking back to what had happened made him shiver and he almost lost control of the car as he took a sharp bend too quickly. He must keep a grip on himself. Although speed was of the essence, he could not afford to take undue risks.

He took another look in the mirror, half-expecting to see a black Wolseley in his wake. But there was still nothing there. Switching back to the road ahead, he then felt like cheering. At last, alongside the approaching junction, a three-way signpost stood resplendent on his side of the road.

He glanced again in the mirror. Still nothing there and he slowed to a virtual stop. To the left, which must be to the north, the sign pointed to Marden, with Goudhurst signposted the other way. He certainly did not want to go south, so he turned towards Marden and hoped the next junction would take him west and on to London.

Within a few minutes, he reached the outskirts of Marden. Civilization, at last. But it was far too busy; eyes on every pavement and corner. Moving towards them was a risk too far. He desperately needed to see a junction which would take him left on to some minor road towards London. And, sure enough, as he crawled forward, there it was, a few hundred yards ahead of him.

He then let out a gasp and slammed on the brakes.

Cars had clearly been halted at the junction and two bobbies appeared to be quizzing the drivers. A roadblock? Now? A full two days after Lamberhurst?

What the hell was going on?

Whatever else, it was patently clear he could not continue along this particular road and, as luck would have it, he had stopped just before a turning into what looked like a housing estate. He immediately made the turn, thankful he was far enough away from the junction for the police not to have noticed his car.

But what was he to do now?

He slowly moved through the estate which was built in a crescent, turning right towards the centre of the village. To where those policemen were at the junction? But the road then straightened out and appeared to be heading for another road which his sense of direction told him was the one turning left at the junction. In which case, this crescent had effectively bypassed the hub of the village and had taken him to the route he had been seeking.

Was this to be his lucky day?

Possibly. At Marden, anyway. But if the police had set up a roadblock here, it would hardly be a one-off. There must be others all over the county. In which case, how was he going to get back to London? One thing for certain, it would be madness to try and do this in broad daylight.

He would have to lie low somewhere. But where?

He now approached a signpost telling him he was heading

towards somewhere called Collier Street. Goodness knows where that might be. It was clearly farming country around here, but the thought of holing up in another barn appalled him – even if he were able to find one. What about a large car park? The Oxford could prove to be anonymous among a horde of other cars. But there would only be a suitable car park in a large town and where would that be? And to get there, he would probably encounter another road block.

He felt well and truly trapped. What was he to do?

But what was this? An answer to his prayers?

A roadside sign told him he was approaching a golf club. And what did golf clubs have? A large car park. And at this time of the day, it could be packed with other cars – particularly if Wednesdays were set aside primarily for ladies or so-called veterans.

In his excitement, he almost missed the turn into what was a narrow lane which would take him well away from the main road. This was getting better and better. And, suddenly, a large car park stretched out in front of him, packed with other cars. But would there be a space for his Oxford?

He drove slowly between two rows of cars, getting more and more concerned. Then, just before the end of the row on his left, there was a vacant space. He decided to drive straight into it, rather than reverse in. He now faced on to an open field, away from the actual golf course and clubhouse. If he then lay slumped in his seat, it would be unlikely that anyone would notice him – apart from the golfers returning to the cars parked on either side of him. Even then it should not be beyond his wits to bluff his way out of any possible predicament.

For the first time this morning, he could relax and take stock. If he waited until dark he must, surely, have a better chance of making it back to London. Would the rozzers really continue to man roadblocks into the night?

As he slumped back into his seat, he again realized how hungry he was. Yet there would be food in the clubhouse. So near, but so far.

But he knew he could not take such a chance. And as each hour in this car park passed by, his hunger did not abate.

Then, what he hoped to have been his master plan hit the buffers.

He had overlooked one simple fact: golfers eventually finished their rounds and went home. And, unlike town centre car parks, the spaces left by departing cars were not filled by others.

Slowly but surely, the car park started to empty. It would not be long before his car would be the only one there. The remaining cars would be those parked nearer to the clubhouse and owned by employees. These people would be bound to question one solitary car remaining in the car park – especially if the police had gone public with its description.

He would clearly have to change his plan and make a break for it. Perhaps any roadblocks might, in any case, have been dismantled by now. It was nearing five o'clock and the police might think it was more trouble than it was worth to operate roadblocks when people were jamming the roads to get home.

Yes, it was certainly a chance worth taking.

Templeton started the car and was soon back on the road. Almost immediately, he reached Collier Street. It appeared to be little more than a hamlet, but he soon saw what he was looking for: another signposted junction. This new road clearly headed north and south, with north being his only possible option.

After making the turn, he checked his rear-view mirror and then nearly steered the car into the nearside ditch. He felt his worst fears had been realized. A black Wolseley saloon car was parked in a lay-by some five hundred yards behind him. He had not seen the car at the junction itself. A bend in the road had obscured it from view. It was almost as if the driver had parked there deliberately. But the car was now very much in his line of sight. Which meant its occupants also shared this unobstructed view.

As if on cue, the car eased forward.

And even though it was so far behind him, the shrill sound of a reverberating bell reached him loud and clear.

Panic may have grabbed him when that stubborn guard had resisted his demands, but it was nothing compared to his present state of mind. He could feel the blood draining from his unshaven face and his whole body started to shake. He seemed to have no control over his limbs. And although his hands were clasped to the steering wheel, they felt as ineffective as two fillets of wet fish.

He could hardly drag his eyes away from the mirror, but then adrenaline kicked in. He forced his limbs into action and thrust his right foot down hard on the accelerator pedal. But, once again, he rued his purchase of such a heavy, unwieldy car. It did its best to surge forward, but Templeton knew it was to no avail. The Morris Oxford could never be a match for a high-powered Wolseley.

But, by heavens, he would give it a try.

He had to.

Although this winding road was not conducive to a high-speed chase, he soon found the Oxford did not stand a chance of keeping pace ahead of the more manoeuvrable police car. There might not be any opportunity for that car to overtake, but there was no need. All it had to do was to sit on the Oxford's tail and wait, no doubt, for a radioed reinforcement car to arrive and head it off.

Unless, before then, Templeton crashed his car.

And with the Oxford now reaching sixty, Templeton knew this was a more than probable outcome. He had never before driven at such speed on such an unsuitable road.

Then it happened.

Another black Wolseley came round the next corner towards him. The Oxford was already straddling the middle white line and he had to heave the steering wheel to the left, braking hard at the same time. But the front wheels failed to respond. They lacked all traction and the car continued in a straight line towards the oncoming bend in the road. Although the ditch had disappeared, the adjacent hedge looked to be as solid as a brick wall. As the police car passed by on the other side, the front of the Oxford hit the hedge full on, the car then flipping backwards on to its roof. Templeton first hit his head on the windscreen and the roof then caved in, flattening him across the steering wheel. As the car came to rest, he realized the impact of the crash had wrecked the car from front to back, the boot lid having been clearly wrenched from its hinges.

Unconsciousness then took hold of him, just after he had witnessed bank notes of every denomination flying through the air like confetti at a wedding.

CHAPTER 33

The station platform was packed. Could you believe it? It was only a quarter past seven. David looked around him. Many were city gents. Most bore the same uniform: dark overcoat, rolled umbrella and black briefcase. How regimented was that? There was even an occasional bowler.

David shook his head. The every day life of a commuter.

How could they do it? Day after day? Thank goodness he was an inspector, able to reach his place of work by car. He could even manage it on foot when it came to getting to Tunbridge Wells branch. Yet, he might not always be so fortunate. If he did his present job too well, promotion might result in a job in London. But he had a subtle plan to prevent that happening: keep upsetting Angus McPhoebe. Otherwise, he could end up joining this rolled-umbrella-brigade. Heaven forbid.

He had only commuted to London a couple of times and had not yet mastered the required tactics. Positioning himself properly on the platform was the main objective. The trains comprised twelve coaches, with doors at the end of each carriage. The driver always stopped at the same position: just short of the signal at the end of the platform. In anticipation of this, groups of passengers would huddle together where the carriage doors would end up. On his first rush hour journey, David had discovered this wide open space on the platform where no one else was waiting. But his perspicacity was soon dented; he became the last person to board the train.

Today, he joined one of the groups. But he was not confident of the outcome. He had still to learn the art of elbow-manipulation. His problem was that he still liked to think of himself as a gentleman.

A buzz of anticipation arose at the rumble of the approaching diesel unit. Most of the Southern Region was electrified, but not the line from Tunbridge Wells to Hastings. The tunnels were too constrictive to take the normal rolling stock. Instead, straight-sided, narrower carriages were needed, the end ones incorporating diesel power units. It meant noisier, smellier trains for the dignitaries from Royal Tunbridge Wells.

As it happened, David did get a seat this Thursday morning. Many others were less fortunate. Most stood dutifully in the corridor, but David was surprised to see several businessmen withdraw small folding fishermen's seats from their briefcases. He could understand Mr Grimshawe using such a seat while he dangled his rod and line, but here in the railway carriage, it seemed a rather forlorn attempt to make the hour's commute a little more bearable.

His destination was Cannon Street station, about a five-minute walk from the bank's Head Office in Lombard Street. He had already forewarned the staff department there of his visit and he hoped he would get immediate access to the records he needed to examine.

He could not obtain the information he required from the day-to-day staff records which were maintained in Tunbridge Wells branch. The more confidential files, particularly for management and senior staff were either kept at the regional staff office in Haywards Heath – or in Head Office, itself. The one David needed to see was held at Head Office. At least that meant not having to go to Haywards Heath. His next meeting with Angus McPhoebe would come soon enough, without it happening today.

The train drew into the terminus at eight-fifteen. David allowed everyone in the carriage to get out first and then made his way across the station concourse into Cannon Street. He crossed the road into St Swithin's Lane which led directly to Lombard Street. As on previous forays to London, he was struck by the sheer number of pedestrians making for the heart of the City. He could hardly believe that a staggering half a million people were employed in the City's so-called 'Square Mile', the country's headquarters for banking and insurance. The jostling and bustling on the narrow pavements certainly brought this home to David. He was relieved not to be a regular statistic within that half-million.

As he fought his way up St Swithin's Lane, he pondered on his reason for being up here and the contrast between working in London and in Tunbridge Wells. And he would not be the only person to think in this way. Colonel Fawkes-William would hate to be such a small cog in such a large business machine. For him, it would be far better to be a big fish in the much smaller Royal Tunbridge Wells pond. Yet, perhaps, that was his basic problem.

David reached the lower end of Lombard Street and made his way past the imposing head office of Lloyds Bank. National Counties occupied a smaller building nearer to Gracechurch Street, but, once inside, David knew he would be surrounded by the pomp of a typical bank headquarters.

The staff department was housed on the third floor and a uniformed messenger guided him to a wrought-iron-gated lift which David judged to be rather incongruous amid its more salubrious surroundings. But it operated efficiently enough and another flunkey greeted him when he stepped out at the third floor.

He was shown to the reception area where he produced his identity card. They were expecting him, which was good news, and a departmental manager took him along to the records' office. The man unlocked the door to reveal a room as large as the back office of the branch in Tunbridge Wells.

Four-drawer metal filing cabinets stood against three of the four walls, tangible evidence of the thousands employed by the bank. David was thankful he only needed to scrutinize one particular file and he cast his eye along the cabinets, each one bearing a single letter of the alphabet, many letters being duplicated over several cabinets.

The departmental manager had left him to his own devices and David was pleased to see tables and chairs set out alongside the wall not adorned by filing cabinets. He had no idea how much information there would be in the particular file he was seeking, but it would be good to sit down while he digested the relevant contents and took notes.

By chance, the first particular file he noticed in his cabinet was for Mr Featherstonehaugh, the Tenterden manager. He had no intention of looking at it. When he eventually returned to that branch to continue his routine inspection, he wanted to assess the manager without any prior prejudice.

But he had to smile.

This file stood out simply because, under the man's name, it was emblazoned in red ink with the words 'Pronounced Fanshawe'. David wondered how many people might have been tripped up on this particular point.

He then thumbed back to the file he needed, withdrew it from the cabinet and sat down at a table.

The file was not as thick as he might have supposed and he quickly scanned through its content. He was a little surprised that there appeared to be no mention of any war service. Although most information within any of the files in this room would be restricted to banking background and assessment reports, other details could give a well-rounded view of a person. Leadership qualities linked to war service could well be influential in a banking career.

But this was incidental to what he was looking for and he now examined each particular document in the file in the hope, and expectation, of being proved right about the suspicions which had been ever-growing in his mind.

Most of the information in the file related to reports and assessments made by Regional Office and visiting officials – including one of his own when he had made that first routine inspection of Tunbridge Wells branch. It seemed strange to see his own name in the file and he briefly scanned his report. He grimaced. It had all the hallmarks of a novice inspector doing his best to appear to be an old hand. These days, he would do much better, now that he had three years' experience behind him.

But these reports were of little interest to him and he went back to the beginning of the file. And, suddenly, it was there, under his very nose. He had missed it the first time he had looked. After all, it was only an apostrophe; that little punctuation mark which could cause so much literary consternation. Especially for Trevor, although, judging from their trip to Tenterden yesterday, the lad did seem to be making progress. But, in this particular case, the apostrophe should not have been there. Not on what was supposed to be official headed notepaper.

It made him examine the rest of the document more carefully. The actual content seemed fair enough, but the address certainly bothered him. And looking even more closely, the quality of the printing appeared to be decidedly questionable.

But this was not something he could simply jot down in the form of a note. Nothing short of a facsimile would suffice.

He took hold of the document and went to the door. The departmental manager had taken away the door's key and, not wanting to leave the room unattended, David attracted the attention of a girl working in an adjoining room.

The girl was happy to take the item to be copied and David also asked her to get the manager to return to the room to lock up.

While he waited, he dwelt upon the repercussions which would arise from what he had found. It really did highlight the dangers of complacency. And in an industry where accuracy was a byword for all that took place, this small matter of an apostrophe should have been picked up by someone. If that had happened, the whole document would have been opened up for scrutiny. What had been overlooked would then have screamed out from the page as being totally out of order.

David shook his head.

The simple overlooking of an apostrophe had resulted in the death of the first cashier, the near death of the guard – if that was not being too optimistic in his case – and the theft of some £200,000 of cash. And was there more to come?

The arrival of the departmental manager with the documents

broke into his thoughts and he took the copy and placed it in his briefcase. He then replaced the original into the file and put this back into the filing cabinet.

The manager then looked at him curiously.

"A call's just come through for you, sir. Our girl didn't realize you were here, but the caller left a number and I've asked her to get him back. You can take it in reception."

David frowned. A call? Here?

Leaving the manager to lock up the filing room, David hurried to reception and heard the phone immediately ring. The receptionist answered the call and then handed over the handset.

"It's me, sir. Trevor."

"Trevor?"

"Yes, sir. Sorry to interrupt, but when can you come back? Will you be finished soon?"

Trevor had made no pretence at disguising the urgency of his call. That was ominous.

"What's going on, Trevor?"

"I've had a call from Chief Inspector Maxie."

"Oh?"

"Yes, sir. He didn't really want to tell me anything. But I got an inkling, sir. I think they might have caught the gunman."

"Really?"

At last. Some positive news. But still more was needed.

"What about Douglas Fairweather? And the money?"

"I don't know, sir. He wouldn't say. But he wants to see you – as soon as possible."

David looked at his watch. It was just after half past nine. Cannon Street station only operated fully during the rush hours and would now be closed for trains to Tunbridge Wells. He would have to get to Charing Cross. That would take twenty minutes or so. His trains from there ran half-hourly, so he should be able to return by half-eleven.

"With luck, I'll be back well before lunch. But I'll also want you

247

to be with me. So, I'll pick you up at the branch. Get back to Chief Inspector Maxie and say we should be with him by noon."

David put the phone down and gathered his things together. If the gunman had been caught, they should soon have the answer to everything. Especially with the help of the evidence in his briefcase.

CHAPTER 34

David got back to the branch by eleven-thirty and located Trevor in the general office. The lad had an air of expectation about him.

"Did you really mean it on the phone, sir? To go with you to the police station?"

David grinned.

"Of course, Trevor. Why shouldn't you share the limelight?"

"I wasn't thinking of that, sir, but ..."

"Call it teamwork, Trevor. But why not? You've been involved from the start. And I might well need your help. But what's happened in the branch this morning? Get your coat on and you can tell me on the way up the road."

They soon stepped out on to the pavement and they certainly needed their coats; a light drizzle was falling. Trevor did not need any pressing about his morning; he was clearly eager to get something off his chest.

"It's been quite a morning, sir. With Colonel Fawkes-William, I mean."

"He turned up, then? The cut wasn't too bad?"

Trevor smiled.

"He didn't look his usual immaculate self. The plaster's quite large. And they must have had a problem getting it to stick on."

"What about Mr Barnett? How's he feeling today?"

"That's a strange one, sir. He seems to have taken on a new lease of life. And I reckon that's down to the manager."

David raised his eyebrows. Mr Barnett being re-invigorated by the Colonel? In the manager's place, it would have been the last thing he, himself, would have done. After being thumped by his sub-manager?

"Tell me more."

"Well, sir, Colonel Fawkes-William's been down in the general office all morning – helping out. First thing – after everyone got in – he called a staff meeting. I did my best to listen in. But I couldn't make it too obvious. Anyway, he said last night had been an eye-opener for him."

"A lip-opener, more likely."

"Be serious, sir. He said he knew how everyone had been under such pressure. And he was going to roll up his sleeves and help out. Those were his very words. And he said he wanted to re-open the Lamberhurst sub-branch tomorrow."

David pursed his lips. Why this apparent character change by the Colonel? What was he up to? And how had he really reacted to the revelation of Mr Grimshawe's murder? On reflection, David felt he should have seen him about this before his trip to London. Instead, he must do it straight after this meeting at the police station.

But re-opening at Lamberhurst? Tomorrow?

"Who's going to man the sub-branch? Is he getting relief staff in?"

Trevor now grinned and seemed to be relishing the telling of the story.

"No, sir. He's going himself. And one of the lads in securities will be acting as guard."

David stopped in his tracks, leaving Trevor to move on ahead until he realized he was on his own. The lad then backtracked and raised his eyebrows.

"Sir?"

"You think I should carry on walking, Trevor? As if nothing has happened? After you've just told me Colonel Fawkes-William, of all people, is leaving his ivory tower to play the part of a sub-branch cashier?"

"But isn't it great, sir? For him to do that?"

More like extraordinary. It certainly appeared to show the man in a different light. But the Colonel would soon have other things on his mind.

"Come on, Trevor," David said, getting back into his stride.

"Let's get today out of the way first. Tomorrow's another day."

Trevor then frowned.

"You've not yet told me how you got on this morning, sir."

"Later, Trevor. It'll all come out in our meeting."

There was certainly no time to brief Trevor now; they were already crossing the road to enter the police station. And there was no need at this stage. Revealing this morning's discovery would best take its course, depending how the meeting progressed.

After they entered the police station, the duty sergeant asked them to wait in the lobby while he phoned Chief Inspector Maxie. He then led them down a narrow corridor to an office which was far more welcoming than the room which had been adorned by those grim prints of prisons. The sergeant then pointed to a couple of chairs on one side of a dark oak table.

"Please take a seat, gentlemen. The Chief Inspector will be with you in a moment."

The moment turned into four or five minutes. The delay had tempted David to put forward his theories to Trevor. But he could easily have been interrupted in midstream. So he stayed silent. As it happened, he would have had time to reveal everything.

The door eventually opened and a grim-looking Chief Inspector Maxie entered the room. That was odd – unless it was tied up with his shingles. He was certainly still wearing his open-neck shirt. But if Trevor's inkling about the gunman had been correct, the Chief Inspector should be beaming. No doubt, all would soon be revealed and David introduced Trevor. After shaking his hand, the policeman took his seat on the opposite side of the desk and then looked at them directly.

"We've got the gunman."

Even though the news was not totally unexpected, David felt a surge of adrenalin. But why the seriousness? This must be a major breakthrough.

"There's just one problem," the Chief Inspector continued. "He's dead."

Trevor actually gasped. David was also shocked. But was he one step ahead of Trevor? If the gunman was dead, and they knew he was armed, had there been a shoot-out? If so, what about Douglas Fairweather?

The Chief Inspector cleared his throat before carrying on.

"Two days had gone by and there'd been no sighting of the man's car. That was really odd. We came to the conclusion he must have holed up somewhere. But that couldn't go on for ever. He'd have to make a break for it sometime. So, we decided to keep all our roadblocks in place. It was a good move. The car was spotted yesterday afternoon – about five o'clock. It was just outside the village of Collier Street. The car was heading north towards Maidstone."

"So, where'd he been?"

"Goodness knows. But our chaps gave chase and he crashed. Going far too fast along the country roads. Anyway, the car flipped over and was completely wrecked. The man didn't stand a chance. He died on the spot."

As David listened, he became more and more concerned. Peter Maxie was only talking about the gunman.

"But what about Douglas Fairweather? What happened to him?"

"We don't know. He wasn't in the car. We're now fearing the worst."

David looked askance.

"You don't mean …"

The Chief Inspector now leaned forward intently.

"Just think about it. The gunman had become trigger-happy – using the butt as far as Mr Grimshawe was concerned. What had he to lose? He'd believed he'd killed two men already. He wasn't to know Barney Wilson's survived. So, why not a third? It would be far easier to make off with all the cash -without Mr Fairweather in tow."

In normal circumstances, David knew the Chief Inspector's reasoning would certainly be sound. Except that nothing had been normal this week, especially after this morning's discovery. David's mind was now in a whirl and his delay in replying encouraged Trevor to step in.

"And had the gunman made off with all the cash?"

The Chief Inspector switched his attention to Trevor.

"You can say that again. But we expected it to be about £75,000 – the Lamberhurst haul and the General's encashments. Yet, there was so much more. When the car flipped over, the boot burst open. Notes flew all over the place. Our chaps seemed to spend hours trying to retrieve it all. They reckon some notes must still be in the adjacent fields. So far, they've recovered nearly £200,000."

Oh dear. David realized he had put up a black. He had omitted to tell Peter Maxie about the other unauthorized cheque encashments. But he had only learnt about them himself last night. He now described exactly what had happened. The policeman was clearly put out and glared at David. Had their previous good rapport come to an end?

"And is there anything else I don't know about?"

David shook his head. It was not the time to reveal what he had discovered this morning.

"Well," the Chief Inspector then added, "at least this revelation must mean the same man carried out all the crimes."

"What about his identity?" David asked, glad to have the chance to deflect matters away from himself.

Chief Inspector Maxie now relaxed slightly, as if pleased to be back on his own patch, one that he was in control of, without the vagaries of outside influences – such as uncommunicative bank inspectors.

"We checked his wallet and the car's registration. His name's Alfie Templeton. He's got a record. Common or garden thieving. He's what you might call a small-time crook. Nothing like this, though. Can't understand how he'd get into big-time stuff – especially with a gun."

"The influence of his partner? You agree he must have had help – from within the bank?"

The policeman nodded.

"That certainly fits. And putting two and two together, I'm even more sure about the obvious candidate."

David raised his eyebrows and waited for the Chief Inspector to elaborate. David then glanced across at Trevor. The lad now looked agog at the developing scenario.

But Peter Maxie simply studied them quizzically, his previous vexation apparently put to one side. He seemed almost to be enjoying himself – as if exercising his prerogative of being the one in charge. That was fair enough. But David could do without any smugness. And he hoped the policeman would refrain from any temptation to tantalize.

"Are you going to keep us in suspense?"

Chief Inspector Maxie smiled and leaned back in his chair.

"People talk about honour among thieves. But don't believe a word of it. That's an old wives' tale. In reality, it's every man for himself. We see evidence of this over and over again. The main aspiration of a villain is to grow rich beyond the dreams of avarice. And he can best achieve this by not sharing any spoils."

David groaned inwardly. The man had, indeed, chosen to tantalize. And David could do without any quotes from Dr Johnson. His previous high regard for the Chief Inspector was at serious risk of waning.

"What I'm getting at," the policeman continued, "is that it's not unknown for partners in crime to fall out. Getting one hundred per cent of any booty can suddenly look far more attractive than only half. It's just the sort of option to exercise the criminal mind. Even to the point of eliminating a partner."

David now knew exactly what was coming. But it was Trevor who responded first.

"It was Mr Grimshawe, then? The gunman's partner?"

Trevor's interjection was laced with genuine disquiet, as if he could not contemplate such an outcome. David glanced at him again and there was no doubting his distress. During the last couple of days, they had dwelt upon in-branch duplicity, but that had all been theoretical. Now, faced with a practical outcome, the apparent reality of what had happened appeared to be hitting Trevor hard.

"Why not?" the Chief Inspector answered. "He knew all the ropes – banking ones, I mean. As first cashier at the branch, he was responsible for all the cash. He knew exactly how much would be there, and when. He was also *au fait* with what happened at Lamberhurst. And with the transport arrangements. And I understand it was you, Trevor, who discovered lapses in security concerning the branch code box. So, he had ready access to that. And lastly, perhaps a big factor, we understand he was hard up."

Trevor now leaned forward, a question clearly hanging on his lips. For now David was happy to sit back. Why not let Trevor, for the moment, anyway, continue to take the lead from their side of the desk?

"That all adds up," Trevor said, " but how would he have come across a small-time crook like this Alfie Templeton?"

Before Chief Inspector Maxie could answer, his telephone rang. He listened intently and actually raised his thumb to David. But after expressing his evident appreciation of some good news, his tone and demeanour then changed.

"No, don't do that. I need him here. Give him something to eat – hot soup I'd say. And then I need to see him. After that he can go there."

He then slammed the phone down and glowered at David.

"Good news and bad news. Good in that your Mr Fairweather's turned up."

David and Trevor looked at each other. Did they share the same anxiety? Had they both latched on to the Chief Inspector's change of mood on the telephone? This change certainly seemed to be the precursor to his good news/ bad news stance. Yet, the good news could not be better. David was mightily relieved that Douglas Fairweather had turned up. So, what was the bad news?

"Unfortunately," the policeman continued, frowning, "he's in a terrible way. He's malnourished and looks as though he's been sleeping rough somewhere. Our doctor says he needs to be hospitalized. But you heard what I said. I can't afford another delay with a witness. It's been bad enough with Barney Wilson. He still can't tell us what happened at Lamberhurst. And with Templeton now dead, I've got to talk to Fairweather. Who knows, he might also have learnt something about Mr Grimshawe."

Trevor leaned forward again.

"You mean Templeton might have let things slip while he held Douglas Fairweather captive?"

Chief Inspector Maxie nodded.

"That could easily have happened. He might have become careless. Or he could have even boasted about what he'd done. And he might have used that as a threat against Mr Fairweather. Anyway, I've pulled rank on our doctor. Once Mr Fairweather's had some food, he can put us in the picture. Then he can go to hospital."

David certainly understood and supported this line of thinking. And he was pleased the policeman had implied that he and Trevor would be included in the forthcoming meeting. But if this meeting was to be delayed for a while, should he first return to the branch? The sooner he saw Colonel Fawkes-William, the better.

CHAPTER 35

In the end, David did not have a chance to get back to the branch. Peter Maxie had invited Trevor and him to lunch in the police canteen. He wanted to know more about the fraudulent withdrawals, so why not do this over plates of ham, eggs and chips? David would have preferred a couple of pints of Harvey's. Oh, well …

Douglas Fairweather must have been having his soup elsewhere; the only other occupants of the canteen were uniformed policemen. David found the place surprisingly civilized. And the police could count themselves most fortunate; it was certainly not a facility enjoyed by local bank staff. In Head Office, yes, and at a few selective large branches around the country. But not here in Tunbridge Wells. He would have to make the most of this free lunch, but he would still have preferred to go to a pub.

They were just finishing their coffee when a young constable approached their table to say they would now be able to meet up with Douglas Fairweather. This was good news, indeed, and it was with an air of anticipation that they made their way back to the room they had used before.

Chief Inspector Maxie drew up an extra chair which he positioned on David's side of the desk, next to Trevor. Perhaps he thought it would be less inhibiting for the cashier to be seated alongside his banking colleagues. David was not convinced. More likely, the man would not register such consideration; his mind must be a blur after what had occurred these last few days.

Almost immediately, a knock on the door heralded the arrival of Douglas Fairweather, accompanied by the same constable.

Three years had gone by since David had seen the sub-branch cashier. He had not been confident about recognizing him, apart from his shock of blonde hair, something which would always draw attention to the man. And having been told that Douglas Fairweather had turned up malnourished and unkempt, David had been unsure of what to expect.

Even though the cashier had now clearly washed and shaved, he appeared to be a shell of the man David now recognized from his previous inspection. And David did not think this was simply because he had probably slept rough for three days, evident from his dark pinstripe suit being rumpled and creased in all the wrong places. There was something disturbing about his general countenance and demeanour. He had natural fair skin, but his face was now ashen, emphasized even more between his flaxen hair and dark office suit. His general pallor was not helped by sunken eyes, devoid of any life, and the overall impression was that of a man who had endured unimaginable trauma these last few days.

David, never mind Peter Maxie, was anxious to resolve matters as soon as possible, yet was this the time to do so? The state of Douglas Fairweather hardly looked conducive to attempt any conversation with him, let alone quiz him comprehensively.

But it had to be done and Chief Inspector Maxie had already made it clear that he also wanted this meeting to go ahead. Yet, his agenda was clearly different from David's as he smiled warmly at Douglas Fairweather and made the introductions. After they had all shaken the cashier's hand, Peter Maxie asked him to take a seat on the vacant chair next to Trevor. The young constable had no option but to remain standing by the door.

"I'm sorry I need to see you so soon, Mr Fairweather," the Chief Inspector said, continuing to smile broadly, a clear attempt to put the cashier at his ease. "I know this can't be easy for you. God knows, it's bad enough for most people to be interviewed by me. But in your case? After what you must have been through?"

Douglas Fairweather nodded and attempted a wan smile. But it did not disguise his clear anguish over his circumstances.

"Anyway," Peter Maxie continued, "I'm not going to keep you long. But I really need to know what exactly happened at

Lamberhurst. I know it's going to be difficult for you – having to re-live such a terrible event. But with Barney Wilson still not able to put us in the picture …"

Douglas Fairweather suddenly sat up, his deadened eyes displaying their first sign of life.

"Barney? You mean he's still alive?"

David felt the whole room come to life. The atmosphere was electric. He could almost smell the air of anticipation. The cashier's question had been so heartfelt. And, despite all that was going through his own mind, David could now understand how desperate the man must have been these last three days, trying to live with his belief that Barney Wilson had been murdered right there in front of him.

Chief Inspector Maxie leaned across the desk and offered his hands to Douglas Fairweather who clasped them with both of his.

"Yes, Mr Fairweather. He's alive. He's in Intensive Care – at the Kent and Sussex. He can't yet tell us what happened, but he's regained consciousness."

"Thank God, thank God …"

The cashier's words tailed off and he slumped back in his chair, releasing the policeman's hands. He closed his eyes, as if giving thanks to the Almighty.

Chief Inspector Maxie waited a few moments before asking what had actually happened at Lamberhurst.

In halting words, Douglas Fairweather described the shooting and how he had been forced into Templeton's car with his sub-branch case. He had been told to lie low on the back seat as the car sped up the hill out of the village. But they had then been stopped by the police in Horsmonden, when he had to feign being asleep. For some reason, they were allowed to carry on, but because of the risk of police roadblocks, they had holed up in a disused barn.

The Chief Inspector listened intently and continued to coax the story out of the cashier.

"So, where was that exactly? How was Alfie Templeton able to find such a place off the beaten track?"

Douglas Fairweather now looked alarmed. He seemed genuinely startled – even frightened – at hearing mention of the gunman's name.

"You've found out who he is?"

Chief Inspector Maxie smiled and was clearly empathizing with the cashier's concern.

"Don't worry. There's no way he can cause you any more problems. You're quite safe now."

Douglas Fairweather's body language appeared to beg to differ. He continued to appear fearful of the man who had captured him at gunpoint.

"You might say that. But he's so dangerous. He's a madman. And he's a killer. You've got to stop him. He might not have killed poor old Barney, but he'd already murdered Mr Grimshawe. He did it on Sunday. I couldn't believe it when he told me. I … I …"

His words tailed off as he collapsed forward on to the desk. His head rested on his arms and he started to sob uncontrollably.

Apart from the blubbering, an uncomfortable silence befell the room. It was as if no one knew what to say. Peter Maxie, presumably wanting to reveal that Templeton was dead, stared sympathetically at Douglas Fairweather, while Trevor simply glanced at David, his eyes filled with compassion for the cashier.

But David now decided to chance his arm. He could understand how the cashier's sobbing was so heartfelt. Templeton must, indeed, have been a madman. And it must have been shocking for Douglas Fairweather to have been cooped up with someone who he believed had murdered two of his work colleagues – men he had worked alongside for some five years.

But enough was enough.

This shilly-shallying had gone on far too long. After all, David was all too aware that his trip to London had not been wasted.

He knew exactly what he wanted to say and he looked past Trevor to Douglas Fairweather whose head was still cradled in his arms.

"What I'd like to know," he said, choosing his words deliberately,

" is how you first got to know this Alfie Templeton?"

A complete hush descended on the room. Fairweather's sobbing now stopped as quickly as it had started. Peter Maxie stared at David, rather than at the cashier, and Trevor's jaw actually dropped as he gaped at his boss's unexpected intervention.

Fairweather simply looked up and across at David, wild-eyed.

David pressed home his point.

"Was it about five or six years ago? Was that when you concocted the idea of having worked for Grindlays Bank? Or was that Templeton's suggestion?"

Douglas Fairweather now close his eyes and slumped back in his chair.

"What's going on?" Chief Inspector Maxie demanded. He did not look at all pleased, as if believing David had been holding back on further information.

David looked at him apologetically and spread his hands out in front of him

"I'm sorry. But I only knew for certain this morning. Before then, I didn't want to put something to you purely on a whim. But now? I think we can all be sure of something. Douglas Fairweather's reaction proves he's not what he's led us to believe."

CHAPTER 36

"But what made you first suspicious?" Trevor asked as they made their way up Mount Pleasant Road towards the hospital. Douglas Fairweather had been dispatched to the cells, his hospitalization now put on hold, and David had decided his next priority was to see how Barney Wilson was progressing. He hoped some encouraging news would be the spur to tackling what would be a far from agreeable encounter with Colonel Fawkes-William.

"It was a combination of things, Trevor. And they only came together last night – while we were talking in the pub. But something had been really bothering me. I just couldn't believe any of the other staff were culpable."

"You mean Mr Grimshawe and Mr Barnett?"

"Yes. And Colonel Fawkes-William. They were really the only possible perpetrators. But when you think about it, it was all pretty flimsy. Mr Barnett didn't seem to be on top of his job and appeared to be married to a young and extravagant wife. So what? Were these criminal matters? Of course not. Mr Grimshawe was in charge of all the branch cash and was hard up. But he and Mrs Grimshawe didn't seem to yearn for a grandiose lifestyle. All he seemed to want to do was to go fishing. As for Colonel Fawkes-William. What was in it for him? Judging by where he lives, he's not short of a bob or two. And his main preoccupation is to nurture his self-importance. That would hardly be enhanced by robbing the bank."

They now stopped at the side of the road before crossing and heading up Grosvenor Road. This would lead them directly to the Kent and Sussex Hospital.

"And then I got round to thinking about Douglas Fairweather." Trevor immediately got on the same wavelength.

"And the huge amount of cash he had in his sub-branch case?"

David nodded.

"Exactly. There was no logical answer to that one. Colonel Fawkes-William certainly didn't have one. And we couldn't query it with Mr Grimshawe, never mind with Douglas Fairweather, himself."

David stopped as they came to a pedestrian crossing and he lowered his voice in the presence of other waiting people.

"And when you think of it, why would a bank robber take a cashier along with him, simply because he was chained to his case? You made that very point yourself, Trevor. Why didn't he get Fairweather to unlock the chain? And then escape with just the case? After all, he had a loaded gun – which he'd already used. It shouldn't have been beyond him to convince the cashier to unlock the chain. We really didn't think that one through. Mind you, the shock of what happened to poor old Barney Wilson didn't help. But we should have thought about it more – and about why there was so much cash in the case."

They made their way across the road and mention of Barney Wilson's near demise clearly triggered Trevor's next thought.

"But what about Mr Grimshawe's murder? Had you worked that one out?"

David shook his head.

"No. There was only one link we really knew about. That he'd had some sort of argument with Fairweather – in the strongroom on Friday evening. Fairweather's kept mum about that, so far. But most other things seem to have come out."

David had certainly been grateful for the satisfactory outcome from the meeting in Chief Inspector Maxie's room. When Fairweather knew the game was up, he came clean about almost everything. Maybe he hoped this would help save his skin.

Trevor fell behind to allow a mother with a sumptuous Silver Cross pram to pass by, but he soon caught up.

"As for his being a hostage, sir …"

"He never was, Trevor – in the true sense of the word. But he was clearly Templeton's prisoner – even though they were partners. And back there in the room he certainly appeared genuinely devastated at Templeton's murderous use of his gun. No wonder he feared for his own life."

"But he never told us why he didn't go straight to the police after he escaped."

"He didn't need to, Trevor. Think about it. Yes, he was Templeton's prisoner. But in law? He must have known he was equally culpable for all they'd done. Giving himself up would have been the last thing he'd want to do."

Trevor nodded.

"But he must have had enough of sleeping rough. Perhaps it was a relief to be picked up."

"Maybe."

"But it was odd how he met up with Templeton."

Yes, indeed. David had been right about it being some five years ago. Fairweather had said it had been on the terraces of Selhurst Park, of all places. The two of them had regularly stood together – at first quite by chance, then by design. The police had been correct in their assessment of Templeton being a small-time crook, but he soon learnt about Fairweather's background. It had then been his idea that they should work together on a plan to carry out a major bank robbery.

"And what about Fairweather having worked at Lloyds, sir? So, why did he say he'd been with Grindlays?"

David almost licked his lips. Thank goodness for such a slip. The lie about Grindlays had been Fairweather's downfall. As for Lloyds, he had admitted to being sacked – as a clerk, not a manager. He had misappropriated funds from a customer's account. In his view, he had only borrowed the money temporarily – just £100 – in anticipation of the sale proceeds of a car. He had just said he had no intention of keeping the cash and had paid it back into the account within a month. The customer never knew it had happened. But the bank found out and operated a strict policy on this sort of thing: they considered it blatant theft. The result? Immediate dismissal, with no references to assist with future employment.

"Grindlays was his big mistake, Trevor. You just heard him say how bitter he'd become – with Lloyds. He then wanted to get his own back against the clearing banks generally. Maybe he thought it was less risky to give Grindlays as his banking background."

"And he was prepared to bide his time."

"Perhaps he'd seen *The Lavender Hill Mob*. Remember that film? For years, Alec Guinness played the dedicated bank clerk and all the time he was planning the perfect robbery. To do the same, all Fairweather needed was a good reference, select a suitable town and find a gullible bank manager."

"Poor old Colonel Fawkes-William."

"Aha. The Colonel was well and truly duped. At least it took Fairweather time to find such a manager – and in the right town. It's comforting, I suppose. That we might not be too vulnerable to this sort of thing in National Counties."

They reached the top of Grosvenor Road and turned left towards the hospital. David was now eager to find out how Barney Wilson was doing. But Trevor was clearly keen to learn more.

"And you had an inkling of this all along?"

David smiled grimly. If only. Yet knowing about it earlier would not have had any bearing on the eventual outcome.

"Not exactly, Trevor. But I was bothered about the Colonel's arrogance. Not just that he looked down on me personally. But he was full of himself about how he got such a good reference for Fairweather. Not to mention how he bamboozled it past the regional staff manager. And he told me about meeting Fairweather in the Conservative Club. He talked about it being a coincidence that two bankers – unknown to each other – had turned up there together. And as you know, Trevor, I don't believe in coincidences."

David could feel the empathy at his side. It would be a good lesson for Trevor. The lad was sure to be sceptical of any future coincidences which might arise during the remainder of his time on the inspection staff.

"As for having such an exceptional regard for Fairweather," David continued, as they turned towards the hospital, "it was simply unnatural – or, at least, naïve. Never mind all that talk about grooming him to be manager at Lamberhurst when the sub-branch got upgraded. So, I decided to do some checking – about his reference from Grindlays. I knew it would be in his staff file up at Head Office. That's why I went this morning. And when I looked through the file, I found what I was looking for. At first I kept missing it. But something just didn't look right. And then it shouted out at me from the top of the page. It was in the printing. Their rogue printer had done a reasonable job – no doubt printing exactly what he'd been told ..."

"Come on, sir," Trevor interrupted, not disguising his frustration. "It's your turn now – dangling me on a string."

David grinned. Sarah would have appreciated that riposte.

"All right, Trevor. But Fairweather's clearly an educated man. And that turned out to be his downfall."

Trevor frowned.

"I don't get it, sir."

"Would you agree that Grindlays was probably founded by a Mr Grindlay?"

Trevor nodded.

"Then think about your grammar, Trevor. And, goodness knows, I keep on at you about apostrophes. It's all about the possessive case. If it was originally Mr Grindlay's bank, there should be an apostrophe between the y and the s."

"But there isn't, sir. I've seen plenty of cheques drawn on that bank and there's never an apostrophe."

"Exactly! But, grammatically, there should be. Yet, for some reason, the bank chose never to include such an apostrophe. But on the reference letter for Fairweather, there it was – loud and clear. A rogue apostrophe!"

Trevor now looked astounded.

"That's most impressive, sir. And after all I've been thinking about you and your apostrophes."

"Now, now, Trevor. Don't be cheeky. But then there was another mistake. The letter was sent from the Calcutta branch of Grindlays. That was where Fairweather had told the Colonel he'd been a manager. But references should always originate from a bank's head office, not a specific branch. And Grindlays head office is here in London."

"So you then knew Fairweather was a fraud?"

David nodded.

"And one other thing had been bothering me. His appearance. His blonde hair. And he was fair-skinned. Yet, he had apparently chosen a career in such a hot country as India. I'm not saying only dark-skinned people should go over there to work, but it seemed to me to be a little odd."

"It's not the thing I'd have done," Trevor agreed.

"Anyway," David continued, "once he was settled into National Counties, he clearly bided his time. He learnt the job. Sucked up to the manager. And then had a bit of luck. Security at the branch was lax, especially with the code box. Because it was left around unlocked, he could get access to it at any time. He hasn't said so yet, but I reckon he copied the code cards. He then made out all those forms 69 himself – probably over a period of weeks. Having coded them correctly, he then forged General Kettleman's signature. Templeton must have duly practised it and then copied it when he cashed the cheques. But with the others, Fairweather didn't even bother to replicate the proper signatures. He might actually have got Templeton to complete them on the forms 69 and then sign the cheques in the same way when he actually cashed them. But the big thing was that, in each case, Fairweather had coded the forms 69 correctly."

Trevor pursed his lips.

"And he also forged Mr Barnett's signature on the forms 69?"

David nodded.

"And by taking advantage of the cheque clearing system, all the cheques cashed on Friday and Saturday would not reach the branch until after the Lamberhurst hold-up. By then, Fairweather and Templeton would be long-gone – with all the money."

David sighed. That was it in a nutshell. Except that it had never been part of the plan to use the gun. Back in Chief Inspector Maxie's room, Fairweather had made that patently clear. When he had been preparing to leave Tunbridge Wells for Lamberhurst, he had been verging on euphoric. The cheque encashments on Friday and Saturday had gone like a dream and their haul was about to be augmented by the £50,000 in the sub-branch case. He might not have thought of himself as being greedy, but even having to divide the spoils, his share would be almost beyond his imagination. As far as David was concerned, that was a clear case of avarice.

Being in such a good mood that Monday morning, Fairweather said that he had even entered into some uncommon banter with Barney Wilson. And the guard seemed to love this rare relaxation in his demeanour.

But Fairweather had utterly failed to anticipate what was to come.

"And it all went wrong," Trevor said, "because of Templeton and his gun. Perhaps he'd always been prepared to fire it – without Fairweather knowing."

"Who's to say? But that's what did it for Fairweather. Especially after the heroics of Barney Wilson – when faced by the gun. And Fairweather clearly liked Barney. Not least for his loyalty. Yet, Barney had been gunned down in cold blood – right in front of him. It could hardly get worse than that."

"And he then found out about Mr Grimshawe – in the barn."

"What a shock that must have been. He now believed two of his close colleagues had been killed. No wonder he wanted to escape. He found himself sharing a hide-out with an out and out killer. A madman, he called him. Yet, if he went to the police, he knew his involvement would come out. But he didn't last long before he was picked up. Then he simply hoped to bluff it out."

Trevor shook his head, as if in wonder at it all.

"Until your intervention, sir. And going back to Mr Grimshawe, and that row Daphne overheard in the strongroom. Was it really significant?"

"I reckon so. As you know, Fairweather's still to spill the beans on that. But I think Mr Grimshawe was suspicious – that Fairweather should want to keep so much money in his till for Monday."

"But how would that lead to Mr Grimshawe's murder?"

"Fairweather must have told Templeton. And Templeton probably said he'd make sure Mr Grimshawe kept quiet until after Monday. He must have been told about the regular fishing arrangement on Sunday. But whether Templeton really intended to kill him, we'll never know. But that would have been another immense shock for Fairweather. When they embarked on their original plan, he could never have contemplated any member of staff being killed."

They were now nearly at the hospital, but as they made for the entrance, Trevor tugged at David's arm.

"Before we go in, sir, there's just one other thing …"

Chapter 37

David frowned. This sounded ominous. Was there something he had missed?

Trevor took an envelope out of his pocket.

"It's nothing to do with the bank, sir. Except that ... well, I wonder if I could leave work early next Friday. I need to be in London – next Friday and Saturday. We should be back at Tenterden by then. Would that be all right, sir?"

Trevor withdrew a letter from the envelope and passed it across. David quickly scanned it. Amazing! He then thrust his hand forward.

"Congratulations, Trevor. Ronnie Scott's? How did this come about?"

"It was last summer, sir. Back in Torquay – at the Walnut Grove. I was playing there one Saturday night and a man approached me at the end of the set. He said he was Pete King and he was opening a new jazz club with Ronnie Scott. It was going to be in a basement in Gerrards Street. It would only be small, but they reckoned it was going to become big-time. They were planning to get Americans to play there. They hoped Zoot Sims would be the first. Can you believe that, sir?"

Zoot Sims? He was the very best; one of David's all-time favourites. But Trevor? Playing there as well?

"Pete King liked my playing, sir. Can you believe that? He then said he wanted me to sit in sometime. Be part of a supporting group. But I never thought it would happen. Then this letter arrived."

David could not be more thrilled for the lad. He certainly had the musical talent. England's answer to Zoot Sims? And there was no question that Ronnie Scott's was a huge step up from the Walnut Grove. But was a big problem now looming? Trevor had come to the London area to improve his playing chances. Was this the start? Was there now a real danger that jazz's gain could be National Counties loss? After Trevor's excellent work these last three months – especially this week – he would be a severe loss to the bank.

And David had another concern.

"I'll agree on one condition."

Trevor looked alarmed.

"What about Katie, Trevor. She must be there for your big moment."

Trevor now grinned in evident relief.

"You think I've not thought of that, sir?"

It was David's turn to be relieved. Yet what was he doing? Matchmaking? That was more in Sarah's line. But it had to be done. Trevor and Katie were made for each other. And they had been apart for too long. Katie's presence should also erase Daphne Simcock from Trevor's mind.

"When we get back to the branch, Trevor, give her a call. If she has trouble getting time off, just let me know."

But now they must move on and David ushered Trevor into the hospital's entrance. He remembered the way to the Intensive Care Unit and he hoped Barney Wilson would be well enough to see them. They would not stay long and then he would have to brace himself to see Colonel Fawkes-William. That would not be an easy interview. The manager had recently shown himself up in a much better light, but he had slipped up badly with Fairweather. David could only wonder what the eventual outcome would be for the Colonel.

After seeing the manager, he would phone the chief inspector at Head Office and would also put Angus McPhoebe in the picture. This might actually be his first ever enjoyable conversation with his *bete noire* at Regional Office.

A nurse was happy to take them immediately to Barney Wilson's room, but she posed a warning: although he was coming along well, he still had great difficulty in talking. She urged David to bear this in mind.

The nurse stayed with them in the room and David introduced themselves to Barney. David was immediately impressed with the guard's handshake. Despite his incapacity, it was strong and firm. It said everything about the man.

David explained that they were the visiting inspectors investigating the case. They just wanted to meet him and see how he was coming along. David had already decided it would not be the time to burden him with details of the investigation, even though it was now more or less resolved. That could come later.

He made sure he did most of the talking, bringing in Trevor now and again to break up the conversation. Barney was able to nod and smile his responses, but as they were about to leave, the door opened and a smiling nurse came in. David and Trevor immediately rose, but the nurse waved them back into their chairs.

"No, please, don't get up. I've only brought a letter for Mr Wilson. It's just been handed in."

She reached across to give it to Barney, but although he was able to grasp it, he was clearly too incapacitated to open the envelope and read its contents. Instead, he held it out towards David and asked him to do it for him.

David was wide-eyed as he took hold of the envelope which had clearly been sent by the local branch of the British Legion. Yet how had they heard about Barney's predicament so soon? Opening the envelope, David withdrew a single sheet of paper. The message was short, but so warmly worded. It wished Barney a speedy, full recovery and commended him on his not-unexpected bravery. Somehow, the news had travelled quickly and it made David's heart swell with pride that such a letter had been sent to a member of the bank's staff.

But it was the envelope which he could still not get over. The bank could never have been made aware of what he was now seeing. What a man! Colonel Fawkes-William had referred to Barney as being 'only a batman'. What would he say now? The envelope had been addressed to Barney Wilson Esq. VC.